HAUNTED HOTELS

SECOND EDITION

HAUNTED HOTELS

EERIE INNS, GHOULISH GUESTS, AND CREEPY CARETAKERS

TOM OGDEN

Globe
Pequot

ESSEX, CONNECTICUT

Globe
Pequot

An imprint of Globe Pequot, the trade division of
The Rowman & Littlefield Publishing Group, Inc.
4501 Forbes Blvd., Ste. 200
Lanham, MD 20706
www.rowman.com

Distributed by NATIONAL BOOK NETWORK

British Library Cataloguing in Publication Information available

Library of Congress Cataloging-in-Publication Data
Names: Ogden, Tom, author.
Title: Haunted hotels : eerie inns, ghoulish guests, and creepy caretakers
  | Tom Ogden.
Description: Second edition. | Guilford, Connecticut : Globe Pequot, [2022]
  | Series: Haunted | Includes bibliographical references.
Identifiers: LCCN 2022005769 (print) | LCCN 2022005770 (ebook) | ISBN
  9781493046928 (paperback) | ISBN 9781493046935 (epub)
Subjects: LCSH: Haunted hotels. | Ghosts.
Classification: LCC BF1474.5 .O33 2022 (print) | LCC BF1474.5 (ebook) |
  DDC 133.1/22--dc23/eng/20220218
LC record available at https://lccn.loc.gov/2022005769
LC ebook record available at https://lccn.loc.gov/2022005770

∞™ The paper used in this publication meets the minimum requirements of
American National Standard for Information Sciences—Permanence of Paper for
Printed Library Materials, ANSI/NISO Z39.48-1992.

For Dylan, Jordyn, Peyton, and Brayden

You can check out any time you like,
But you can never leave!

"Hotel California,"
Don Henley/Glenn Frey/Don Felder
(The Eagles, songwriters)

CONTENTS

ACKNOWLEDGMENTS

It would have been impossible for me to complete *Haunted Hotels* without the assistance and support of many people. My thanks go to Betty Jean Morris (for providing background on the Hotel del Coronado and the *Queen Mary*), Roxana Brusso (for the Marina Hotel), Gary Fitzgerald (for the Hotel Blackhawk), Bonnie Gordon and Nancy Tassin (for the Myrtles Plantation), Barrett Ravenhurst (for the Inn at Jim Thorpe and the Emporium of Curious Goods), Greg Lyczkowski (who first pointed me toward the Knickerbocker Hotel), Kathy Haggerty (for information on the St. James Hotel), Kyle Carter (for an update on the renovation of the Hotel Blackhawk), Jay Matz (for information on railway aficionados), Chris Donovan (the staff historian at the Hotel del Coronado), and the Lake George Chamber of Commerce (for information on Millionaires Row).

Other friends shared their first-person ghost encounters, including Chuck and Bambi Burnes, Shawn McMaster, S. Earl Statler, Kate Ward and Marty Rosenstock, Ian Varella, and Mark Willoughby. Thank you.

As always, my gratitude goes out to Mark Willoughby, Michael Kurland, Linda Robertson, Joan Lawton, and Dustin Stinett for their advice, feedback, and patience.

Finally, thanks to Greta Schmitz, my editor for this second edition; Chris Fischer, my project editor; and copy editor Emily Natsios.

INTRODUCTION

"If only these walls could talk . . ."

Hundreds, perhaps thousands, of American hotels are said to have resident spirits. In some cases, management has embraced and even advertises the spooky tales. Some offer in-house ghost tours. Others have been more circumspect and ignore the claims, afraid they could scare off would-be visitors. A few places outright deny the rumors.

From a business standpoint, there are arguments to be made on all sides. Hotels can debate the wisdom of acknowledging the reports all they want, but meanwhile guests at their accommodations continue to run into ghosts.

All of the ghost stories in this book are based on eyewitness accounts and existing lore. Some are straightforward retellings of long-standing legends, while other chapters contain original, fictional short stories based on the old wives' tales. Hopefully I've wound up with a mix that makes this collection spooky but fun to read. And if I really succeeded, you'll have no choice but to believe the hauntings are real.

It would be impossible to include all of the hotels that are purported to be haunted in one book, so I've carefully picked legends to show the wide variety of accommodations, apparitions, and paranormal activity out there. For those of you might want to visit a few of them, I've split the hotels into four groups by area, roughly organized according to the time zones in which they're located.

A note about courtesy before you go: Remember that hotels are generally not comfortable having strangers casually meander throughout their premises. The merely curious certainly are not allowed to wander in their residential hallways. If you stick to the open public areas, a quick peek inside a hotel may pass unchallenged or unnoticed. If you want to spend any significant time in the building, however, take a room for the night or patronize one of their restaurants, bars, or gift shops.

So pack those bags. It's time to hop in the car and set out on a road trip to some of the most haunted hotels in the United States—where the ghosts check in, but they don't check out.

PART ONE: THE EASTERN STATES

CHAPTER 1: CONNECTICUT CAPERS

Hotels don't have to be huge to be haunted. Many a small inn and B&B have ghosts from their pasts, often their original owners or occupants. Connecticut's accommodations are no exception to the rule.

Captain Grant's
Preston, Connecticut

Litchfield Inn
Litchfield, Connecticut

Captain Grant built the historic bed-and-breakfast that now bears his name as his private residence in 1754. It has served as a hostelry since at least the time of the American Revolution. **Captain Grant's** welcomed members of the Continental Army, and fifty years later it was allegedly a safe house for runaway slaves on the Underground Railroad.

The phantom that's seen most often in the inn is none other than Captain Grant himself! The apparitions of a mother and her two children also show up regularly, usually in the Adelaide Room. Although the identities of the latter spooks are uncertain, one of the youngsters—a ghostly girl—is said to be named Deborah Adams.

Even guests that don't see any spectres sometimes hear soft, disembodied voices and footsteps. Or they may discover that small objects in their rooms have moved from one place to another. Now and then, picture frames on the walls tilt, seemingly on their own.

Carol and Ted Matsumoto purchased the building in 1994 and opened it as a B&B the following year. They live at peace with their Other World occupants, and Carol has written a book about her experiences, *The Ghosts of Captain Grant's Inn.*

Litchfield Inn is located in northwestern Connecticut in the Litchfield Historic Landmark District. Georgian, Greek Revival, and Late Victorian styles are all represented in the village's many well-preserved, period buildings. The two-story Litchfield Inn is found about two miles outside of "downtown."

Visitors to the hotel have reported two different female ghosts. According to one story, a male guest opened the door to his room to find the full-bodied materialization of a woman sitting on the bed. The man immediately shut the door and ran back to the front desk. The receptionist ensured him that the room wasn't occupied, and, sure enough, when the traveler returned, no one was there. The other revenant is the spirit of an elderly Native American who's often present in the kitchen and the dining room.

Captain Grant's
109 Route 2A
Poquetanuck Village
Preston, CT 06365
(860) 303-8748 or (800) 982-1772
https://www.captaingrants.com

Litchfield Inn
432 Bantam Road
Litchfield, CT 06759
(860) 567-4503
https://litchfieldinn.com

CHAPTER 2: APPARITIONS IN THE ADIRONDACKS

The Sagamore
Bolton Landing, New York

At least a half dozen ghostly guests have taken up residence in the exclusive Sagamore Hotel in Bolton Landing, New York. Two ladies and a gentleman each travel alone; an arguing couple turn up in the dining room. Then there's the impish boy whose antics disrupt players on the golf course.

Pam and Johnny needed the getaway more than either of them cared to admit. It had been a rough winter, with almost twice as much snow as usual, and by January, Johnny could be depended upon to defiantly yell out, *"What* global warming?" whenever a new blizzard hit. When the spring thaw finally came, both of them were anxious to get out of the house.

They didn't have to travel far. Living a few miles outside Albany, they already knew where they wanted to go: straight up I-87 into the Adirondacks. The vistas would be incredible at that time of year, what with flowers starting to bloom on the vast meadows and the first melts filling the creeks and waterfalls to capacity, all topped by the stunning white peaks of the mountains. And then there would be the lake.

At nearly thirty-two miles across, Lake George was, in their opinion, one of the most perfect places on Earth. The narrow lake's clear waters, up to three miles deep in places, were perfect for boating, fishing, swimming, or just plain idling along the shore. The region's dense forests and hillsides offered trails for beginner to advanced hikers. And the small lakeside towns exuded all the charm and friendliness that any visitor could hope for.

It's little wonder Thomas Jefferson wrote to his daughter in 1791 that Lake George was "without comparison the most beautiful water" he had ever seen. He described the lake as being "interspersed with islands, its water limpid as crystal, and the mountain sides covered with rich groves."

The first Europeans to see it were Samuel de Champlain and his men. The French explorer mentioned the lake in his personal log on July 3, 1609, but he didn't name it. Thirty-seven years later, a missionary, Isaac Jogues, christened it

Lac du Saint-Sacrement. After the British victory in the Seven Year's War, the lake was renamed to honor King George II.

Pam preferred what the native Abenaki and Algonquin tribes living in the region had called it: Horican, meaning "tail of the lake," perhaps in a reference to its position with respect to nearby Lake Champlain. Horican was also the name used by James Fenimore Cooper, one of her favorite authors, in his 1826 novel *The Last of the Mohicans.* Pam remembered being swept up into the book's tale of romance as a child, and driving through the very region where the story was set brought it all back to mind.

Johnny was a fan of Cooper, too, but he mostly recalled the book's battle scenes, kidnappings, and massacres. He had been amazed when he found out that part of its plot may have been based on a very real event: the 1777 Native American killing of a young woman named Jane McCrea. The attack had happened nearby. She had been traveling to meet her fiancé, who was stationed at Fort Ticonderoga near the north end of Lake George.

Pam and Johnny wouldn't be heading all the way to Ticonderoga that night. They had taken a room at the outrageously luxurious **Sagamore**, which was located on a small island off Bolton Landing. They'd even splurged and taken a veranda suite with a lake view. It cost about twice what they normally spent for rooms when they went on holiday, but the Sagamore was special. It also had a *Mohicans* tie-in! *Sagamore* is an Americanized version of the Algonquian word *sakimawa,* meaning "chief." And Cooper used the word throughout his writings.

Johnny exited the interstate onto NY 9N. After stopping for a light snack in the village of Lake George at the southernmost tip of the lake, he and Pam leisurely began the remaining ten-mile drive to their destination.

By the early 1900s, Lake George had become one of the premier tourist destinations in the Northeast. It was particularly attractive to the super-rich, who built large mansions on a section of Lake Shore Drive (then called Bolton Road) bordering the waters' western coast. The several-mile stretch soon became known as Millionaires Row. The stone houses, which the owners self-effacingly called "cottages," were huge, with up to a dozen bedrooms each and acres of property attached.

The Sagamore hotel was the brainchild of Myron O. Brown, the manager of Mohican House, an early lakeside lodge. He convinced four millionaires—William B. Bement, George Burnham, Robert Glendenning, and E. Burgess Warren—who summered in the Adirondacks—that they should invest in a newer, more lavish hotel. They formed the Green Island Improvement Company and bought a small islet, the seventy-two-acre Green Island, just offshore from Bolton Landing. (Another backer, John Boulton Simpson of New York, joined them soon after.)

The Wilson Brothers, architects from Philadelphia, designed the Sagamore in a Queen Anne style. They built the hotel on the south end of the island, and it opened on July 3, 1883, to rave reviews. From its inception the hotel was intended for wealthy, discriminating patrons only. Riffraff need not apply. The inn was soon filled to capacity—up to four hundred guests—especially during the busy summer season when the well-heeled sought to escape the heat and grit of the cities.

Fire struck the building in 1893 and again in 1914, but each time the damage was repaired and the hotel opened anew. By 1930, the exclusive resort was showing its age, but it was rejuvenated thanks to an influx of capital from two of the hotel's corporate shareholders, Dr. William G. Beckers of New York and William H. Bixby of St. Louis.

Starting in the Depression years, many of those owning houses on Millionaires Row sold off their property. By midcentury, most of the homes had been torn down or transformed into hotels, though three of the estates still exist. By the end of World War II, the clientele who visited Lake George had also changed as middle-class families became more mobile and could afford to travel there.

Through it all, the Sagamore eked by, but eventually it was forced to close its doors in 1981. Two years later, Norman Wolpin, a real estate developer, teamed with Kennington Ltd. of Los Angeles to form Green Island Associates. The new consortium completely restored the fading lady. Since then, additional guest accommodation buildings have been added to the property: several condominiums, the seven Lodges, and even the Tudor-style Wapanak Castle that houses twelve. Taken together, the new units add another 250 rooms to the one hundred available in the main historic building. Today, the hotel is managed by Ocean Properties of Delray Beach, Florida.

Johnny and Pam drove across the short bridge connecting the village of Bolton Landing to Green Island. Though the two weren't frequent guests at the hotel, the familiar building with its glimmering white facade, red tiled roof, and gables was always a welcome sight.

After checking in, the pair headed toward the elevator. They entered the lift, signaled for their floor, then turned to the front as the doors closed. Slowly they became aware that they weren't alone. They looked over their shoulders and were startled to see a man standing behind them. Odd that they had hadn't noticed him when they entered. They must have been so excited about getting to their suite that they had been completely oblivious to the fact that someone was already in the car.

The fellow was portly but fashionably dressed in an expensive brown suit with a gold watch fob attached to his vest. His most distinguishable feature was his huge handlebar moustache—a style that was popular at the turn of the nineteenth century.

"Oh, I'm sorry. I didn't see you there," Pam gasped.

The stranger met her gaze as a wry smile crossed his lips. No sooner had he nodded a silent acknowledgment than the elevator slowed to a halt. It was Johnny and Pam's floor. The young couple stepped out of the car, and the doors gently slid shut.

The rest of the afternoon passed peaceably enough, but for some reason they just couldn't get the man they had seen in the elevator out of their minds. That night, as they headed for dinner at La Bella Vita, one of the hotel's six restaurants, they decided to inquire about him at the front desk. His wardrobe and grooming were so unusual that they figured the staff would know him. Perhaps he was one of the employees, hired to wear period costumes and mingle among the guests to enhance the hotel atmosphere. It was then that Pam and Johnny got the shock of their lives. The man they had seen was a ghost. And he had a name: Walter.

The startled couple was told that the first person to see the apparition was a female staff member who entered an empty elevator only to bump into an invisible presence lurking inside. As the young woman stared, a male figure slowly became visible. The phantom looked exactly the way Johnny and Pam had described. He also reeked of cigars, which the pair had noticed, too. In time, employees had decided that the phantom was probably trying to find his way down to the Trillium bis, a restaurant that used to be a gentlemen's smoking lounge. They also named him Walter, even though all attempts to truly identify the spectral visitor had been in vain.

Intrigued by the ghostly legend, Johnny and Pam decided to ask around. By the time they left on Sunday, they discovered that the Sagamore is home to at least five other spirits. Two of them were married, and their apparel suggested they came from the first decade the hotel was in operation. The spectres would come down from the second floor and make their way into the Trillium bis. Some accounts say that they would sit patiently for a few moments in the restaurant's reception area before completely disappearing. Most versions of the story have them entering the dining room and breaking into a fight. The husband would violently throw his wife to the floor. Then, as she reached up to grab at him, they both faded into nothingness.

There haven't been many reports of the arguing couple—and fewer of Walter, as well—since the wing in which the Trillium bis was located was converted into guest rooms. But that doesn't mean the spirits aren't around somewhere.

Pam and Johnny should be very happy they didn't run into one of the other phantoms at the hotel, because it shows up in people's suites in the middle of the night. The spectre is a woman, but nobody knows who she is—or was. Dressed all in white, she materializes by people's beds and leans over them. When the startled guests awaken, she blows her icy breath onto their faces. Other tenants never see the phantom, but they are aware she's in the room. Many are so uncomfortable that they're being watched by invisible eyes that they toss and turn throughout the night and are unable to get to sleep.

Another story concerns a sous chef who, several years ago, suddenly quit after making an almost unbelievable claim. He said he was at his station in Mister Brown's Pub when a tall blonde woman, dressed in elegant white evening attire, came into the kitchen. She marched up to the chef, spoke with him briefly—what was said has not been recorded—then stepped forward and walked right through him. Shocked, the chef looked behind him just in time to see the mysterious creature vanish from sight. He turned in his apron on the spot.

Finally, there is the boy. The Sagamore has an eighteen-hole, par 70 championship golf course that was designed by Donald Ross in 1928. The spectre of a mischievous young lad dressed in 1950s clothing has been seen sneaking around the course, which is located across the causeway on the mainland. According to legend, when the boy was alive he used to earn spare change by finding lost balls and turning them in at the pro shop. Unfortunately, one day he didn't check before he ran out into the street, and he was struck and killed by a car. Death doesn't seem to have slowed the boy down, however. These days, he doesn't wait for the balls to go astray. He'll pick them up as soon as they hit the fairway and hide behind a tree. Then when the players approach, he'll laugh and throw the balls at their feet.

Sightings of all six of the Sagamore's ghosts have occurred often enough that their tales have become part of the hotel's legacy. Although the resort doesn't necessarily encourage the reputation, some sources place the Sagamore on the list of Top Ten Haunted Hotels in America. What better reason to visit Lake George and the Sagamore for oneself?

The Sagamore
110 Sagamore Road
Bolton Landing, NY 12814
(518) 644-9400 or (800) 358-3585
www.thesagamore.com

CHAPTER 3: THE BOHEMIAN SPIRIT

Hotel Chelsea
New York, New York

The legendary Chelsea Hotel calls itself "a rest stop for rare individuals." And what's more "rare" than a ghost? At least three famous phantoms are known to walk the hotel's halls.

Meagan couldn't believe it. She was finally in New York City! She had dreamt about this moment for years.

She hoped to see her name in lights on the Great White Way one day, but she was still Midwestern sensible. Before moving lock, stock, and barrel to the Big Apple, she thought it would be best to first take a wee bite. She wanted to make sure she liked the place. But if the energy and excitement that overwhelmed her as she stepped out of Port Authority were any indication, the city had already won her over.

She decided that for her first weeklong foray she would overnight at one of the city's old, historic hotels rather than in some bland, faceless Hilton or Sheraton. Something with a little more character, a trifle off-kilter, yet clean and safe for all of that. As soon as Meagan saw the hotel's name pop up on Travelocity, she knew where she had to stay: the **Chelsea**.

Even back in Nebraska, Meagan had heard about the fabled hotel. It was impossible for any real performer *not* to know about it. Dozens upon dozens of artists, designers, writers, directors, and musicians, some of them the top in their fields, have stayed there over the decades.

As she walked into the lobby, Meagan was immediately struck by the offbeat ambience of the place. The cacophony of furnishings and mismatched furniture screamed bohemia; the walls were filled with artwork, from oil paintings and sketches to sculpture. (She would discover that the art continued up the walls, lining the winding staircase as well.) After a minimum of fuss, she made her way up to her room—she had chosen a cozy one-bedroom for her short exploratory visit of the city—and began to unpack.

As the mid-eighteenth century approached, the "city" of New York was confined to the southern tip of Manhattan. In 1750, Capt. Thomas Clark, an officer in the French and Indian Wars, settled along the Hudson River about two and a half miles farther north. His homestead, which he named Chelsea, was located near what is today Twenty-third Street between Ninth and Tenth Avenues.

The city continued to expand. Meanwhile, the Clarks' daughter, Charity, married Benjamin Moore, the Episcopal bishop. Their son, Clement, became famous as the author of the poem "A Visit from St. Nicholas," or, as most people know it, "The Night Before Christmas." Clement took advantage of the burgeoning demand for real estate, and by around 1850 he had subdivided and sold off the family's property to form the district known as Chelsea to this day.

In 1884, the Hotel Chelsea opened on West Twenty-third Street between Seventh and Eighth Avenues in the thriving theater district. It was the first co-op apartment building in New York City, designed for long-term residents, although some rooms were available for short-term lease. At the time of its construction, the twelve-story building was the tallest in Manhattan, and it remained so until 1902.

Several features made the place highly attractive. The building had a striking Queen Anne–style redbrick facade. Hallways on the guest floors were tiled in marble. No two apartments were alike; some were particularly spacious, with up to seven bedrooms. Many had balconies with wrought-iron railings. All had tall doors and windows, and some had ceilings that reached ten to twelve feet high.

Meagan tested her bed. It was comfortable, with a bright, new comforter on top. Many of the room fixtures, such as the bathroom taps, were certainly mid-twentieth century, but there was a modern flat-screen TV on the bureau and Wi-Fi.

And the walls seemed particularly thick. No wonder musicians—and perhaps more pointedly, their neighbors—loved the rooms. No sound would bleed between them. If it weren't for the noise of the city coming through the windows, the place would be quiet as a morgue. (As the thought came to mind, Meagan shuddered. Could she be any more ghoulish?)

The original hotel cooperative was short-lived. The company went bankrupt in 1903, and the building was put up for sale. Two years later it reopened as a hotel. The Chelsea continued to welcome long-term tenants, however—a tradition that remained until very recently. (Today the maximum stay at any one time is three weeks.)

Soon there was an ever-changing whirlwind of guests passing through. The hotel's reputation as a haven for artists started almost immediately. Early visitors included actresses Lillie Langtry and Sarah Bernhardt (who traveled with and slept in her own coffin rather than use hotel beds) as well as writers O. Henry and Mark Twain.

The parade of performers and artisans who have called the Chelsea home beginning in the 1950s really cemented its reputation as a sanctuary—and even asylum—for creative souls. Willem de Kooning, Robert Mapplethorpe, Jasper Johns, and Diego Rivera were just a few of the visual masters who had lived and worked there.

Stage and film personalities who have darkened its door include Jane Fonda, Milos Forman, Elliott Gould, Ethan Hawke, Dennis Hopper, Eddie Izzard, Elaine Stritch, and Uma Thurman. Some of Andy Warhol's "Superstars," including Edie Sedgwick, frequented the hotel, and the artist directed his 1966 film *Chelsea Girl* to chronicle their time there. Author Arthur C. Clarke was rooming at the Chelsea when he met with Stanley Kubrick to collaborate on the screenplay for *2001: A Space Odyssey.*

The hotel's musical heritage is even more amazing: Bob Dylan wrote "Sad-Eyed Lady of the Lowlands" while living there. A stay prompted Joni Mitchell to write "Chelsea Morning." Dee Dee Ramone took up residence and wrote songs for the Ramones in his near-soundproof room. His time there also led to his writing a novel, *Chelsea Horror Hotel.* Then there's Leonard Cohen, who composed "Chelsea Hotel No. 2" about his tryst in his apartment with an unnamed woman, though the lyrics almost certainly refer to Janis Joplin.

Others from the music industry to choose the Chelsea were Canned Heat, Alice Cooper, the Grateful Dead, Jimi Hendrix, Madonna, Edith Piaf, Patti Smith, Virgil Thomson, Rufus Wainwright, Tom Waits, and Frank Zappa. The list goes on and on.

But the most notorious musical couple to stay there were Sid Vicious, the bass guitarist for the Sex Pistols, and his girlfriend, Nancy Spungen. Theirs was a dictionary definition of a codependent, destructive relationship, and it ended, eventually, in both of their deaths.

The English punk rocker was born Simon John Ritchie in 1957. His friend John Lydon gave him the stage name Sid Vicious partly as a joke when Lydon's pet hamster, Sid, "vicious"ly bit Ritchie. After working with two other bands, Vicious was hired to replace Glen Matlock, who left the Sex Pistols in 1977. His first performance with the group was in April that same year.

Sometime in November, Vicious started seeing American groupie Nancy Spungen. She was a heroin addict, and soon the rocker was also addicted. Their unstable antics ultimately destroyed the group, which disbanded in January 1978. Vicious continued on a solo career, but by then his body was clearly falling apart.

On the morning of October 12, 1978, Vicious awoke in his apartment, Room 100, at the Chelsea Hotel. Spungen lay dead on the bathroom floor, having bled to death from a wound to her stomach caused by Sid's knife. Vicious was arrested for her murder but somehow managed to be released on bail. Ten days later he attempted suicide, and in December he was sent to Riker's Island for fifty days for assaulting Patti Smith's brother Todd.

By the time he got out on February 1, 1979, Vicious had gone through rehab and was clean. But between that night and the next morning, he died of an overdose, having shot up with almost pure heroin.

Despite the fact that his time with Spungen was marked by bouts of extreme violence, Sid Vicious denied to the end that he had killed her. He swore that he had no memory of the night because of the amount of drugs he had taken, but he offered several alternate possible explanations for her death: Perhaps she fell on the knife during their argument. Maybe some unknown outsider stabbed her during an attempted robbery or a bad drug deal gone wrong.

Meagan knew Sid Vicious's ghost was rumored to be back at the Chelsea. His highly identifiable spectre has been seen in and lingering around the elevator. He doesn't engage with strangers, though, so no one can be certain about the true reason for his return. Maybe he is trying to find the real killer. And Vicious isn't the only spectre said to haunt the halls!

The Chelsea has been a temporary sanctuary for numerous famous writers, including Brendan Behan, Charles Bukowski, William S. Burroughs, Quentin Crisp, Simone de Beauvoir, Allen Ginsberg, Edgar Lee Masters, Arthur Miller, Jean-Paul Sartre, Gore Vidal, and Tennessee Williams. In one of the apartments, Jack Kerouac wrote much of the original manuscript of *On the Road,* famously on a single, long roll of paper. Charles R. Jackson, author of *The Lost Weekend,* ended his own life in his Chelsea Hotel room on September 21, 1968. But the two writers who have chosen to return to the Chelsea after death are Thomas Wolfe and poet Dylan Thomas.

Wolfe was born October 3, 1900, in North Carolina. His form was the autobiographical novel, and he's best remembered for his magnum opus *Look Homeward,*

Angel. (The work is now just as well known for its theatrical adaptation by Ketti Frings.) Wolfe first visited New York City in 1923, when he made his first attempt to have his plays produced on Broadway. The following year, he accepted a brief position teaching English at NYU, and he was in and out of Manhattan for the rest of his life. His pied-à-terre was often the Chelsea Hotel. The celebrated author developed pneumonia while visiting his brother in Seattle in July 1938, and that September he was admitted to Johns Hopkins in Baltimore for military tuberculosis of the brain. He died there on September 15, 1938, just shy of his thirty-eighth birthday.

Wolfe obviously developed some strong connection with the Chelsea—enough to draw him back from the Afterlife. Perhaps his transparent figure has come back to walk the hallway on the eighth floor because he stayed in Room 831 while he was in Manhattan working with his editor, Scribner's Maxwell Perkins, on the manuscript for *Look Homeward, Angel.*

Dylan Thomas probably spent less time at the hotel than Wolfe, but who knows how much of it he was able to recall? By the time the Welshman first toured the United States to perform poetry readings, he was already a major alcoholic. It's well documented that upon returning to Room 206 at the Chelsea after a night of binge drinking at the White Horse Tavern on November 3, 1953, Thomas proclaimed, "I've had eighteen straight whiskies. I think that is a record." (He exaggerated, according to eyewitnesses, but not by much.)

The poet's most enduring work is *Under Milk Wood,* which was originally presented as a radio play on the BBC. Thomas performed it solo for the first time at Harvard on May 3, 1953. Just eleven days later, he read the play with other actors at the Poetry Centre in New York. He went home to England for four months, then came back to Manhattan.

He was already sick—he had lifelong respiratory problems—when he returned to America on October 20. He managed to get through a series of personal appearances, including more readings at the Poetry Centre and a recorded symposium at Cinema 16. Thomas was suffering severely by the night of his bender at the White Horse Tavern. The unhealthy air quality in New York did him no favors, and Thomas begged out of social obligations on November 2 and 3. By midnight on November 5 he was unable to breathe. Thomas was rushed from the Chelsea Hotel to St. Vincent's Hospital about two o'clock, where doctors discovered both acute bronchitis and pneumonia. The poet died there on November 9, 1953. Though it's widely assumed the cause was alcoholism—and it was certainly a contributing factor—he actually died of a swelling of the brain due to a lack of oxygen from the pneumonia.

Dylan Thomas may be buried back in Wales, but for some reason his soul has stayed at the Chelsea. Guests will catch his translucent figure careening down the corridors throughout the hotel. To paraphrase his most famous single verse, perhaps he does not want to "go gentle into that good night."

(Some say that he also haunts the White Horse Tavern, where he'll buy people a round of drinks at his favorite table in one of the corners. Sometimes an empty beer or whiskey glass will show up there, thought to be a sign of his presence. Staffers have also heard noises down in the basement that they credit to Thomas.)

According to some residents, playwright Eugene O'Neill and industrial titans J. P. Morgan and Andrew Carnegie also roam the Chelsea halls, and unidentified apparitions have been reported in the lobby bar, the Star Lounge.

There are other paranormal phenomena in the hotel as well. People stumble upon unexplainable cold spots or feel a sudden chilly breeze. Objects move on their own, and the lights, TV, and bathroom water taps turn on or off by themselves. Disembodied voices and footsteps echo in the roomy apartments and down empty hallways. And a few visitors feel the hand of an unseen spirit touch them. Some of the anomalies might be explained away by the expected creaking of an old building. But the rest?

Given the amount of passion, drama, and tragedy that the hotel has seen, it's surprising that even more spectral activity doesn't occur. During her short stay, Meagan never encountered anything otherworldly. She certainly didn't see any ghosts—that is, unless the long-haired rock-and-roller with the purple fingernails standing by the lift was Sid Vicious back from the dead.

But she didn't care one way or the other. She'd be coming back to the Big City—maybe even staying at the Chelsea Hotel again. And, if she did, she'd be happy to share it with the spooks.

Hotel Chelsea
222 W. Twenty-third Street
New York, NY 10011
(212) 243-3700
www.hotelchelsea.com

CHAPTER 4: ENTITIES AT THE INN

The Inn at Jim Thorpe
Jim Thorpe, Pennsylvania

The pastoral settings of the Lehigh Valley, the gateway to the Pocono Mountains, belie the number of apparitions that inhabit Jim Thorpe, Pennsylvania. Tourists usually visit for a day or two, but many spirits have taken up permanent residence in the mid-nineteenth century Inn at Jim Thorpe.

Russell burst through the door, and as he barreled into the room a cold blast of November air swept in behind him, hitting the shop owner square in the face.

"Barrett, you're not gonna believe it. I saw one! I just saw one of the ghosts over at the hotel."

Barrett Ravenhurst, the proprietor of the Emporium of Curious Goods in Jim Thorpe, Pennsylvania, looked up, bemused. He had known Russ for a long time, and the young man had been trying to see one of the spectres said to haunt the Inn at Jim Thorpe for years. If he finally spied one, or thought he had, well, it was a big deal indeed.

Ravenhurst and his store were well known in those parts. He was raised in Lehighton, six miles down the road. For thirty years, he made his profession as a magician, and it was his interest in the relationship between magic and faith that led to his earning a doctorate in comparative religion. His study of Wicca—the earth-centered belief most commonly identified with witchcraft—led Ravenhurst to annual pilgrimages to Salem, Massachusetts. While there, he visited a friend's New Age store and decided that a similar one might thrive in the arty, laid-back community of Jim Thorpe. (The Salem shop—The Cat, The Crow and The Crown—is owned by Laurie Cabot, who in the 1970s was made the Official Witch of Salem by decree of Governor Michael Dukakis.)

In 1987, with partner Rick Brong, Ravenhurst opened his own shop in two connecting storefronts on Broadway, the main street through Jim Thorpe. Within just a few years, the Emporium had become the largest boutique of its kind in northeastern Pennsylvania. And just what does it carry? Books, of course—more than five hundred titles on all sorts of metaphysical subjects, such as alchemy, spell casting, and the Kabbalah. Soothing oils, pungent incense, aromatic plants. Antiques. Wiccan items, ceremonial athames, and ritual wear including robes and capes. All in all, it was an eclectic, eccentric collection suited to the tastes of occult enthusiasts.

And, as if that weren't enough, the shop is haunted, home to a large, gray ghost cat. For sixteen years, before buying an elegant twenty-two-room Victorian mansion in Lehighton, Ravenhurst lived in an apartment above the Emporium. Frequently he would catch the phantom feline out of the corner of his eye, but whenever he would turn to directly face it, the cat would disappear.

The eerie animal didn't keep to the upstairs, however. It showed up almost as frequently in the shop itself. Brong has spied the cat as well—sort of. While looking at a curtain hanging in a passageway, he saw the bottom edge of the cloth lift up, then drop again, just as if something had crawled under it.

They've nicknamed the otherworldly entity "Spooky."

Now, when the shop is opened in the morning, if anything has been knocked over or fallen off a shelf, the owners simply chalk it up to Spooky. Ravenhurst and one of the clerks have both felt the invisible creature rub up against their legs at one time or another. Many customers have also commented on it over the years. More than a few have seen it lying on the counter and gone over to pet it, only to be startled by having the cat vanish right before their eyes.

One time Ravenhurst was surprised to hear four teenage boys who had wandered into the store calling out to the cat. When it ignored them and walked away, they called out to Barrett, "Hey, mister, do you know you have a cat in here? It went behind the counter." Ravenhurst didn't bother to explain what they had actually seen. That particular counter was up against a wall, and the ghostly cat had walked straight through it.

It wasn't a sighting of the phantasmal kitty, though, that Russell wanted to share with Barrett. It was his unexpected detection of an apparition in the 150-year-old hotel catty-cornered across the street.

Jim Thorpe is nestled along the Lehigh River in the southern foothills of the Pocono Mountains. Anthracite coal was discovered nearby around the turn of the nineteenth century, and in 1818 the Lehigh Coal and Navigation Company founded the small community as a railroad hub and shipping center. It was originally named Mauch Chunk, a derivation of the words for "sleeping bear" in the language of the Lenni-Lenape tribes that lived in the area.

By the middle of the twentieth century, the easily accessible coal had been mined, and the region fell into an economic slump. Fortunately, there was a budding tourism industry. Aficionados of fine period architecture sought out the preserved mansions that industrialists had built just outside of town. Hikers, cyclists, and rafters came for the mountainsides, trails, waters, and clean air. It was only ninety miles from New York City, seventy from Philly, and a mere twenty miles—a hop, skip, and a jump—to Allentown.

The hamlet also became a mecca for artisans—painters, sculptors, crafts-people, and weavers galore. And with the New Age thinking that arose in the 1970s, it had also become a perfect place for Barrett Ravenhurst to set up his shop.

By then the town was known as Jim Thorpe. After the death of the celebrated athlete in 1953, Thorpe's widow agreed to bury the Olympic legend in Mauch Chunk, even though he had never visited the place. The town erected a large granite monument over his grave and renamed itself Jim Thorpe in his honor. The tomb stands there to this day and has, indeed, become one of the town's major tourist attractions.

Thorpe's grave isn't haunted, but the hotel in town that bears his name is decidedly so. It dates to 1833, when local businessman Cornelius Connor built the White Swan Hotel to cater to the needs of the region's increasing number of visitors. At the time of its construction, it was one of several large hotels in Mauch Chunk.

Sixteen years later, in 1849, a massive fire swept through downtown, destroying many of the buildings, including the White Swan. Connor immediately rebuilt the structure, this time naming it the New American Hotel. Its exterior had a New Orleans look about it, including first- and second-story verandas with wrought-iron railings and potted plants hanging from the eaves. Among the notables to stay in this new facility were President William H. Taft, Gen. Ulysses S. Grant, John D. Rockefeller, William "Buffalo Bill" Cody, and Thomas Edison.

The economic downturns of the mid-1900s were difficult for the hotel, and the inn fell into disrepair. By the 1960s and 1970s, many residents were staying there on a reduced-cost, month-to-month basis.

Enter John Drury. In 1988, he bought the New American Hotel. Having previously renovated the Chestnut Hill Hotel outside Philadelphia and the Keswick Theatre in Glenside, he completely restored the New American. He kept the basic French Quarter exterior and Victorian interior but fully modernized the forty-five rooms and suites.

Drury rechristened the hotel the **Inn at Jim Thorpe**, and his son David was made the general manager. An outstanding combination of old and new, the Inn at Jim Thorpe has been placed on the National Register of Historic Places.

With as many incarnations as the hotel has had, it's only fitting that the inn is haunted. Were the spirits awakened by all of the hubbub during the reconstruction? Or have they been there all along? The rumors of their presence have only become common knowledge recently—thanks in large part to the new owner's willingness to publicize guests' claims on the hotel's website.

Certainly all of the locals, like Russell, had heard the legends for years. Finally on that chilly afternoon, his efforts were rewarded. He didn't know why, but that day on a whim, he poked his head into the lobby. He wasn't thinking about the spirits. Don't they only show themselves at nighttime? But something had compelled him to go inside.

A friend working the front desk waved hello as Russ quietly strode into the room. She knew why he was there; he had once confided that he hoped to someday see one of the phantoms. Russ smiled sheepishly at her, passed to the far side of the room, looked around, and then turned to walk back out the entrance. He thought he heard his friend call, "See anything?" But his eyes were glued to a spot on the foyer wall. An indistinct but definite shadow had appeared, a human shape.

Russ jerked his head around to see if there was anyone standing behind him or a light source that could be causing the shadow. But no, except for him and the young lady on the other side of the check-in counter, the place was empty. There didn't seem to be anything that could be causing the shade's appearance.

Russ turned back to the shadow. Surprisingly, it was still there. Then the hazy image started to move, slowly, floating across the bare wall. As Russell stared at it in wonderment, the figure faded away to nothing. Just before the image vanished, however, he had the presence of mind to quickly raise his cell phone and snap a picture.

"Russell. What's going on?" called the girl from behind the desk.

Russ rushed out without answering. He knew the first person he had to tell was Barrett. He would accept what he had to say without question or reservation. Seconds later Russell was in the Emporium.

Barrett tried to calm Russell down, told him to take a deep breath or two, and then listened carefully to his tale. Although Barrett had never been fortunate enough to spy one of the inn's apparitions himself, many, *many* people had told him similar stories. Usually the paranormal activity in the rooms are the typical things that go bump in the night: cold spots, objects moving on their own, or the faint scent of smoke (thought by locals to be a ghostly reminder of the White Swan fire). On the second floor, people hear the sound of invisible children laughing, and the odor of cigar smoke lingers in the air. Towels find their way into the toilets to stop up the plumbing.

A few of the inn's rooms are particularly haunted. In 211, for example, the television switches itself on and off. It's been reported that one man woke in Room 203 to discover his cell phone had relocated itself to the inside of the mini-bar. (Men, for some reason, are particularly susceptible to having their personal property moved about by spirit hands.)

Pesky shadows and orbs turn up in 305, and Room 315 is subject to chairs turning themselves over. Then there's Room 310. According to an old story, a nurse attended her long-term patient there, and she's been known to get upset when guests climb into bed. Some occupants have felt her invisible, icy fingers closing around their limbs, but on occasion her shimmering spectre, dressed all in white, has also appeared. And she's not the only phantom to show up in 310. There's also a tall man with greasy, combed-back hair who materializes from time to time.

There's one apparition who allows herself to be seen all over the hotel. It's a woman dressed in late-nineteenth-century clothing, but her identity is unknown because she has no facial features. She'll drift down hallways or turn up inside guest bedrooms, but if she realizes she's being watched, she'll quickly pass through the nearest door, even if it's closed and locked.

Visitors who have success in spying a full-form spirit are few and far behind, however. Most people, if they spot anything at all, are like Russell and only glimpse shadows or capture a ball of light in one of their photographs.

As Russ prattled on to Barrett about his ghostly encounter, he finally remembered taking a picture of the shadow with his phone. He scrolled through the photos to see what, if anything, had turned up. Dim but definitely there in front of the hotel wall, a tiny globe of light was floating about five feet off the floor.

Russell slowly turned the screen to Barrett. The two stared at the remarkable image. Barrett had seen several such photos before, but never one from just across the street. Right then and there, he made a mental note to pick up a small pocket camera on his way home. Next time, he thought, if anyone brought evidence of ghosts cavorting at the inn into the Emporium, it was going to be him!

There is one more haunting in Jim Thorpe that's worth noting: Cell 17 of the Old Jail.

In the 1860s and 1870s, the Molly Maguires was a secret, militant organization of Irish coal miners that operated independently of their union. Conditions in the mines were deplorable; safety measures were lax or nonexistent. Every day, the men risked their lives down in the hole for a miniscule salary. The Molly Maguires used violent means, including arson, kidnapping, and murder, to draw attention to the coalmen's plight and to force owners to fix the problems and raise the workers' pay.

Instead of acquiescing, the mine keepers brought in the Pinkerton Agency to infiltrate the mob. Many of the criminals were arrested, and ten were sentenced to die. On June 21, 1877, six men were publicly hanged in the Carbon County prison in Pottsville. Another four were hanged in Jim Thorpe (still Mauch Chunk at the time) for the murder of two mine bosses.

Among the quartet was Alexander Campbell. Before he was led to the gallows, he pressed his hand against the wall of his cell, number 17, and laid a curse of sorts on the building. He swore on his innocence that his handprint would never go away. It would stay there as an eternal reminder of the injustices done to the miners. Indeed, all attempts to remove the mark have been futile. Although it has faded, visitors to the prison, which now operates as the Old Jail Museum, can still make it out.

The Inn at Jim Thorpe
24 Broadway
Jim Thorpe, PA 18229
(570) 325-2599 or (800) 329-2599
www.innjt.com

The Emporium of Curious Goods
15 Broadway
Jim Thorpe, PA 18229
(570) 325-4038

Barrett Ravenhurst and Rick Brong, proprietors. The Emporium is open daily 11:00 a.m. to 5:00 p.m. Closed on major holidays.

The Old Jail Museum
128 W. Broadway
Jim Thorpe, PA 18229
(570) 325-5259
www.theoldjailmuseum.com

CHAPTER 5: DELAWARE DISTURBANCES

Delaware is famous for its dune-backed beaches on the Atlantic Ocean, but for ghost hunters it also offers plenty of places to set up shop. Some of its haunted lodgings date back to colonial times—Delaware was the first state to ratify the US Constitution—while other spook-filled accommodations are significantly newer on the scene.

Addy Sea
Bethany Beach, Delaware

David Finney Inn
New Castle, Delaware

Addy Sea, which now operates as an oceanfront bed-and-breakfast, was built by John M. Addy, a Pittsburgh plumber, in 1901 as a summer getaway home on the Atlantic Ocean. The Late Victorian style house, complete with a red, cedar-shingle roof and gingerbread trimming, stayed in the Addy family until 1974, when it was sold to a neighbor, Leroy T. Gravette III. The new owner renovated and updated the facilities, and the hotel remains in Gravette family hands to this day.

Three of the inn's thirteen rooms are haunted. Room 1 purportedly has a bathtub that sometimes shakes for no reason. Guests in Room 6 have heard the sound of an organ playing in the middle of the night, which is doubly surprising because there isn't one of the instruments anywhere in the hotel or in any of the homes nearby. (Faint, strange music played by other instruments has been heard throughout the building.) A male ghost that appears in Room 11 is thought to be Paul Delaney, a former employee of Addy Sea.

In addition to these room-specific hauntings, overnight guests have reported hearing disembodied footsteps coming from the corridors and the roof. The latter sounds are believed to be those of Kurty Addy, who died from a fall off the roof. Also, now and then the scent of perfume inexplicably drifts through the air.

Ghost legends are murky enough, but there's much that's uncertain about the early years of the **David Finney Inn** (also seen as the Historic David Finney Inn and the Old David Finney Inn). Many believe that Finney, a popular and affluent lawyer, built the three-story structure sometime in the 1680s, with the year 1685 being seen most frequently. Located just blocks from the Delaware River waterfront, it became his private residence, but Finney reserved the third floor for his law practice. Some sources suggest his father, Dr. John Finney, actually built the place and always intended it to hold a tavern and rooms for rent as well as son's law offices.

Regardless, in the 1730s, Dr. Finney constructed a house of his own, today known as the Amstel House Museum, directly across the street from the inn. An underground tunnel connected the two homes so that family members could pass back and forth during inclement weather.

The hotel has had several different owners over the years. Currently, there's an eatery, the Sonora at David Finney Inn, on the ground floor. People claim that Dr. Finney's spirit can be felt in the bar and restaurant.

A law firm occupies the second story of the David Finney Inn, but no hauntings have been reported there.

Almost all of the creepy stuff takes place on the third floor. The story has five guest rooms, at least two of which can be rented through Airbnb. Doors and windows open and shut by themselves, faucets turn on and off, and personal objects go missing, only to turn up elsewhere in the room. The ghost activity is usually blamed on David Finney, who spent so much of his time there.

Interestingly, similar activity is said to take place on the third story of the Amstel House Museum. In fact, many people believe that the hauntings in the David Finney Inn either originate in or emanate from the museum. The invisible trickster in the doctor's former house is thought to have been someone in the Finney family.

Addy Sea
99 Ocean View Parkway
Bethany Beach, DE 19930
(302) 539-3707
https://www.addysea.com

Amstel House Museum
2 East 4th Street
New Castle, Delaware 19720
(302) 322-2794
www.newcastlehistory.org

David Finney Inn
(also seen as Historic David Finney
Inn and Old David Finney Inn)
216 Delaware Street
New Castle, DE 19720
(302) 322-1233
www.airbnb.com

CHAPTER 6: DC DENIZENS OF THE DARK

Hay-Adams Hotel, Mayflower Hotel, Omni Shoreham Hotel, Willard Intercontinental Hotel
Washington, DC

The nation's capital, a hornet's nest of politics, scandal, and intrigue, is no less a hotbed of haunted activity. With so many colorful characters having passed through the doors of its famous hotels, it's no wonder that many of their spirits have returned to take up residence.

The fact that Marian "Clover" Hooper's ghost haunts a hotel she never visited —the **Hay-Adams Hotel**—is unusual but not unique. What's more interesting is that she first haunted one of the houses that was demolished to build the hotel.

Hooper, who may have been Henry James's inspiration for the title character of his novel *Daisy Miller*, was married to Henry Brooks Adams, an acclaimed author, journalist, historian, and Harvard professor. Adams also happened to be the grandson of John Quincy Adams, the sixth president of the United States, and, of course, the great-grandson of the second US president, John Adams.

The couple moved to Washington, DC, in 1877 and soon became great friends with John Hay and his wife Clara. Hay had been a personal secretary to President Abraham Lincoln and served as Secretary of State under both William McKinley and Theodore Roosevelt.

Adams and Hays decided to build adjacent houses on Lafayette Square, and while construction was underway the Adamses took up residence nearby on H Street. In April 1885, Marian's father died, and she fell into a deep depression. Then, on December 6, she committed suicide in her bedroom by ingesting potassium cyanide, a chemical she used as a hobbyist photographer. Her husband found her body lying on the rug in front of the fireplace.

Adams, who was devoted to his wife, was so grief-stricken that he became reclusive, destroyed all of Marian's letters, seldom talked about her publicly, and only vaguely referred to her in his autobiography, *The Education of Henry Adams*. Whether Marian's spirit ever returned to the house in which she died is unknown, but when the new mansion was completed and Adams moved in, Marian apparently came, too. For many years, neighbors and passersby reported hearing a woman's voice inside the house, wailing and deeply sobbing, late at night when there were no female domestics present.

Meanwhile, the Hays' daughter Alice inherited her parent's house after their deaths, and she and her husband purchased the Adams house next door when Adams died in 1918. They leased it to the Embassy of Brazil, and it's said that Marian's hauntings continued at the property. Not only was she responsible for a stubborn cold spot in front of a fireplace, but on rare occasions her apparition would materialize in one of rocking chairs. She'd glare at the interloper before suddenly vanishing.

Harry Wardman, a DC-based developer, bought both the Hays and Adams houses in 1927 and razed them to build a luxury accommodation, the Hays-Adams Hotel, in their place. When it opened the following year, Marian Clover Adams immediately moved in—to stay. The hotel has changed hands, been refurbished, and undergone complete renovations over the past near-century, but Adams is still there as its resident ghost.

Almost all of the paranormal activity occurs on the fourth floor. Phenomena include locked doors that open and shut by themselves and electronic devices that turn on and off unexpectedly. A female voice has been heard crying inside various rooms as well as in stairwells, often whispering, "What do you want?" Although the spirit is never seen, hotel staff have it call them by name or even briefly hug them. Manifestations are frequently accompanied by a whiff of mimosa (Marian's favorite aroma) or almonds (which can take the same scent as potassium cyanide). The apparition is most active during the first two weeks of December, the anniversary of Marian Adams's death.

Amateur ghost hunters, be forewarned: The lobby and restaurants are accessible to the public, but the five-star hotel does not encourage casual sightseers.

The **Mayflower Hotel**, also located in Washington, DC, opened in 1925. It was named to commemorate the 300th anniversary of the *Mayflower* landing at Plymouth Rock in 1620. Built a cost of about $11 million, the ten-story hotel has at least 500 guest rooms and around 70 suites, and its lobby and mezzanine are filled with antiques, marble statuary, and gold leaf. The hotel is listed on the US National Register of Historic Places and has also been named a US Historic Site.

Due to the number of elite overnight guests and visitors it has hosted over the years, the Mayflower has acquired a number of nicknames, including the "Grande

Dame of Washington, DC" and the "Hotel of Presidents." It was Harry Truman, who stayed there many times, that allegedly dubbed her the city's "Second Best Address"—after the White House, of course.

No end of political events have been held there, one of the first being Calvin Coolidge's inaugural ball in 1925. Coolidge was already president, having assumed the office after Warren G. Harding's sudden death from a stroke in 1923, but Coolidge easily won election on his own merit the following year.

In the midst of his campaign, however, tragedy struck. In July 1924, Coolidge's younger son, Calvin Jr., died of sepsis at the age of sixteen. The president was heartbroken, but he dutifully went back on the road to greet voters. He was still in mourning at the time of his inauguration on January 20, 1925. Although he attended the swearing-in ceremony, Coolidge skipped the celebratory ball at the Mayflower Hotel that evening.

It's said that now, every year on January 20, all of the lights in the hotel flicker or dim at 10 p.m.—the exact time Coolidge was scheduled to enter the ballroom. Also, one of the elevators supposedly gets stuck on the eighth floor for about fifteen minutes about the time the president would have descended from his suite.

The **Omni Shoreham Hotel** has been a central part of DC's social and political life since developer Harry Bralove built it in 1930. (Omni Hotels and Resorts acquired it in 1983.) Franklin Delano Roosevelt's first inaugural ball was held there on March 4, 1933, and it has hosted an inaugural ball for every president since, although not all of them were "official" galas planned by the Inauguration Committee or visited by the new Chief Executive. President Bill Clinton famously played the saxophone at his Shoreham Hotel party in 1993.

Henry L. Doherty, the founder of Cities Service Company (later the Citgo Petroleum Corporation), was one of the original financiers and minority stockholders of the hotel, and shortly after it opened he moved into an eighth-floor apartment with his wife Grace and their daughter Helen. Doherty had long suffered from acute arthritis, and Grace had been his nurse for several years before they married she was widowed.

While staying at the Shoreham Hotel, Doherty employed a full-time housekeeper, Juliette (sometimes seen as Julia) Brown, but it's unclear whether she was already working for the family prior to their arrival or whether she had been part of the hotel's staff as an Executive Housekeeper. In either case, just a few months into the Doherty's tenancy, Brown suddenly died in the Doheny apartment of natural causes. She had telephoned down to the front desk around 4 a.m. saying that she wasn't feeling well and needed assistance, but by the time help arrived, she had already passed. (An alternate version says she attempted to make the call to the desk but died before it went through. A hotel engineer was sent up to fix what was assumed to be a disconnected line, but instead he found the housekeeper dead and the telephone lying on the floor.)

Whatever the reason for their departure, the Dohertys moved out shortly thereafter, and suite remained unoccupied until 1973, all the while remaining in the Doherty family hands. Some accounts mistakenly report that the family continued to stay there. There are even claims that Helen died in the room, too, shortly after the maid's demise, and a few versions of the old wives' tale say that Grace also passed away in the room. But by 1936, Henry Doherty was near bedridden and residing in a Philadelphia hospital, where he died three years later. Grace passed away in 1949, a decade after her husband, and Helen died in Denmark in 1964.

Eventually, of course, the former Doherty apartment was fully renovated for rental, and it was numbered Suite 870. Almost immediately, overnight guests began to notice that doors sometimes swung open or shut without being touched, and the TV and lights would turn themselves on or off. There were inexplicable cold breezes. Room service and housekeeping carts would move by themselves, and guests would return to the room to find that furniture had shifted while they were away. Now and then, there were unmistakable sounds of disembodied murmuring and whispers. Folks staying in adjacent rooms occasionally complained of hearing noises coming from Suite 870, only to be told the room wasn't occupied. Soon people began to refer to the apartment as "the Ghost Suite."

The **Willard Intercontinental Hotel** stands on the site that Colonel John Tayloe III built six small rental houses in 1816. A man named Henry Willard leased them from Tayloe's son in 1847 and combined the units into a single, four-story building that he eponymously named the Willard Hotel. It stood until 1901 when it was replaced by a twelve-story hotel.

The Willard Hotel closed in 1968 and sat unoccupied for almost twenty years until the Intercontinental Hotel Group acquired it. After a complete renovation, the stylish hotel, commonly referred to today as "the Willard," reopened in 1986.

Because of its location just one block away from the West Wing of the White House, almost everyone in DC politics has visited the hotel at one time or another. Abraham Lincoln, a personal friend of Henry Willard, stayed there with his family the week before his first inauguration.

The Willard Hotel was a favorite of President Ulysses S. Grant, too. It being simpler times, Grant would often saunter over to the hotel in the early evening and enjoy a cigar and brandy in the lobby. His habit soon became an open secret, so people seeking favors or who wanted to the president to endorse some issue would show up at the hotel to "accidentally" bump into him. The unwelcome intrusions occurred so often that Grant started to refer to these uninvited guests as "lobbyists."

These days, people sometimes feel Grant's unseen presence in the hotel's foyer, and some have caught the unmistakable scent of his cigar, even though smoking is no longer permitted in the building.

Hay-Adams Hotel
800 16th Street NW
Washington, DC 20006
(202) 638-6600
www.hayadams.com

Mayflower Hotel
1127 Connecticut Avenue NW
Washington, DC 20036
(202) 347-3000
www.marriott.com/hotels/travel/
wasak-the-mayflower-hotel
-autograph-collection

Omni Shoreham Hotel
2500 Calvert Street NW
Washington, DC 20008
(202) 234-0700
www.omnihotels.com/hotels/
washington-dc-shoreham

Willard Intercontinental Hotel
1401 Pennsylvania Avenue NW
Washington, DC 20004
(202) 628-9100
www.intercontinental.com/
Washington

CHAPTER 7: SALT LICK SPECTRES

French Lick Springs Hotel
French Lick, Indiana

Thomas Taggart, a former owner of the French Lick Springs Hotel, has never really let go of the property, even after death. And now he's joined at the lodgings by a cacophony of fellow phantoms.

A hotel has stood on the site of today's French Lick Resort Casino since the mid-nineteenth century. Its name (as well as that of the town) comes from natural salt licks that drew forest animals to the spot, which in turn led to the area becoming a major hunting ground for Native Americans. French trappers and traders were the first Europeans to the pass through the region and eventually inhabit it, lending their nationality to the settlement's moniker as well.

Recognizing the potential value of the real estate once it was developed, Dr. Thomas Bowles bought 1,500 acres there in 1832. The land included three mineral springs, the largest of which was called Pluto's Well. Bowles built the first inn on the property sometime between 1840 and the official opening date of 1845. The hotel was repeatedly enlarged and had several different owners, even as it gained a reputation for the medicinal qualities of the waters in its spa.

In 1901, **French Lick Springs Hotel** was purchased by a consortium headed by Thomas Taggart, a three-time mayor of Indianapolis and former U.S. senator. By 1905, Taggart had become the sole owner, and it was under his guidance and that the facilities became a first-class hotel and resort. It was listed on the National Register of Historic Places in 2003.

Taggart died in 1929, but employees and visitors alike claim he has never really left the premises. Taggart's spirit, although usually unseen, lingers near the service elevator. People know he's nearby when they smell his particular tobacco or when the lift suddenly begins to operate on its own. He also apparently likes grand receptions in the ballroom, because staff have heard the sounds of a party in full swing behind the closed doors of the unoccupied hall. Reportedly Taggart even once appeared inside the empty ballroom riding a horse.

There's other paranormal activity going on in the French Lick Hotel as well, especially on the sixth floor. Folks see dark shadows, and they hear ghostly footsteps and disembodied laughter. Distinct cold spots occasionally materialize, and a sudden gust of wind sweeps down a corridor now and then. Finally, although the room number is kept secret, a blood-colored stain repeatedly shows up in a bathtub where an abandoned bride killed herself.

French Lick Springs Hotel
Part of the French Lick
Resort Casino
8670 Indiana Highway 56
French Lick, IN 47432
(812) 936-9300
https://www.frenchlick.com

CHAPTER 8: THE MARSHALL MANIFESTATIONS

The Marshall House
Savannah, Georgia

Spirits from the past engage the living at the Marshall House. Some of them come from its days as a hotel, others from its time as a temporary hospital during two pandemics and a war.

The **Marshall House** was opened in 1851, making it Savannah's oldest hotel. It's named for Mary Marshall, who had championed the belief that the city needed a first-class hotel for visitors. Although the accommodations have undergone several renovations over the years, many features of the original design are still in place, including brick walls, wooden floors, doors, claw-foot bathtubs, wrought-iron verandas, fireplaces, and staircases.

The sixty-five-room hotel was transformed into a makeshift hospital three times—twice during yellow fever outbreaks in the eighteenth century and again during the War Between the States, first for the Confederate wounded, then later for the Union army. Dozens if not hundreds of soldiers died in the hotel. Countless amputations also took place, and it's believed that human bones discovered under the floorboards during one of the hotel's facelifts were from some of the operations.

Today, staff and visitors sometimes encounter the phantoms of men wearing Civil War–era garb throughout the hotel. One of the spectres is a young man holding his severed arm.

People have reported hearing disembodied voices and screams as well as the sound of children running down the corridors. Other hauntings include doorknobs jangling without being touched, flickering lights, and faucets turning themselves on and off.

The Marshall House
123 East Broughton Street
Savannah, GA 31401
(912) 644-7896
https://www.themarshallhouse.com

CHAPTER 9: THE FELLOW ON THE THIRTEENTH FLOOR

Biltmore Hotel
Coral Gables, Florida

Thomas "Fatty" Walsh was no stranger to violence. A hit man for the mob, he moved to Florida and became part owner of a Jazz Age speakeasy on the thirteenth floor of the Biltmore Hotel in Coral Gables, Florida. Despite being killed there, he's apparently decided to stick around to schmooze with hotel guests.

"The strangest thing just happened to me."

The concierge looked up. Midforties, dressed in a smart pantsuit, with her hair styled in a severe corporate cut, and wearing just the smallest hint of makeup, the woman was clearly a no-nonsense type. Her statement, neither defensive nor demanding, was a simple statement of fact. And she wanted answers.

She had taken one of the suites in the hotel's signature ninety-three-foot tower, which had been modeled after the Giralda Tower in Seville, Spain. Accompanied by the bellman, she had entered the tower's private elevator and pressed the 10 button. The doors silently slid shut, and the lift started its smooth ascent. She watched patiently as the floor numbers lit up as the elevator rose: 7, 8, 9.

But then, rather than stop at ten, the lift took on a mind of its own. It passed her floor without slowing down, continuing on to eleven, then twelve. Finally, at thirteen, the elevator came to a standstill. The doors parted.

A suite took up the entire level, but it was completely dark, save for what light was coming through the windows. The room was dead silent, and an almost eerie, uneasy calm filled the space.

The woman glanced over at the bellman standing beside her. Was she seeing a hint of fear in his eyes? Why was he concerned about a small elevator malfunction? Or was he bothered by where it stopped? Very few hotels have a thirteenth floor because of superstitions associated with the number—or rather the hotels *have* them but just don't *number* them thirteen.

What was more puzzling: The doors stayed open for what became an uncomfortably long period of time. Just as the woman was about to step across the threshold into the foyer of the suite, the doors finally began to close. The bellman, who had recovered his composure, quickly punched the 10 button, the elevator made its short descent, and within seconds it stopped at the correct floor.

It was only after she had settled into her apartment that the woman made her way down to the lobby to ask the concierge about the odd behavior of the elevator and the staff member's reaction. What she heard made quite a story.

It all dated back to the early 1900s, when Florida was undergoing a rapid land boom. George E. Merrick, a speculator and developer, was one of the men at its center. Besides founding the University of Miami, he also laid out many of Miami's surrounding suburbs, including Coral Gables.

The upscale residential hamlet, nicknamed the City Beautiful, was planned from the start as a haven for the well-to-do. Huge mansions soon sprang up beside the wide, palm- and banyan-lined boulevards. Merrick realized that a showcase luxury hotel was necessary to cater to the needs of affluent visitors to the resort town.

In 1924, he convinced John McEntee Bowman, head of the Biltmore chain, to join him in building a landmark hotel in the community. The project was announced at a gala dinner on November 25, 1924. It would be glorious even by Biltmore standards. Plans called for a $10 million, four-hundred-room hotel on 150 acres that would also feature ten tennis courts, a polo field, an eighteen-hole golf course designed by Donald Ross, and a 23,000-square-foot, 700,000-gallon swimming pool—the largest hotel pool in the continental United States.

Bowman entrusted the job to the architects Leonard Schultze and S. Fullerton Weaver, who had previously designed New York City's Grand Central Station and Biltmore hotels in Atlanta and Los Angeles. (The last of these would become a haunted hotel after the notorious 1947 murder of the so-called Black Dahlia. See chapter 28.) The sprawling Coral Gables structures would be Mediterranean revival, a blend of Spanish and Italian influences. And it would have a signature tower. Each of the suites located there would take up an entire floor and have several bedrooms and bathrooms as well as access to a private elevator.

The Biltmore made its debut on January 15, 1926. For the opening, railcars dubbed the Miami Biltmore Specials ferried members of high society from the Northeast down to Florida. Fifteen hundred guests rode up the arched driveway to the hotel and gasped as they entered the breathtaking lobby. There was a high vaulted ceiling covered with frescoes, tall marble columns, travertine and terrazzo floors, mahogany railings, leaded glass chandeliers, and a lushly decorated courtyard and fountain. Three orchestras, including one led by Paul Whiteman, were engaged for the festivities.

The Biltmore was an immediate success, and from the Roaring Twenties up to the war years, it was one of the most fashionable destinations in the entire country. Notable guests included royalty (the Duke and Duchess of Windsor), presidents (Franklin Roosevelt), magnates (the Vanderbilts), and Hollywood celebrities (Bing Crosby, Judy Garland, Ginger Rogers).

It also drew its share of shady underworld figures, perhaps most notably Al Capone, who liked to entertain on the thirteenth floor, now known as the Everglades Suite. Also, in 1929, Thomas "Fatty" Walsh was gunned down in that very room. Police files of the subsequent investigation seem to have disappeared, but here's what happened according to the general consensus:

Walsh was already well known in crime and law enforcement circles by the time he moved to Florida from New York. He was into the narcotics trade and was an "associate" of gangsters Dutch Schultz and Charles "Lucky" Luciano. For a time he and Jack "Legs" Diamond were bodyguards of Arnold "The Brain" Rothstein. Not long after Rothstein was murdered in 1928, Walsh made his way to the Sunshine State.

There, he quickly fell into the scene at the Biltmore Hotel, where police were turning a blind eye to an illegal speakeasy and casino being run on the thirteenth floor by Ed Wilson. For a time Walsh and Wilson became partners, but the collaboration was short-lived. The suite was packed and business was in full swing on the night of September 7, 1929, when a heated argument broke out between the two men.

Walsh was an "enforcer" himself, so he should have known better than to turn his back on another mobster—even if he was his partner. But Walsh didn't fear for his life. He was in the middle of a roomful of people. What was the guy gonna do? Shoot him?

Apparently that's what happened. When Walsh turned to walk away, Wilson pulled out a gun and shot him twice in the back at point-blank range. Walsh staggered a few steps to the coral rock fireplace and dropped to the floor, dead.

Some guests may have used a secret escape route that had been installed behind a bookcase. Or perhaps the shocked onlookers waited patiently as the single elevator made the several trips that would have been necessary to vacate the premises. Regardless, the room was emptied in minutes. Walsh's body was later discovered where it fell, covered with a sheet. Despite the fact that there must have been several witnesses to the murder, no one was ever arrested.

Though the 1930s brought the Depression years, the hotel managed to remain open. Just as ballrooms turned to the novelty of dance marathons to draw in visitors, the Biltmore found unusual ways to stay afloat, made possible in large part by its famed swimming pool. Sunday afternoons were set aside for aquatic shows that drew crowds of up to three thousand. The programs featured little Jackie Ott, who dove into the pool from an eighty-five-foot platform, and synchronized swimmers, one of whom, Esther Williams, would become a star in Hollywood. (Although he didn't perform in the shows, a pre-*Tarzan* Johnny Weissmuller was a swimming instructor at the hotel at the time.) The Biltmore also sponsored golf tournaments, beauty pageants, fashion shows, and, believe it or not, alligator-wrestling exhibitions.

During World War II, the War Department took over the hotel and converted it into the Army Air Forces Regional Hospital. Most of the windows were covered with concrete for their protection, and, fortunately for future generations, the marble floors were covered with linoleum. It remained a veterans' hospital until 1968, and during those last years, the University of Miami's School of Medicine operated out of the building.

The city of Coral Gables took possession of the Biltmore in 1973, but the edifice sat unoccupied for a full decade until the decision was made to do a full $55 million restoration. The hotel's grand reopening took place on New Year's Eve, 1987.

In 1992, the Seaway Hotels Corporation was granted a contract to manage the facilities. As part of their commitment, the celebrated property underwent a complete $40 million refurbishment, raising it to contemporary world-class standards. A spa and fitness center were added, and as part of the repair and modernization of the legendary pool, Ott's old high-dive tower was replaced with a stunning waterfall. The city spent an additional $3 million upgrading the golf course. Today the Biltmore Hotel has 275 guest rooms, 130 of which are suites. In 1996, it was given National Historic Landmark status.

It was during the decade the magnificent lodgings stood vacant that it gained its reputation for being haunted. Dennis Hauck, author of the indispensable *Haunted Places: The National Directory,* cites the rumor that townsfolk standing out on the hotel's golf course supposedly were able to see weird, unexplainable lights in the deserted tower and that spooky noises, including macabre laughter, would echo from within the uninhabited building.

Surprisingly, a few psychics and paranormal groups were allowed to enter the premises to investigate. They never spotted an apparition, but at least one team captured heavy breathing, a loud sigh, and the sound of tapping, like an elderly person walking with a cane, on audiotape.

Sightings and reports of paranormal activity began in earnest after the hotel was reopened to guests. And what tales they are!

A phantom couple repeatedly appears and disappears as the pair dances to the strains of unheard music in the ballroom. In the clubhouse, a spectre wearing a top hat has been spotted playing the piano. A Woman in White—paranormal jargon for a female spirit dressed all in white—has shown up in several rooms throughout the hotel. It's believed that she committed suicide by leaping from a high window in the tower.

Doors in the hotel will open and shut by themselves (especially for servers heading back into the kitchen), lights operate on their own, and lampshades go missing. Now and then mysterious, illegible handwriting will show up in the condensation on steamy bathroom mirrors.

Most of the paranormal activity that takes place on the thirteenth floor is attributed to none other than Fatty Walsh. Fortunately, despite his occasionally brutal livelihood, the gangster was a rather convivial man in life. He's never been destructive or hurt anyone in death.

Guests catch the unexplainable scent of his cigar smoke in the air, and the room is prone to sudden cold spots. Items left on shelves or tabletops fall to the floor or shift without being touched, and those staying overnight have heard muffled laughter or sensed an unseen entity moving around in the room after the lights are turned out.

It's said that the most famous person to experience one of the room's anomalies was President Bill Clinton. He was attempting to watch a football game on a television in the suite, but at first the set seemed to have no signal. Then it started to switch on and off by itself. The president didn't attribute the experience to the paranormal, but he did choose to go elsewhere to watch the game.

Walsh really likes to play tricks with the private elevator to the tower—or perhaps he just wants visitors. Guests have said the lift will bypass their own floor and go up to the thirteenth floor, even though a special key is now required above the eleventh floor. On one occasion, the doors stayed open at the thirteenth floor for such a long time that the couple inside decided to investigate. As soon as the woman stepped out of the car, the doors slammed shut behind her, and the elevator immediately started back down to the lobby with her husband inside. She was rescued, but not until after several panicked minutes standing alone in the haunted suite.

According to Sarah Parvis, who wrote the children's book *Haunted Hotels,* the elevator once came to an abrupt halt when a guest inside opined aloud that Fatty Walsh deserved the end he got. Only after the woman profusely apologized did the elevator start up again.

Finally, a few guests on the thirteenth floor have stated that they encountered a female apparition there. Fatty Walsh had the reputation of being a real ladies' man. Has he been lucky enough to find a companion in the Hereafter? Perhaps all it will take is a night in the Biltmore Hotel to find out for yourself.

Biltmore Hotel
1200 Anastasia Avenue
Coral Gables, FL 33134
(305) 913-1926 or (800) 727-1926
www.biltmorehotel.com

CHAPTER 10: THE DEMON DOLL

The Artist House
Key West, Florida

Sometimes horror movies that claim to be "based on a true story" really are! There are certainly enough creepy legends about killer puppets and demonic toys. Meet one of the devil dolls: Robert of Key West, which has been frightening families and terrifying tots since the early 1900s.

The Colonial Queen Anne–style cottage in Key West known as the **Artist House** was built as a private residence by Mr. and Mrs. Thomas Otto between 1890 and 1898. They had a son, whom everyone called Gene, in 1904. Both parents were busy with careers, so a staff was hired to care for the boy during his early years.

When Gene was about five years old, the daughter of a Bahamian servant gave the youngster a large doll her mother had made for him. (In some tellings of the story, the woman was Gene's nurse.) The doll stood three foot tall, was stuffed with straw, had a wig of synthetic wool hair, and was costumed as an American Naval officer. The doll so resembled Gene that it was named Robert, which was the boy's given name. Sometime later, the nurse was let go, and that's when the weird stuff started happening.

Gene began having vivid nightmares, and people would walk into his empty room to find it inexplicably in complete disarray. Occasionally when the boy was young and alone in his room, the house staff would overhear him giggling or talking to himself. The only thing unusual about that? The voice wouldn't be his. But whenever such events took place, Robert—the doll—was in the room as well.

Some of the servants insisted that the woman who made the doll practiced voodoo and had placed a curse on it after she was fired. A few visitors to the house admitted that they felt Robert had an evil aura, but it wasn't until one of Gene's aunts told the parents she also believed the doll was bewitched that they packed it away. Allegedly, the next day the aunt died.

Gene grew up to become an author and painter. He inherited the house after his parent's death, and he moved there with his wife, Anne. Robert remained stored in an attic or the cupola on the roof. Both Gene and Anne passed away in the 1970s, and the house acquired new owners—but the forgotten doll had been left behind.

Before long, neighbors became aware of a child's giggling coming from the cupola as well as the sound of someone rustling about. And they swore that from time to time they saw a little boy—Robert!—peeking out of the dome on the roof and an attic window. In the end, the demon doll was removed and put on display in the nearby Fort East Martello Museum.

Almost as soon as Robert was gone from the Artist House, which is currently operated as a bed-and-breakfast, a new haunting started there. Anne's spirit returned to the premises, dressed in her wedding dress and as beautiful as she was when alive. She's most often seen on the turret staircase in the cupola, some say to keep Robert from returning. Anne's apparition is also spotted in the back bedroom on the second floor. Some authorities on Key West ghosts claim that the house is also visited by the spectre of a little girl, who occasionally materializes on a rear staircase. She has never been identified, and her connection with the home is unknown.

By the way, just because Robert's safely out of the Artist House, that doesn't mean the doll's no longer possessed. Visitors to the museum have claimed they heard Robert tap on the inside of his display case. People who try to take his photo sometimes have their camera freeze up or, if they do succeed in snapping a picture, have found the doll's image blurred or blackened out. Legend has it that before you take Robert's photo, you have to politely ask for permission. If for some reason he declines, he'll tip his head to one side to let you know. If you then take a photo anyway, the doll will curse you and your family for eternity.

But here's one old wives' tale that can be debunked: Repeat visitors to museum have sometimes noted that the small toy lion sitting on Robert's lap has moved from one knee to the other. It's not witchcraft. The stuffed animal isn't attached to the larger doll in any way and was added to dress up the exhibit. No doubt the staff occasionally switch the little lion inadvertently during periodic cleaning. Unless, of course, Robert does it himself when no one's looking.

The Artist House	**Fort East Martello Museum**
534 Eaton Street	3501 South Roosevelt Boulevard
Key West, FL 33040	Key West, FL 33040
(305) 296-3977	(305) 296-3913
http://www.artisthousekeywest	https://www.kwahs.org/museums/
.com	fort-east-martello/visit

CHAPTER 11: MEDIUMS AND MORE

Hotel Cassadaga
Lake Helen, Florida

The existence of life after death has been a tenet of most major world religions, possibly dating back to prehistoric times, but the doctrine is at the very foundation of Spiritualism, a faith that didn't come into being until the mid-nineteenth century.

The two central creeds of the religious or philosophical belief known as Spiritualism are that a person's spirit survives physical or bodily death and that it's possible for the living to communicate with those Beyond the Veil. Often this contact between realms is facilitated by a medium, or a person described as a "sensitive," whether it be in a private reading or with several participants gathered together (often around a table) for a séance.

The Spiritualist movement began in 1848 when two sisters, Kate and Maggie Fox (aged eleven and fourteen, respectively), purportedly started receiving messages from the Other Side in their parents' farmhouse in Hydesville, New York. The coded missives arrived at night, in the dark, in the form of ghostly raps on the walls or furniture. The girls' simple demonstrations—which they later confessed they had faked—led to other people claiming to have ability to contact the dead as well, and within a few short years Spiritualism had adherents and practitioners worldwide.

In 1875, a New York medium named George P. Colby moved to central Florida, claiming that he was psychically led to the location by his spirit guide, Seneca. About two decades later, members of a Spiritualist community named Lily Dale in upstate New York began to show interest in founding a winter haven in Florida. To that end, Colby donated thirty-five acres of land to found the Southern Cassadaga Spiritualist Camp, or simply Cassadaga, in 1895. It has grown to encompass fifty-seven acres with about fifty-five homes being occupied year-round.

The Cassadaga Spiritualist Camp is still active and is the largest Spiritualist retreat in the southern United States. It was added to the National Register of Historic Places in 1991. Several of the town's residents are working psychics or mediums and are available for consultation.

Overnight visitors often stay at the small but quaint **Hotel Cassadaga**, also seen as the Cassadaga Hotel. It's said to be haunted by an Irish phantom named Arthur. Although remaining unseen, his presence is always accompanied by the aroma of cigars or gin. He's also known for noisily rearranging furniture when no one's looking.

Hotel Cassadaga
355 Cassadaga Road
Lake Helen, FL 32744
(386) 228-2323
http://www.hotelcassadaga.com

PART TWO: THE CENTRAL STATES

CHAPTER 12: WINDY CITY WRAITHS

Congress Plaza Hotel
Chicago, Illinois

It's little wonder that so many of the world's inns, hostels, motels, and hotels are haunted. People come and go in an endless stream, each bringing his or her story to the lodgings. At the Congress Plaza in Chicago, the spirits of some of the hotel's former guests have returned for another stay.

The **Congress Plaza Hotel**, located on Michigan Avenue facing Lake Michigan, was opened to cater to the crowds that would be drawn to Chicago for the World's Columbian Exposition of 1893. The hotel was designed to be harmonious with the Auditorium Building, which already stood directly to the north on the other side of Congress Street (now Congress Parkway). In fact, the original name of the Congress Plaza Hotel was the Auditorium Annex. The facades of the two structures matched, and they were connected by an underground walkway called Peacock Alley.

The twelve-story hotel had five hundred rooms and cost a million dollars to build. In 1898, a squarish, four-story block of rooms was attached to the hotel's south side. Then, between 1902 and 1907, a further extension—a fourteen-story South Tower—was added on to serve as apartments. Before long, the original part of the hotel was being called the North Tower.

The South Tower contained a massive banquet hall, now known as the Gold Room, which featured the first air-conditioned ballroom in the United States. In 1909 a second ballroom, the Florentine Room, was installed in the North Tower. By the time the complex was rechristened the Congress Plaza Hotel (due to its location on Congress Street and its proximity to the Congress Plaza in Grant Park), the place had more than a thousand guest rooms.

Over the next half century, from the Jazz Age to the Swing Era and on through World War II, the hotel had a remarkable history and cemented its sterling reputation. Today, it offers 871 guest rooms in addition to the suites.

It also has its ghosts. Doors open and close throughout the hotel without human help, and the knobs will become inexplicably hot or frigid. Photos and artwork on the walls tilt—and supposedly sometimes spin—on the own. Visitors have reported hearing disembodied voices and whistling, and staff members as well as guests sometimes sense an unseen "someone" watching them. The twelfth floor of the North Tower is said to have the most spirit activity in the Congress Plaza Hotel. There are unmistakable cold spots galore and finicky TVs that go on and off by themselves, sometimes even when they're not plugged in! As if that weren't enough, the full-form ghost of a small boy runs up and down the North Tower corridors, and a female phantom is said to manifest in one of its rooms, although no one seems to be able to pin down which one.

Congress Plaza Hotel
520 South Michigan Avenue
Chicago, IL 60605
(312) 427-3800
www.congressplazahotel.com

CHAPTER 13: PFISTER RETURNS

The Pfister Hotel
Milwaukee, Wisconsin

The Vinoy Renaissance
St. Petersburg, Florida

Charles Pfister, who founded his eponymous hotel in Milwaukee back in the 1890s, never seems to have left. But his spectre may not be alone. Unseen spirits play tricks in many of the rooms. In fact, at least one visiting baseball player has refused to stay there overnight ever again.

Ira found the place amazing every time he walked in.

He had lived in Milwaukee for only about a year, but work had already taken him to the **Pfister Hotel** to attend more meetings and banquets than he could remember. Nevertheless, every time he entered the foyer he was once again stunned by the hotel's opulence. Ira had stayed in any number of luxury hotels during his travels, but the Pfister had a certain elegance few others could match.

Of course, that was Charles Pfister's plan from the very beginning.

In 1818, a French Canadian explorer named Solomon Juneau founded a small village near present-day Milwaukee. Two more pioneers, Byron Kilbourn and George H. Walker, went on to establish their own hamlets along the Milwaukee River, and in 1846, the three towns merged to form the present city. By that time, German immigrants were flooding into the area, so much so that the city got the nickname Deutsches Athen, or "German Athens."

One of those immigrants was Guido Pfister. Born in Hechingen, Germany, in 1818, Pfister was a tanner by trade. He came to the United States in 1845, settling in Buffalo, New York, before moving to Milwaukee in 1847. He set up his own tanning and leather store, which was immediately successful. In 1872, he partnered with Charles Vogel, and within just a few years their tanning company, Pfister and Vogel Leather, was producing more leather than just about any other manufacturer in the Midwest.

Pfister had many interests besides the tanning trade. He became president of the German Exchange Bank and a trustee of the Northwestern Mutual Life

Insurance Company. He was also a director of the Milwaukee and Northern Railroad Company, the Northwestern National Insurance Company, and the Milwaukee Merchandise Insurance Company.

He also believed that Milwaukee needed a first-class—a world-class—hotel. He wanted a magnificent building, indeed, someplace where people would feel privileged to stay: a "grand hotel of the West." But he also hoped that folks from every social stratum would feel free to mix and mingle there.

Guido Pfister didn't live to see the hotel. He died in 1889 at the age of seventy-eight before a single stone was laid. His son, Charles, shared his vision, however, and he and his sister, Laura Vogel, immediately set about to fulfill their father's dream.

Charles hired architects Henry Koch and Hermann Esser to design an eight-story Romanesque Revival structure to be located on East Wisconsin Avenue just three blocks off Lake Michigan. Guido had estimated that the hotel would cost $500,000. Charles authorized $1.5 million—in 1890s dollars!

Pfister insisted that, wherever practical, Milwaukee workers be employed and Wisconsin materials be utilized in the building, including the distinct cream-colored brick on the exterior. (In 1843, two brothers, George and Jonathan Burnham, had opened a brickyard in town using a particular local yellow clay. Other factories followed their lead, and, soon, so many buildings were constructed with the pale blocks that Milwaukee got a second sobriquet: Cream City.)

The exterior of the limestone-and-brick Pfister Hotel is almost plain. The interior is anything but. The front doors open into an enormous, three-story lobby topped by an Italian-style fresco on the ceiling. Many of the staircases, the decorative pillars, the huge fireplace, and the floors are faced with marble. As a final touch, Pfister filled the lobby, hallways, and other public areas with dozens of pieces of Victorian artwork from his own collection—more than eighty in all, making it the largest display of Victorian art in any hotel.

The Pfister Hotel had its grand opening on May 1, 1893. At the time, it was arguably the most luxurious hotel in the country. It was also one of the most modern. The Pfister was one of the first—if not *the* first—hotel to run completely on electricity (provided by its own generator), and there were individual thermostats in every room. It also had the most up-to-date fireproofing available.

The hotel was only one of Charles Pfister's many endeavors. He was an even better businessman than his father. He started working in his father's tanning company in 1876, and he eventually became president and treasurer. He also followed in his father's footsteps in railroad, insurance, and banking. He became a power broker in city and state politics, too, almost always on the side of the Republicans. In 1900, he became the owner and publisher of the *Milwaukee Sentinel,* and he used the newspaper to boost his own interests as well as the image of the city. He finally sold the journal to William Randolph Hearst in 1924.

Pfister died just three years later. But he's never really gone. Pfister's pride and joy was his namesake hotel, and he's apparently stayed there to make sure that everything is kept in tip-top shape.

Ira didn't know about Pfister's ghost when he crossed the main lobby heading toward the ballroom. His mind was on the upcoming event. He had been asked to provide a few words after dinner, and he hated public speaking. But he was one of the managers of his company, and making presentations came with the territory.

As he passed the grand staircase leading to the upper atriums, he couldn't help but notice the two large Italian bronze lion statues, nicknamed Dick and Harry, at the foot of the steps. For the first thirty-three years of the hotel's existence, they had stood silent guard outside the main entrance.

Ira's eyes crept heavenward toward the amazing frescoed ceiling, but for some reason he found his attention being drawn to a portly gray-haired gentleman, elegantly dressed in a business suit, who was staring down from the first landing. As Ira studied the stranger, he realized the man was not looking at him at all, at least not specifically. Rather, he was smiling benignly, surveying the entire surroundings in a single, fixed gaze, taking in all three levels of the atrium at one time. And he was content.

Ira wondered who the old guy was. He certainly wasn't the concierge. Ira had passed him as he came in. And the cut of the unknown gentleman's clothes wasn't quite modern enough for him to be the manager of such a prestigious hotel. *Oh, well,* Ira thought as he hurried toward the Imperial Ballroom. *It's not my concern.*

The cocktail hour was over, and seating for the banquet was beginning as Ira rushed into the room. He instantly felt guilty. He thought he had arrived in plenty of time to schmooze: Heck, that was half the point of coming to these things. How long had he been staring at that man in the lobby?

Ira was quickly greeted by the host and hostess, who showed him to his seat at one end of the head table. He made small talk throughout much of the dinner and then began to collect his thoughts as the first speaker began. *Thanks for inviting me. It was an honor to work on behalf of such a fine organization.* And so on and so on . . .

Ira's mind drifted. *I bet this room has seen some amazing things,* he pondered. Indeed, the hall had been inaugurated with a banquet honoring President William McKinley and his cabinet.

Unconsciously, Ira's eyes once again glanced skyward. The gold and beige ballroom was built on two levels, with its ornate ceiling towering thirty-two feet over the dance floor. Halfway up was the minstrel's gallery, where, in past times, musicians would have been seated to play.

There he is again! Ira's eyes froze as he caught sight of a solitary figure standing in the musicians' alcove. It was the same man he had seen just an hour or so earlier on the staircase. The kindly intruder said nothing; he just hovered there, fixedly, looking down at the crowd, with the same slight grin on his face. The man *had* to have something to do with the hotel!

Curiosity finally got the better of him. Ira tapped the shoulder of the gentleman seated next to him, someone he knew to be a longtime resident of Milwaukee.

"Excuse me, Stan, do you happen to know who that person is standing up there on the mezzanine?" As Ira pointed, both men looked up at the railing. Whoever had been standing there was gone.

The episode was quickly forgotten as the speeches progressed, and the evening finally drew to a close. It was only on his way out of the hotel that Ira noticed a portrait hanging in the lobby. It was the same person Ira had seen on the stairs and in the gallery niche. Why would the hotel have an oil painting of *him?*

Ira rushed over to the concierge desk. "Excuse me, could you tell me who's in that painting over there?" he asked as he gestured toward the artwork.

"That?" the man replied incredulously. "You must be new to Milwaukee. That's Charles Pfister, who founded the hotel. Why do you ask?"

Ira didn't know how to answer.

Almost every U.S. president beginning with McKinley has either stayed at or visited the Pfister Hotel. It's also been home away from home for such notables as Sarah Bernhardt, Bob Hope, Elvis, Bruce Springsteen, and Jay Leno, just to name a handful.

In 1962, Ben Marcus (of the Marcus Corporation) bought the Pfister Hotel and immediately set about refurbishing it to its original stately grandeur. In the mid-sixties, he added a modern, twenty-three-story tower adjoining the north side of the hotel, raising the guest room count from 200 to 307. The entire structure was once again renovated in 1993. The building is now registered as a Historic Hotel of America by the National Trust for Historic Preservation.

So far, Pfister's phantom has not shown up in the tower where the new rooms are located. But there have been many, many reports of Charles's ghost appearing on the hotel's original marble staircase, the musicians' gallery in the ballroom, and in a storage area on the ninth floor. A few have seen him in one of the elevators and walking his dog. Pfister never interferes with visitors or staff. Instead, the spectre appears to be politely overseeing operations, making certain that everything is running smoothly.

Pfister may not be the only spirit haunting the hotel. Guests have reported hearing knocking sounds in the walls, and TVs and air conditioners have a habit of turning themselves on and off. A phantom dog has been heard yapping and racing up and down the corridors. Is it the same one that's been seen with Pfister?

People from every walk of life have experienced ghosts around the hotel. Interestingly enough, some of the most recent reports of paranormal phenomena have come from baseball players when their teams come to town to play the Milwaukee Brewers.

An incident that occurred to Carlos Gomez, the Minnesota Twins outfielder, was widely reported by the Associated Press in July 2009. A few years back, while coming out of the shower, the ballplayer was sure that he heard voices in the other room. But when he went to investigate, he found the place empty. Then, as he started getting dressed, his iPod, which was sitting on a tabletop, came to life and started to vibrate. Every time Gomez turned it off, it would start up again. In another version of the story, the ballplayer heard the iPod playing static as he came out of the washroom. When he picked up the iPod to examine it, music started playing, but only for a few moments. It then switched back to static.

When Gomez's team returned to the Pfister on their next road trip to Milwaukee, he made sure that he had a roommate—and brought a Bible. Now, he just wishes the team would stay at a different hotel.

Gomez isn't the only one who has insisted on doubling up. At least two different pairs of teammates playing for the Florida Marlins also opt for sharing rooms when they're at the Pfister.

Pablo Sandoval, the Venezuelan-born player for the San Francisco Giants, is said to have encountered strange anomalies at the hotel as well. When Jim Tracy was managing the Los Angeles Dodgers, he would often hear suggestions from his players that it might be best to move to a less-spirited hotel. It's said that Adrian Beltre of the Dodgers, for instance, was known to sleep with a baseball bat by his side when he stayed at the Pfister because of all the strange noises in the dark. (For whatever reason, the Dodgers no longer use the Pfister Hotel when they're in town.)

Brendan Ryan, shortstop for the St. Louis Cardinals, was witness to a strange light orb that floated through his room. He was also subject to another common ghost phenomenon: The room got inexplicably chilly.

In an AP interview, Phil Rozewicz, the Brewers clubhouse manager, related a story about an unnamed out-of-town rookie who was put up at the Pfister along with the rest of his team. The new player woke up in the middle of the night to find that his blinds were up and the window was open. He shut them both and went back to bed, but early the next morning he awoke to find them open again. The next night he slept in the lobby. Eventually he moved to a different hotel.

To this day some of the Brewers won't overnight at the Pfister if business requires that they stay downtown.

Do *you* dare visit? Why not? The spectres, whoever they are, have never done anyone any harm. And, in a way, it's comforting to know that the founder of the hotel is still there, watching over the staff and making sure guests have a pleasant stay.

The Pfister Hotel isn't the only lodgings where pro baseball players encounter ghosts when traveling out-of-town. **The Vinoy Renaissance** in St. Petersburg, Florida, has long been a popular choice for visiting teams playing the Tampa Bay Rays. Many of the athletes staying there have seen the spectre of a man in full tuxedo walking the corridors, only to see it vanish before their eyes. Pitcher Scott Ryan Williamson claimed that during one of his visits he felt invisible eyes watching him as he prepared to turn in for the night. Once settled into bed, he felt an inexplicable pressure against his body as if someone were sitting on top of him. Williamson also caught a faint glimpse of a male spirit standing by one of the room's windows. A strength coordinator for the Pittsburgh Pirates reported that a translucent male apparition—who may or may not be the same phantom—materialized in his hotel room as well. Finally, the wife of a Toronto Blue Jays player claimed bathroom faucets in their room at the Vinoy Renaissance turned themselves on and off.

The Pfister Hotel
424 E. Wisconsin Avenue
Milwaukee, WI 53202
(414) 273-8222 or (800) 558-8222
www.thepfisterhotel.com

The Vinoy® Renaissance St. Petersburg Resort & Golf Club
(commonly referred to as The Vinoy Renaissance)
501 5th Avenue NE
St. Petersburg, FL 33701
(727) 894-1000
https://www.marriott.com

CHAPTER 14: COLD COLD HEART

The Redmont Hotel
Birmingham, Alabama

Everybody loves a ghost story, especially if it involves someone famous. Well, in the country and western music world it doesn't get more famous than Hank Williams.

When the fourteen-story **Redmont Hotel** in Birmingham, Alabama, opened in 1925 it was advertised as "Birmingham's Most Modern Hotel." One of its big selling points was that every guestroom had its own bathroom—an uncommon amenity for the time. The Redmont is the city's oldest operating hotel and was added to the National Register of Historic Places in 1983.

The building has many of the usual phenomena that traditionally occur in haunted hotels, such as doors that open and shut by themselves as well as furniture and baggage that move on their own. In addition, it has at least four ghosts. One of them is a small dog that's been spotted in the corridors, but the other spectres are human. An unidentified Woman in White only appears on the ninth floor, where it's assumed she died, but Clifford Stiles, a former owner of the Redmont Hotel, turns up all over the place.

The hotel's most famous ghost is country legend Hank Williams Sr., who stayed at the Redmont one of the last nights of his life. Williams had a rapid rise to stardom and is remembered for such songs as "Your Cheatin' Heart," "Hey Good Lookin'," "I Saw The Light, "Cold Cold Heart," and "I'm So Lonesome I Could Cry."

Williams's career was in trouble by the time he was thirty, however. His health had deteriorated from his dependence on painkillers that had been prescribed to him following back surgery, compounded by his excessive drinking and the use of chloral hydrate to sleep. His resulting unreliability and erratic performances had forced the Grand Ole Opry to reluctantly drop Williams from its main stage roster.

But Williams still had fans who wanted to hear him sing. He booked a concert in Charleston, West Virginia, for New Year's Eve 1952, followed by a gig in Canton, Ohio, the next day. Knowing he was in no shape to operate a car, Williams convinced a friend to let his college-freshman son, Charles Carr, drive him to the shows.

Carr picked up Williams in Montgomery, where the singer was living, and headed north. They stayed overnight on the second floor of the Redmont Hotel in Birmingham on December 30 with plans to start out fresh the next day. They left the hotel early, but by the time they reached Chattanooga, a snow and ice storm had settled over the area. With more than 400 miles still to go, Williams decided to fly from Knoxville to get to his show on time.

Unfortunately, the plane had to turn back mid-flight due to bad weather. The performance in Charleston was canceled. Williams and Carr checked into the Andrew Johnson Hotel in Knoxville, but they only got about three hours rest before the Ohio concert promoter called, telling Williams he would have to leave immediately if he had any hope of making it to Canton. Williams and Carr set off at 10:30 p.m. When Carr stopped for gas in Oak Hill, West Virginia, sometime early on New Year's Day he found Williams dead in the back seat of the car. The singer had died of heart failure sometime during the night.

Williams's last full overnight in a hotel was at the Redmont but, other than that, he had no personal connection with the place. Apparently that was enough, however, for his spirit to return there for its eternal rest.

The Redmont Hotel
2101 5th Avenue North
Birmingham, AL 35203
(205) 957-6828
www.redmontbirmingham.com

CHAPTER 15: A CONVERSATION WITH . . .

Hotel Blackhawk
Davenport, Iowa

Who would suspect the unassuming Hotel Blackhawk in Davenport, Iowa, of harboring ghosts? Yet it does. Several. One of them, "the Whistler," is only heard in the dead of night. Another spectre plays the piano in the ballroom. A third, an ethereal woman, walks the corridors. And is it possible that the other hallway haunter, a mature, well-attired apparition, is none other than Cary Grant?

Another night out of town on business. When Susan took the job as the regional manager of a sales firm in Decatur she knew she'd be on the road. She just didn't know how much.

In an era of teleconferencing, she hoped that most of her work could be done behind her desk, making calls, answering e-mails, and only attending conventions when absolutely necessary. She hadn't fully appreciated that, as the public face of her company in that part of the country, meeting clients face-to-face was an essential part of doing business.

So here she was in Davenport, Iowa. The city was established in 1836 and named for George Davenport, an army officer in the War of 1812 and an early settler in the region. The town became the county seat in 1840 and was Iowa's military headquarters during the Civil War. The city really began to blossom economically just after the turn of the twentieth century, and several of the downtown structures were built at that time—including the **Hotel Blackhawk**, where Susan was staying.

It's nice now and then to get into an old, historic place like this, she thought as she made her way up to her room. Most of the places she stayed were sleek, bland, and interchangeable, so it would fun to overnight in a quirky spot with a little character.

The Hotel Blackhawk dated to 1915. It originally had just seven stories, but four more floors were added the following decade. In all, there were about four hundred guest rooms and suites.

During its heyday, the Hotel Blackhawk was the best lodgings in town. Bandleaders such as Stan Kenton and Guy Lombardo were attracted to its ballroom, the finest in the Quad Cities (as several towns in the area straddling the Mississippi River are collectively known). The hotel was also the stopping point for every celebrity or notable politician that came through, including Jack Dempsey, Carl Sandburg, Herbert Hoover, and Richard Nixon.

When Susan visited in the late 1980s, the Blackhawk was pretty much the only game in town. And it certainly had a pedigree. Hadn't Cary Grant stayed there less than a decade earlier?

The iconic film star was born Archibald Leach in Bristol, England, in 1904. He came to America with the Bob Pender company of acrobats and physical comedians in 1920. With their tour over, the Pender Troupe appeared in the cast of a musical, *Good Times,* on Broadway. Afterward, the Pender group returned to the United Kingdom, but Leach stayed. The handsome, charming youth was soon back on the Great White Way, where he performed in five more musicals over the next eight years. He then joined a repertory company at the Muny in St. Louis, performing in at least seven shows there in 1931 alone.

That same year Leach moved to Hollywood, where Paramount Pictures put him under contract and gave him the name by which he's known today. Over the next thirty-five years, Cary Grant made more than seventy movies and became one of Tinseltown's biggest box office stars. He retired when he was still on top, cementing his debonair image in the public's hearts and minds forever.

In 1982, sixteen years after he'd retired from films, Grant stunned his friends by announcing that he was returning to the stage, albeit in a one-man theatrical reminiscence complete with Q&A called *A Conversation with Cary Grant.* Over the next four years, he made thirty-six appearances with the show.

Grant was to appear at the Adler Theatre in Davenport, Iowa, on November 29, 1986. Unlike the old show business adage, that show would *not* go on.

The night before it was scheduled, Grant and his fifth wife, Barbara Harris, checked into their suite on the eighth floor of the Hotel Blackhawk (some sources give the room number as 907) and spent a relaxed evening alone. The next afternoon, the couple strolled through downtown Davenport with Doug and Vicki Miller, who had codeveloped and financed the show. Then, shortly after four, Grant arrived at the theater.

The Adler Theatre, less than a block away from the Hotel Blackhawk, started life in November 1931 as the Orpheum Theatre. It had been planned by the Radio-Keith-Orpheum vaudeville chain (RKO) as far back as 1926. Somehow, despite the Depression, the $2 million movie palace got completed. The interior was decorated in the Art Deco style then in vogue. The lobby was replete with ebony and marble furnishings, and the ceiling was covered in gold leaf.

The Orpheum Theatre lost its luster and appeal as audiences fled to the suburbs in the 1950s and 1960s. It showed its last movie in 1973 and only managed to stay open through the rest of the decade by booking an occasional touring show or concert. In 1983, the performance space was incorporated into RiverCenter, a massive new convention-meeting complex. Over the next three years, the playhouse, renamed the Adler Theatre, was restored top to bottom, from its original crystal chandeliers down to its English carpets.

The Adler Theatre had its grand reopening on April 16, 1986, with a Burt Bacharach concert featuring the Quad City Symphony Orchestra. It was into that space that Cary Grant sauntered on November 29.

A first run-through went fine. The show would open with an eight-minute film montage, ending with a clip from the 1970 Academy Awards telecast in which the actor received his honorary Oscar from Frank Sinatra. Mirroring what was happening on the screen, Grant would leisurely walk onto the stage. He'd take his place on a stool situated far downstage (at his request) so that he could be as close as possible to his fans.

While a few technical adjustments were being made, Grant retired to his dressing room. Once there, he unexpectedly became ill. He thought his headache and nausea would pass, but when it worsened it became clear he had to be taken back to his hotel. Ever the professional, Grant refused to go to a hospital because he didn't want to cancel that night's performance. But when his condition didn't improve, two doctors were summoned. They alerted St. Luke's Hospital immediately. By the time the ambulance arrived, Grant was already in a coma. He was taken first to the emergency room, and then to the Intensive Care Unit, but he never regained consciousness. Cary Grant, eighty-two years old, was pronounced dead from a stroke at 11:22 p.m.

His body was flown back to Los Angeles by chartered jet, but some say he's never left the Blackhawk.

Susan had heard as much. Supposedly the misty outline of an elderly, gray-haired man appears from time to time in the halls. No one's ever gotten a good look at the spectre's face to identify him, but legend has it that the apparition may be Cary Grant. Perhaps he's returned to the hotel until he take a proper final bow.

Susan wasn't about to let some silly old wives' tale keep her from getting a good night's sleep. The long drive into town and the afternoon meetings had gotten the better of her. She had more people to see the next day, so she decided to turn in early, around nine. After a few pages of light reading, she reached over and turned off the light on the bedstand. Within minutes, she was sound asleep.

Normally, she went through the entire night without stirring. For some reason, however, that night she woke with a start. She was so surprised to find herself awake at 4:00 a.m. that it took her a few moments to remember where she was. Right—she was in Davenport, in the Hotel Blackhawk.

As she sat there, puzzled, she realized that the room was unnaturally cold. She pulled the blankets up around her shoulders. Were September evenings always this chilly in Iowa?

Then, off to one side of the room, she heard a faint noise in the darkness, like radio static. And, underneath the buzzing, there were two just barely audible voices. They were soft enough that she couldn't make out words, but it was definitely people talking.

Curious, Susan stepped out of bed and tip-toed toward the door. The murmuring was coming from the hallway! Susan gently wrapped her fingers around the knob, gave it a jerk, and thrust her head out into the corridor. The place was deserted.

Susan was confused. She was sure the sound had come from outside the room, but perhaps she had been mistaken. She shut the door, crossed to the window, and peeked out. There was enough illumination from the streetlights that she could clearly see that the sidewalks were empty. It was only then that she realized the buzzing had stopped.

Susan closed the curtain and climbed back into bed. She had barely laid her head on the pillow when the delicate droning and hushed tones started up again. She tried to put them out of her mind when, without warning, a sharp, loud whistle, like a master summoning his dog, cut through the dark.

That did it! In a flash, Susan jumped out of bed, changed into street clothes, grabbed her iPod, and headed down to the lobby. She had been planning to get up in an hour or so anyway to get an early start. She'd come back to the room to change after it got light.

Later, after breakfast, Susan struck up a conversation with the girl behind the front desk. She told her about the strange experience she had in the middle of the night and asked whether anyone else had ever reported anything similar. Keeping a tight smile and without answering her directly, the clerk said she was sorry there was a problem with the room and offered to change it. Susan replied that she'd consider it, but for now she'd stay where she was.

Whether the front desk clerk knew about any purported ghosts in the hotel, Susan had no way of knowing. The girl certainly wasn't saying anything one way or the other. But when Susan got back in the late afternoon, she found out everything she wanted to know. The shift had changed, and a young man was on duty. Susan figured it wouldn't hurt to ask him, and she got a mouthful.

"Oh, you heard the Whistler."

The Whistler? Susan wondered.

"Well, that's what we call him. He was some kind of scientist who lived in the hotel during World War II. He worked in a shop across the street and used a walkie-talkie to communicate with someone back in the hotel. But sometimes he'd just lean out the window and get the guy's attention by whistling."

To illustrate, the clerk spread his lips and made a crackling through his teeth, imitating the sound of a walkie-talkie, followed by a crisp whistle. It was eerily similar to what Susan had heard the night before.

The Whistler didn't return to visit Susan on her second night in town. But if she had stayed a bit longer, she might have seen one of the other two ghosts that inhabit the Hotel Blackhawk.

The wraith of a woman, dressed in a red or blue evening gown—she apparently has a choice of ensembles on the Other Side—often appears drifting down hallways throughout the hotel. Because of the woman's attire, it's assumed that she's probably heading toward the ballroom—which is where the other spirit hangs out. Guests at the Blackhawk sometimes hear piano music floating out of the ballroom when it's not being used. But the phantom musician, whoever it is, has never been seen.

In the 1990s, a gaming consortium called Isle of Capri bought the Hotel Blackhawk and rechristened it the President Casinos Blackhawk Hotel. By then, the inn was starting to look a little long in the tooth, and the company agreed to upgrade the facilities. They also promised to build another hotel down on the waterfront.

But the new hotel never came to pass, and (if truth be told) not much was done to old place, either. In the dead of winter, February 2006, a fire broke out in the Blackhawk when a meth lab that had been secretly set up in one of the rooms exploded. Although the flames were contained to that story, other floors suffered severe water and smoke damage. Soon thereafter, several water pipes froze and burst, causing the hotel to close down completely.

It took almost three years of political wrangling for a renovation proposal to be approved. In the end, Isle of Capri sold the building to Restoration St. Louis. Work on the rechristened Hotel Blackhawk began in January 2009, and it re-opened in December of the following year. In March 2013, the hotel became part of Marriot's Autograph Collection of luxury accommodations.

So far there have been no authenticated reports yet of the ghostly guests' return, but the hotel has only been back in business for about a decade. That's a blink of the eye in eternity. Only time will tell.

Hotel Blackhawk
200 East Third Street
Davenport, Iowa 52801
(563) 322-5000 or (855) 958-0973
https://hotelblackhawk.com

CHAPTER 16: TAKING THE CURE

1886 Crescent Hotel & Spa, Basin Park Hotel
Eureka Springs, Arkansas

Arlington Resort Hotel & Spa
Hot Springs National Park, Arkansas

Hot natural springs have drawn thousands of tourists to Arkansas, many of them looking a cure for (or at least relief from) their aches and pains. Three of the state's best known spa hotels also have otherworldly guests, but they don't come for the waters.

When Wendy decided she needed to get away for a long weekend, all her girl-friends said she *had* to go to Eureka Springs. Located about thirty-five miles from Fayetteville in the Ozark Mountains, the small town—it only has about 2,500 permanent residents—is set on a steep hillside. The place is known for its winding roads and quaint Victorian homes, and many of the buildings now house boutiques, art galleries, and crafts shops.

Across the valley from downtown is the Christ of the Ozarks, a seven-story-tall, white concrete statue of Jesus, and the city plays host to an annual production of *The Great Passion Play,* which draws thousands of visitors each spring.

Wendy wasn't heading there for spiritual healing, though. She was giving herself a three-day retreat to undergo another type of renewal. She planned to pamper herself with massages, facials, body wraps—you name it—at the New Moon Spa located in the **1866 Crescent Hotel**.

The town owes its existence to the cool mineral springs located throughout the region. In the mid-1800s, a doctor by the name of Alvah Jackson was convinced that his son's enflamed eyes were healed by rinsing them with the waters of one pool named Basin Spring. During the Civil War, the doctor operated a "hospital" in a local cave and later bottled and sold the springwater as Dr. Jackson's Eye Water.

Then, in 1879 a friend of his, Judge J. B. Saunders, claimed that by bathing in the pools he had cleared up a chronic and debilitating skin disease. Within weeks, the word was out, and people flocked to the area for the springs' restorative powers. Is it any wonder that, when a town was founded there on February 14, 1880, it was named Eureka Springs? Within a year, the hamlet grew to a city of more than ten thousand.

Former Arkansas governor Powell Clayton moved to Eureka Springs in 1882, and he tirelessly began to promote the site's bucolic air and scenic beauty. To attract tourists and settlers, the Eureka Springs Improvement Company, spearheaded by Clayton, was established to bring the railroad to town.

His campaign worked. Soon the streets were lined with fashionable houses and hotels. Perhaps foremost among the lodgings was the Crescent Hotel, which Clayton built with several partners in 1886. Architect Isaac L. Taylor was selected to design the hotel, which would sit on twenty-seven acres a mile north of and overlooking the city. The walls were constructed of magnesium limestone quarried from the banks of the White River, and the eighteen-inch-thick blocks were fitted so precisely that no mortar was needed between them. Modern conveniences such as Edison lamps, steam heating, and an elevator were incorporated into the interior, and guests could make use of the hotel's attached stables, which had room for a hundred horses.

The exuberance of the hotel's early years was short-lived. By 1901, it had fallen on hard times, and seven years later it was transformed into the Crescent College and Conservatory for Young Women. But the school couldn't sustain itself either, and it closed in 1924. For four years, from 1930 to 1934, the building housed a junior college. For the next two summers, it was run as a seasonal hotel. The Crescent Hotel's outlook was uncertain when, in 1937, it was purchased by Norman Baker.

If ever there were a man who deserved being called a huckster, it was Baker. He was born on November 27, 1882, in Muscatine, Iowa, the youngest of ten children. His hometown, located on a bend of the Mississippi River, was a center of commerce, and after quitting school at sixteen, Baker began work as a tool and die maker. But machinist work wasn't in his blood. Sometime around the age of twenty, Baker saw Doctor Flint, an itinerant magician, perform a mind-reading act, and the young man decided right there and then where his future lay.

In 1904, he framed his own traveling show, fronting a pseudo-psychic named Madame Pearl Tangley. When she quit after five seasons, Baker hired a college girl, Theresa Pinder, as her replacement. She and Baker were married the following year.

The couple returned to Muscatine in the summer of 1914. During the break from the road, Baker came up with an invention that would make him rich. He perfected a new type of calliope run by compressed air that was a vast improvement over the more dangerous and less tuneful models powered by steam.

Baker gave up the mentalism act, and in 1915 he divorced his wife. He concentrated on marketing his Tangley Calliaphone, which he built and sold for the next seventeen years. His other business interests weren't so legitimate. In 1920, he started a mail correspondence course to teach drawing—even though he had virtually no artistic ability or background himself.

Baker knew that the best way to reach the widest possible audience was on the airwaves. In 1925, he founded radio station KTNT, which he said stood for Know the Truth. In exchange for a promise to promote Muscatine, city fathers provided the station free electricity and water, and they waived its taxes. Baker used KTNT to broadcast his personal views, but one in particular struck a chord with the common man in rural Iowa: distrust of big business, whether it be government, Wall Street, or the American Medical Association.

In 1929, to boost ratings, KTNT investigated a cancer clinic run by Dr. Charles Ozias in Kansas City. Based on what he saw—and despite having had no medical training whatsoever—Baker came up with his own version of the Ozias "cure" and opened a clinic in Muscatine.

The treatments at the Baker Institute consisted of a series of injections (five to seven a day) of what today would be considered holistic medicine—except that it had no possibility of effecting a cure: a liquid solution containing alcohol, glycerin, carbolic acid, and essences of watermelon seed, corn silk, and clover.

In the spring of 1930, the American Medical Association went on the attack. Tired of the shyster slandering them nonstop on the radio, worried that his denunciations of cancer surgery would be taken seriously, and concerned for the people who were losing their lives from what they called "Baker's cancer cure quackery," the AMA called on state licensing boards, Iowa prosecutors, and the Federal Radio Commission to put him out of business. Baker returned fire by suing the AMA for libel and defamation.

But in 1931, the tide turned against Baker. First, the FRC refused to renew his radio license. He lost his court case against the AMA, and he was indicted for practicing medicine without a license. To escape arrest, Baker went to Mexico, where he remained for six years. Finally in 1937, he returned to Muscatine to face justice. His sentence was a slap on the wrist: a single day in jail.

Baker knew that he had no future in Iowa. But a tiger doesn't change its stripes. It just moves on to a new hunting ground. And Baker found one in Eureka Springs, a place already renowned for miraculous healings. The charlatan took over the Crescent Hotel in 1937, renamed it the Baker Hospital, and basically started up the same scam he had operated back at the Baker Institute. For two years he got away with it.

But his actions had not gone unnoticed by authorities. What finally led to Baker's downfall were seven letters he sent through the U.S. mail to advertise his clinic. He was arrested for mail fraud, and in a January 1940 trial he was found guilty on all charges. He was sentenced to four years in the Leavenworth Federal Penitentiary and was fined a mere $4,000. (It was believed that he had bilked cancer patients out of an estimated $4 million.)

Baker was set free on July 19, 1944. He moved to Florida, where he died of cirrhosis of the liver in 1958. His body was returned to Muscatine for burial.

The sanatorium was closed after his imprisonment. In 1947, a Chicago consortium acquired the property and turned it back into a hotel. Guests were once again visiting the "Castle in the Air High Atop the Ozarks," as it was advertised. In 1972, the Crescent Hotel got a long-overdue makeover when two businessmen from Wichita, Kansas, bought it and restored the grande dame to its Victorian splendor. Today the hotel is owned by Marty and Elise Roenigk.

Wendy knew little of the hotel's history. She was just happy it was her turn to enjoy the Queen of the Ozarks, as the 1886 Crescent Hotel & Spa is often called.

It was a late autumn dusk as she pulled up the drive, parked her car, and entered the foyer. Minutes later, she was slipping her key into the door of Room 419. Anxious to get settled in, Wendy swung open the door and . . .

Standing there, midway across the room, was a woman, her back to the door. The stranger slowly, silently, spun on her heels and stared directly at Wendy. She parted her lips and pleasantly smiled, as if happy to see a new face.

"Oh! I'm sorry," Wendy cried out in surprise. "I thought, I mean, I didn't know this room was still occupied. The clerk must have made a mistake."

The stranger approached Wendy cautiously, seemingly unsure about how to explain her presence. All she said was, "Are you here for the cure, too?"

"The cure? You mean the spa. Yes. It's my first time." Wendy glanced over her shoulder as she gestured into the hallway. "Perhaps I should head down to the front desk to see about a different room."

She turned back into the room to apologize once again for her intrusion. But the woman had vanished. More puzzled than frightened, Wendy closed the door and went downstairs. She spotted the staff member who had checked her in and started to explain what had just happened.

The young woman's eyes visibly widened. "Really?" she almost squealed. "You actually met Miss Theodora?"

It was *not* the reaction Wendy expected. A manager, overhearing the exchange, glared at the clerk and asked Wendy to step with him to the end of the desk where they could talk discreetly. What she learned in the next few moments was equally thrilling and disturbing: The person she had spoken to in 419 wasn't a guest at all, at least not in the last sixty-some years. It was a ghost, thought to have been a cancer patient during the time the hotel was the Baker Hospital. Her identity was uncertain, but the staff had named her Theodora, and her appearances—and subsequent sudden disappearances—always followed the same routine. Guests have also discovered they shouldn't say anything to upset her: She's been known to toss people's belongings into the hall if they indicate they don't like the room.

Wendy was dumbfounded. At first she was uncertain whether she wanted to stay in the hotel anymore. But she had been planning the weekend for some time, the sympathetic manger offered her a very nice alternate room, and, in the end, she decided that no spook was going to come between her and her exfoliating scrubs!

The rest of the holiday was blissfully uneventful, in part because Wendy didn't find out until after her return to Fayetteville that the entire hotel was haunted—by more than a dozen documented spirits, making it one of the most ghost-infested hotels in the United States.

The apparition that Wendy encountered was not the only one from the facility's two and a half years as a hospital. A nurse, dressed in a Depression-era white starched uniform, has been seen on the second floor and, to a lesser extent, the third. She's often spied wheeling an empty gurney down the corridor. The nurse never interacts with any of the living, so she remains anonymous. Interestingly, although the cart is also an apparition, guests hear its wheels turning.

By far the hotel's most notorious phantom is Norman Baker himself. Although he left the grounds in disgrace, some part of him no doubt remained attached to the place. It was, after all, the site of his greatest and most lucrative con. He has been seen shuffling all over the hospital—or hotel, rather—most notably outside of what is now the recreation room, wearing a befuddled expression. He's almost always dressed in a white linen suit with a lavender or purple shirt.

There are resident spirits from every incarnation of the Crescent Hotel. A lone girl, presumed to have been a student during the building's days as a conservatory, strolls through the gardens behind the hotel. According to legend, she died when she jumped, fell, or was pushed from the roof. She may or may not be the same phantom as a secretive "Lady in White" who shows up in the garden and on balconies.

A male spectre occasionally descends the main staircase, suddenly appears at the bottom of the steps, or shows up in the lobby bar. He's a mutton-chopped man dressed in a Gay Nineties black swallowtail tuxedo jacket, gray striped formal pants, a high-collared shirt, ascot, white gloves, and top hat. The ghost is often mistaken for a specially wardrobed member of the staff or a costumed strolling actor. Many now think that he was Dr. Ellis, a one-time house physician.

Several spirits are connected with the hotel's main dining room and kitchen. A gracious but ghostly gentleman in 1890s attire makes the rounds during dinner, chatting with patrons. One moment, he's telling them that he's waiting for his lady friend to join him; the next moment, he's vanished from sight.

Both staff and visitors have peeked into the Crystal Dining Room when it was closed and have seen a party of phantoms, all dressed in Victorian-era clothing, supping at one of the corner tables. Not only that: There were spectral servers attending them. Even when the ghosts don't materialize, sometimes their reflections appear in the mirrors.

A chef has reported seeing the apparition of a little boy in knickers and wearing old-style, wire-rimmed glasses running through the kitchen. At times, pots and pans come to life and move about on their own.

At least one group of teenagers has reported being followed into the elevator by a waiter dressed in turn-of-the-twentieth-century garb. They assumed he was from room service because he was carrying a tray of butter. He stood quietly, expressionless, not acknowledging the youngsters' presence, but when the lift stopped on the third floor and the kids got out, so did the waiter! He followed them partway down the hallway, but when the teens gathered up the courage to turn and confront him, the ethereal image had evaporated.

Then there are the apparitions that don't seem to be pegged to a particular point in time. A tall man with a beard knocks on random doors and, when they're answered, asks, "Are you waiting for me?" just before popping off into the aether. Colored lights and floating orbs streak through the North Penthouse, which was once "Dr." Baker's private residence. A Native American has been spotted roaming the fourth floor, and a crying woman carrying a baby blanket aimlessly wanders the passageways throughout the building. Visitors have rushed up to a man in his late teens or early twenties who has collapsed onto the lobby floor, only to have him fade away at their feet. Overnight guests have felt invisible hands tugging at their sheets and blankets in the middle of the night. And there's even a phantom house cat scurrying about.

Everyone agrees that the second floor is the most haunted area of the hotel. Unexplainable wisps of cold wind often whip down the long hallway on the second level. Many believe the chill emanates from Room 218, which seems to be the most haunted room of all. It has an ephemeral intruder thought to be Michael, an Irish stonemason who died after falling several stories and crashing to the floor of the unfinished room during the hotel's construction. Mostly he stays in the room out of sight, but some have seen his hand emerge from the bathroom mirror or heard his mournful wail.

Room 218 is plagued by other paranormal activity, which may or may not be caused by Michael's ghost. The lights and television turn on and off without assistance. Doors and windows swing open and closed, and the toilet flushes on its own. Disembodied footsteps can be heard in the room. The most frequent anomaly, pounding noises, comes from inside the walls.

(Michael is also thought to be the entity haunting Room 202 and, for some reason, 424. A very few people have also seen the worker outside the hotel, wandering throughout the property.)

Ancient tales suggest that the Shawnee and other indigenous tribes were aware of the medicinal powers of the nearby mineral springs and considered the spot to be sacred. There are those today who believe the pools and underground aquifers have a mystical aura or spiritual energy that attracts supernatural elements to the Ozark valley.

Is that why the ghosts return, or are they drawn back to the hotel itself? Heaven knows the place has seen its share of joy and sorrow, celebration and death. No doubt many souls formed deep emotional ties to the Crescent Hotel, and some of those links may have been strong enough to allow the spirits to transcend death. The truth may never be known.

While visiting family in nearby Fayetteville in 1997, Marty and Elise Roenigk of East Hampton, Connecticut, dropped by Eureka Springs. Delighted by what they saw, the couple wound up purchasing not only the 1886 Crescent Hotel & Spa but the equally historic **Basin Park Hotel** (also seen as the 1905 Basin Street Hotel). The Roenigks were devoted preservationists, so they immediately began to refurbish both hotels, making sure that any modern renovations didn't detract from their period restorations.

By the time the Roenigks bought the hotels, it was common knowledge—at least among paranormal aficionados—that the 1866 Crescent Hotel was haunted. But as it turned out, the Basin Park Hotel was full of ghosts, too.

The Basin Park Hotel had opened on July 1, 1905, with one hundred guest rooms. The eight-story structure was built up against (and partially into) a mountain, a fact mentioned in "Ripley's Believe It or Not." The hotel had a main staircase and a cage elevator, and there was an exit on each floor that allowed guests to access the hillside's wooded paths without passing through the lobby. In an odd sense, that meant every room could be described as being on the "ground level."

The Basin Park's most colorful period was from 1944 to 1955 when it was under the ownership of Joe Parkhill. He expanded the hotel's offerings so that, in addition to town's famous "healing" spring waters, his guests could enjoy regular dances, fishing trips, horseback riding, and even hayrides. It became an open secret that the so-called Rooftop Billiards Room on the sixth floor also had slot machines and served liquor by the drink—activities that were illegal at the time. (The bar and slots could be quickly stowed away and hidden if need be.)

Once the Chicago underworld got wind of what was happening in Eureka Springs, a new type of clientele began to "vacation" at the Basin Park Hotel, which Parkhill did nothing to discourage. By 1955, the criminal activity was tarnishing the town's reputation, so much so that police (headed by a proverbial "new sheriff in town") finally raided the hotel. Joe Parkhill and several others were arrested, and the slot machines were destroyed. With the pecuniary lure of the hotel gone, "the boys" stopped coming down from Chi-Town, and the sudden loss of revenue resulted in the hotel having to be sold. It changed hands several times until it finally began the property of the Roenigks.

Throughout all of this, the Basin Park Hotel accumulated a wide array of apparitions, but it's been impossible to link any of them to a specific person, time, or event. For example, there's the shining, translucent spectre of an adult woman with piercing, blue eyes and long, blonde hair and a gentleman in a nondescript brown suit. The pallid phantom of a little girl with ponytails and wearing a yellow dress has been seen all over the hotel, although she also occasionally surprises hotel guests by walking through the wall into their rooms. Spectral dancers are spotted whirling away in the Barefoot Ballroom, and folks have reported seeing the ghosts of a dog and a lion. Other paranormal phenomena include objects moving on their own and the presence of glowing orbs of light.

The Basin Park Hotel is quite comfortable with its ghosts and even conducts in-house paranormal investigations on Wednesday through Saturday nights from March through November. Amateur ghost hunters: See the hotel's website for details.

In 1832, the Arkansas Territory asked the U.S. government to put a cluster of natural thermal springs and adjacent mountains about 135 miles north or Eureka Springs under federal protection. The preserve would become Hot Springs National Park in 1921.

The original **Arlington Hotel** opened in 1875, offering its guests access to the nearby hot springs that gave the town its name. By the time the lodgings were built, the healing mineral waters had already been drawing tourists for more than fifty years.

In 1893, to accommodate the increasing number of visitors to Hot Springs, the Arlington Hotel replaced its three-story, wooden structure with a larger, more elegant Spanish Renaissance building. The new, five-level hotel featured three hundred guest rooms, wrap-around verandas, a rotunda, a glass dome in the lobby, and a grand ballroom.

Sadly, fire gutted the Arlington hotel on April 5, 1923, but it managed to reopen on December 31, 1924, with a festive party to usher in the New Year. Guest rooms were stylish and spacious, and they offered all the most modern amenities.

Not only did this third incarnation of the hotel have its own bath house (with sections modestly separating the men and women, of course), but hot mineral water could be directed into fifty of its rooms.

Even though the Arlington Hotel doesn't like to discuss whether it's haunted—in fact, they'll downright deny it—many paranormal enthusiasts claim that it is.

Guests have reported flashing lights in their rooms and water faucets that turn on or off without human assistance. Bottles fall off shelves for no apparent reason. Several hotel visitors have felt an invisible entity brush up against them or heard disembodied laughter. Folks who overnight in Room 824 often sense a dark, brooding, even sinister presence while staying there.

For skeptics who must see a ghost to believe in them, there are a number of apparitions roaming the place. A woman in a wedding gown has been spotted standing at windows, peering outside expectantly. A phantom bellman confines himself to the fourth floor, and little girl in a pink dress materializes in the lobby. There are other spectres, too, all wearing clothing from the late 1800s or first decades of the twentieth century.

1886 Crescent Hotel & Spa
75 Prospect Avenue
Eureka Springs, AR 72632
(479) 253-9766 or (877) 342-9766
www.crescent-hotel.com

The five-story hotel (with additional penthouses) sits on fifteen acres in the Ozark Mountains. There are seventy-two rooms and suites in the original main building, plus thirty-eight new two-bedroom cottages on the grounds. The 1886 Crescent Hotel & Spa is listed as a Historic Hotel of America by the National Trust for Historic Preservation.

Basin Park Hotel
12 Spring Street
Eureka Springs, AR 72632
(877) 456-9679
https://basinpark.com

Arlington Resort Hotel & Spa
239 Central Avenue
Hot Springs National Park, AR 71901
(800) 643-1502
https://www.arlingtonhotel.com

CHAPTER 17: THE BELLE OF NEW ORLEANS

Le Pavillon Hotel, Dauphine Orleans Hotel, Chateau Bourbon Hotel, Hotel Monteleone, Omni Royal Orleans Hotel, Hotel Maison de Ville, Place D'Armes Hotel, Andrew Jackson Hotel, Lafitte Guest House, Hotel Provincial, Le Richelieu Hotel

New Orleans, Louisiana

It was quite a day for Dana as she undertook the Herculean task of visiting ten haunted hotels, all within a few blocks of each other. The surprise didn't come until she returned to the hotel where she was staying, where she literally bumped into the apparition of a lost teenage girl.

Dana made her list and checked it twice. She had devised a walking tour of the French Quarter that encompassed almost a dozen different hotels. What made this expedition so special was that virtually every one of the lodgings was supposed to be haunted.

New Orleans was founded on the banks of the Mississippi River in 1718 by Jean-Baptiste Le Moyne de Bienville (also seen as Sieur de Bievnille), and it's believed to be one of the most haunted cities in America. Much of the reputation, no doubt, came from its being the unofficial home of voodoo in the United States. The mysterious belief, a blend of religion, magic, and superstition, arrived in the Crescent City with the importation of Caribbean slaves. Soon, it was established in the Cajun culture.

Rumors persist that one of its most famous practitioners, Marie Laveau, the Voodoo Queen, who died in 1881, still walks down St. Ann Street in the Vieux Carré. Her spirit also comes back to her old house as well as the area around her mausoleum in St. Louis Cemetery No. 1. In the graveyard, she appears in the form of a large black crow or, on occasion, a coal-black hellhound.

Dana would try to stop by the cemetery if she had time, but first: the hotels. She made her plans carefully. She was staying at **Le Pavillon**, nicknamed the Belle of the South. But she didn't choose it for its plush furnishings and accommodations. She picked it because it was reputed to be the most haunted hotel in the city.

One of its most reliable phantoms is a ghostly middle-aged couple, dressed in 1920s-era finery, who are seen holding hands or walking arm in arm as they wander through the hotel, although they're not believed to have been married. They are easy to recognize: The man has a mustache, wears a hat, and sometimes carries a cane or umbrella. There's also always the scent of a strong cigar when he's near. The woman has dark hair, wears a blue gown, and carries a purse. Her perfume is sometimes detected in the third-floor room where she used to stay, and the odor of a cigar lingers on the fourth floor, where he roomed. The scent of tobacco is especially strong between the evening hours of seven and midnight.

Their story is a sad one. The two used to meet at Le Pavillon surreptitiously. On one of their trysts, the man died of a heart attack while walking back to the hotel. His spectre showed up in the building almost immediately; hers joined him after her death in the 1960s. They are sometimes seen separately, but they always seem to be together throughout the afternoon.

There are other apparitions in the hotel as well, including a resident hippie. The guy wears 1960s or 1970s clothing: a bright shirt with billowing sleeves, bell-bottom pants with a large belt buckle . . . and no shoes. The young man, in his late teens or early twenties, runs down the corridors and sometimes vanishes as he walks through walls. Now and then people catch a glimpse of him in the hotel mirrors as well. He's also a bit of a Peeping Tom. Guests have seen him staring at them from outside the window—even when they're staying on the upper floors. He's the one who's usually blamed when personal objects in the rooms move about on their own or guests feel their bedding being pulled by invisible hands in the middle of the night.

Then there's the ghost of a little old lady in a flimsy black nightgown who sits down on the bed next to guests—mostly men—while they're trying to get to sleep. Holy succubus!

Dana thought that, with so many ghosts at Le Pavillon, she might get lucky during her two nights there and see one of them. But she also had a backup plan. She had picked up a map at the city's visitor center and pinpointed ten hotels in the French Quarter that were supposed to be haunted. (Le Pavillon is located just a few blocks outside the Quarter.) By starting first thing in the morning, Dana would be able to get to all of the hotels in one day.

She knew that she was probably on a fool's errand. The chances of catching a spook were slim to none. Spirits don't appear on any schedule, and they're least likely to show up in broad daylight. But she figured it was worth a shot. With so many hotels and so many ghosts purported to be haunting them, who knew?

Bright and early the next morning, Dana was up and out. First on her list: the Dauphine Orleans Hotel. She walked the half block up Poydras to Baronne, then turned right. In just five blocks, she hit Canal Street and the beginning of the French Quarter. As Baronne crossed Canal, it became Dauphine. Just three more blocks, and she was at her first stop.

This was going to be easier than she had imagined. Realizing that the farthest hotel on her list was only about twelve blocks away, Dana relaxed. There was no need to rush. She could take her time and recheck her notes along the way. She reached into her bag, pulled out her journal, and began to read:

Dauphine Orleans Hotel, 415 Dauphine St. The first buildings on this site date back to 1775. The main building was constructed in the 1800s. Like most houses from this time period, it was laid out around a central courtyard. James Audubon is said to have stayed in a cottage on the grounds around 1821 or 1822 while painting part of his *Birds of America.* The hotel bar was once an infamous house of ill repute known as May Baily's Place, which dates back to, at the latest, 1857.

The phantom of a woman—May Baily?—has been spotted moving the bottles behind the bar, and customers sometimes mistake the spectres of ladies dressed in typical nineteenth-century bordello attire for costumed performers. The shade of a Civil War soldier meanders through the courtyard outside the former saloon, and the beds in the guest rooms sometimes shake or bounce on their own, primarily in the very early morning or late in the afternoon.

Dana strolled through the foyer and out into the center court. She looked from end to end, but, as she suspected would be the case, there were no military men there, real or imagined. She could pinpoint Baily's, though: There was a symbolic red light hanging from the wall out front. But it was too early in the day for *any* kind of activity to be going on inside the bar. Unfortunately, there was no way for Dana to check whether the beds were minding their manners in the guest rooms, so it was back out onto Dauphine Street.

She backtracked two blocks toward Canal Street, then turned left onto Iberville. One block down she was at number 800, the **Chateau Bourbon Hotel**. Now a Wyndham Hotel, the Chateau Bourbon started life as the Orleans Ballroom, built by John Davis in 1817. Plantation owners and other members of high society would dance away the evening on the gleaming floor, with chandeliers of European glass sparkling high overhead. Beginning in the 1820s, masquerade balls were held there, presaging the modern Mardi Gras celebrations.

The Civil War years took their toll, and by 1881 the building was owned by the Sisters of the Holy Family, an order of African-American nuns. They transformed the facilities into a convent, a school for girls (the St. Mary's Academy), a small hospital, and an orphanage. When the sisterhood moved out in the 1960s, the place was once again repurposed, this time into the hotel we see today.

The Chateau Bourbon is far from squeamish about its purported ghosts, and it celebrates them on its website. At least seventeen different apparitions have been identified over the past half century. First there is the spectre of a female dancer who twirls all alone on the dance floor of the ballroom, which is now on the hotel's second floor. Her period dress suggests that she is a holdover spirit from the building's earliest days. She's not alone in there, however. The catering staff has been known to see and hear tablecloths and glassware moving by themselves.

The wraith of a Confederate soldier, nicknamed simply "the Man," walks the third, sixth, and seventh stories. Then, too, there are spectral children and women who most likely date to the time the hotel was a convent and school. The young-sters materialize all over the hotel, including inside guest rooms. Even when they remain out of sight, their disembodied voices have been heard. One little girl in particular likes to roll a ball down the sixth-floor hallway. There's one person the spectral children try to avoid: They are said to be afraid of an adult female ban-shee who often shows up in the elevator.

Women have felt an invisible set of lips (thought to belong to a male spirit) kiss them on the cheek. Gentlemen who curse aloud might get slapped on the face by an imperceptible spirit hand.

The ghost whom Dana hoped to meet, and one who seems to be a frequent visitor, is an old man who sits all by himself in the lobby reading a newspaper. He's always smoking a cigar, and people are able to smell the tobacco burning. But if you try to engage the Southern colonel in conversation, he evaporates.

Dana scanned the reception area. There was a young couple checking out of their room and a teenage girl chatting up one of the bellboys. A few folks were sitting in the foyer, but, unfortunately, the elderly entity was not among them.

Reluctantly, Dana stepped out onto the sidewalk. She only had to travel one block down Iberville toward the river until she hit Royal Street. Close to the intersection, she found **Hotel Monteleone**. Dana was amazed by its size. With six hundred rooms, it was probably the largest hotel in the Vieux Carré, and some of America's top writers have been guests: William Faulkner, John Grisham, Ernest Hemingway, Anne Rice, and Tennessee Williams, among others.

It also plays host to about a dozen ghosts. To mention just a few, guests have heard a jazz singer vocalizing inside an empty room and two ten-year-old boys playing hide-and-seek in the hallways. Another youngster who appears to be lost walks up to people and take their hands before vanishing completely. A workman tinkering with the grandfather clock in the lobby during both daytime and nighttime hours turns out not to be real. In addition, doors, especially those of the restaurant, become unlocked on their own, and the elevators will stop on floors where they haven't been called.

But did Dana get to experience anything spooky at the Monteleone? Sadly, no.

Three down, seven to go, she thought to herself as she stepped out the door. At least the rest of the hotels were either on or just a block to one side of Royal. It was time to head into the heart of the Quarter.

By this time, Dana had resigned herself to the fact that she probably would not be having a ghoulie jump out at her. But she was on a mission, and she was going to see it through. She checked her notebook as she breezed through the next four hotels in short order.

Omni Royal Orleans Hotel, 621 St. Louis St. The primary ghost seems to be that of a housemaid dressed in eighteenth-century clothing. The hotel building doesn't date back to that period, so she must be a lingering spirit from an earlier time. She'll show up in guest rooms, switch on the lights, run a bath, or flush the toilet.

Hotel Maison de Ville, 727 Toulouse St. In addition to the main house, the boutique hotel has nine guest cottages that are refurbished former slave quarters. Anomalies on the premises include tapping sounds, voices, wet footprints, shifting objects, and invisible hands pulling off bedsheets or grabbing at people's feet as they lie in bed. There are also occasional full-form materializations of both male and female phantoms.

Place D'Armes Hotel, 625 St. Ann St. There are eighty-five guest rooms in the various buildings making up the property, located just off Jackson Square. The hotel was built on the site of a schoolhouse that burned to the ground, killing many children and the teachers. Some of their souls have been emblazoned onto the scene. The ghost of one girl in particular appears quite often. But the spectre that's probably seen the most frequently is an aged, bearded man from the 1800s who will suddenly appear, acknowledge the visitors, and then just as quickly vanish.

Andrew Jackson Hotel, 919 Royal St. The inn, with twenty-two guest rooms and suites on two levels, is named for the former president who, as a major general in the War of 1812, defeated the British in New Orleans. Legend has it that the hotel was built on the grounds of an all-boys' school that was razed in the fire that destroyed much of the Crescent City in 1788. Five youngsters died in the flames, which may explain the sound of phantom children playing in the central courtyard in the dead of night. Some guests have claimed that the ghost of Jackson himself has wandered through the building. Various other apparitions have been seen, heard, and felt in the hallways on the first and second floors as well as on the stairwell.

It was time for lunch. Past time. Dana had been so excited about getting under way first thing in the morning that she didn't have a full sit-down breakfast. Instead, she had grabbed a croissant, some fruit, and juice at a convenience store midmorning. But now it was well into the afternoon, and she was starving—and exhausted.

Besides, she needed a break. The hotels, the second-story patio balconies, the wrought-iron railings, and the eighteenth- and nineteenth-century furnishings were all starting to blur together in her mind. She had to let what she'd already seen settle in her brain before she tried to cram in anything more.

Dana headed a block up to Bourbon Street and plopped down in the first inviting restaurant she could find. She didn't even look up to see its name as she entered. She just needed a place to sit down and rest for a few minutes. That, and a po'boy.

So far, it had been a disappointing morning for her. Well, she *had* gotten to see some amazing architecture, and everyone she talked to was very nice and helpful. In many places, staff members had been more than happy to show her around their premises once they heard why she was there. But Dana had yet to see anything, well, otherworldly.

She had just three more hotels to go before making her way back to her own hotel. Fortunately, the **Lafitte Guest House**, on Bourbon, was just steps away. The land where the bed-and-breakfast now sits was first deeded to Charity Hospital by the Spanish king in 1793. When the building burned down in 1809, a small combination brick-and-wood house was put in its place. Paul Joseph Gleises replaced it in 1849 with a three-story showcase mansion with an attached annex for the slave (and, after the war, servant) quarters.

Gleises and his wife, Marie, had six children, two of whom died in what is now Room 21. One daughter was felled by yellow fever; the other youngster hanged herself. Although the family moved before the Civil War to Philadelphia, then on to New York, they retained ownership of the property until 1866, when it was sold.

Marie never got over the loss of her girls, and her ghost has returned to keep vigil in the room where they passed. Many guests who stay there are temporarily overcome with unexplainable feelings of intense hopelessness and unfathomable sadness. Visitors to the guest house know when Marie is walking around the inn because lights flicker in her wake. The girl who died of fever hasn't traveled far, either. Her reflection is trapped in a mirror mounted just outside her former room.

Dana snuck onto the second floor and stared into the mirror. Nothing there. Room 21 was occupied, so she couldn't ask to go inside. But it didn't matter. It was getting late, and she still had two more places to cover before dinner.

Next on her list was the **Hotel Provincial**, which was about two blocks away on Chartres Street. The many buildings (as well as the courtyards and two pools) that make up the lodgings lie on what was a land grant from King Louis XV in 1725, just six years after the founding of the city. The land passed through many hands over the two-and-a-quarter centuries until the first two structures of the present hotel, the 100 and 200 buildings, opened in 1961. The 300 building, added six years later, dates to 1825, and the 400 building was a retail store, built in the 1830s, before being acquired in 1964.

Perhaps the most interesting section of the hotel, at least for paranormal purposes, is the 500 building, which was made part of the hotel in 1969. Originally, a military hospital stood on the site in the 1720s. The land then passed to the Catholic Church. In 1831, the property transferred back into private hands, and the old structure was replaced by two new buildings that were used for shops and a boardinghouse. They stood until a fire razed them in 1874, when they were replaced by the building found there today.

But here's the spooky part. For some reason, the long-gone hospital has imprinted itself onto the area as a residual haunting. Guests have walked into their rooms in the 500 building and been startled to see blood on the bedcovers or wounded soldiers crying out in pain. On at least one occasion, people stepped out of the elevator onto the second floor to see the ghostly tableaux of the eighteenth-century hospital in full operation before their eyes. As they started in disbelief, the fantastic vision seemed to quiver and then fade away, until all that was left in its place was the present-day, nondescript hallway.

(Paranormal experts call this last type of spirit phenomenon "retrocognition" or "postcognition." It's an ultra-rare occurrence in which there is a sudden shift or displacement in time, and the past and present briefly touch. Those who experience the anomaly don't actually travel into the past, nor can they interact with it. But they can momentarily see it, almost as if they were watching it from afar or through a window.)

The most frequently repeated story about the Provincial concerns a phantom solider, dressed in a 1930s-era khaki uniform complete with hat and military ribbons. He appears in various rooms and supposedly loves country music. But the story goes on to say that he likes a particular station. If anyone leaves a radio playing, the dial will mysteriously shift to WTIX-FM 94.3.

The tale about the country-music-loving soldier who haunts the Provincial is particularly interesting because there's a similar legend attached to Cottage 4 at the Hotel Maison de Ville. Is it possible that, sometime in the past, storytellers got the two venues mixed up and the mistake has been perpetuated ever since? Stranger things have happened.

The specific radio station the soldier enjoys also raises some questions. At the time of this writing, WTIX-FM 94.3 plays oldies rather than country-and-western music, but perhaps the old wives' tale that identifies the station is a holdover from a time when WTIX had a different format and playlist. Dana stood quietly, hoping to catch a few strains of music floating through the air. But all she heard was the gentle buzz of the French Quarter waking up for the long Saturday night ahead.

She headed the two blocks down Chartres to her final destination, **Le Richelieu Hotel**. The buildings were part of a private home, which the owner renovated into guest quarters in 1969. Several Spanish soldiers were purportedly executed in 1802 right where Le Richelieu Hotel now stands. Their tortured souls haunt the bar area and the swimming pool. But none of them was taking a dip as Dana passed through the courtyard.

With her quest complete and far from her hotel, Dana decided to hail a cab to head back to her room for a relaxing soak in the tub, to be followed by a light dinner—if there can be such a thing in New Orleans. Then, if it wasn't too late, she'd drop in at the cemetery to pay her respects to Marie Laveau. If she had any energy left after that, she'd head back to the Quarter to experience Bourbon Street at night. And who knew? Maybe if she ducked into one of the hotels she had visited earlier, a ghost or two might pop out under the cover of darkness.

As Dana stepped out of her taxi and headed toward the entrance of Le Pavillon, she unexpectedly felt a jolt at her elbow. She turned to come face-to-face with a young girl. She was about fifteen to seventeen, pretty, with pale white skin, doe-like brown eyes, and long brown hair pulled back from her face. The girl was dressed in vintage clothing, all in black: a full dress that fell to her ankles, a broad-brimmed hat, and a shawl, and she held onto a small clutch purse for dear life. If Dana hadn't known better, she'd have thought Blanche DuBois from Tennessee Williams's immortal play *A Streetcar Named Desire* had come to life.

"Pardon me," the girl said with a heavy French accent, "I am . . . lost." Dana watched as the sprite floated down to the cab she had just left, spoke briefly with the driver, and stepped inside. In a moment, the car was off.

Dana was halfway across the lobby when, on a whim, she turned and walked back to the concierge. Something—she couldn't tell what—was troubling her about the girl.

"Excuse me, sir," she ventured. "Did you by any chance see that lady in black who just passed by?"

The man smiled broadly. "Oh, you mean our *petit fantôme*? Our little ghost?"

Dana was stunned. When, that morning before setting out, she had mentally ticked off all the spirits who made their home in Le Pavillon, she had completely forgotten that the hotel was also allegedly haunted by a teenager by the name of Adda (or Ava or Eva, depending where you pick up the story). The girl is said to have lived in the 1840s and was rushing to the docks to meet her family to board a ship when she was killed by a runaway carriage. *No wonder she seemed confused*, Dana thought. *She doesn't know what happened to her or where she is, and she can't find her parents*.

"Yes," the concierge continued, "the poor girl bumps into guests all the time as she wanders through the lobby. Did you smell her perfume? Some people catch a strong whiff of roses or lilacs as she goes by. The ones I pity, though, are the poor cabdrivers. Think what it must be like for them when she disappears from the backseat halfway to the cruise ship terminal."

Dana smiled, slowly at first, then with a broad, contented grin. After years of trying, she had finally seen a ghost, and she wouldn't have known it if she hadn't stopped to ask the concierge. Sometimes you *do* have to rely on the kindness of strangers.

Is there a hotel, inn, or bed-and-breakfast in the New Orleans French Quarter that *isn't haunted?* Here's the contact information for the eleven lodgings mentioned in this chapter.

Le Pavillon Hotel
833 Poydras Street
New Orleans, LA 70112
(504) 581-3111 or (800) 535-9095
www.lepavillon.com

Dauphine Orleans Hotel
415 Dauphine Street
New Orleans, LA 70131
(504) 586-1800 or (800) 521-7111
www.dauphineorleans.com

Chateau Bourbon Hotel
(formerly the Chateau Sonesta Hotel)
800 Iberville Street
New Orleans, LA 70112
(504) 586-0800
www.wyndhamchateaubourbon.com

Hotel Monteleone
214 Royal Street
New Orleans, LA 70140
(504) 523-3341
www.hotelmonteleone.com

Omni Royal Orleans Hotel
621 St. Louis Street
New Orleans, LA 70140
(504) 529-5333
www.omnihotels.com

Hotel Maison de Ville
727 Toulouse Street
New Orleans, LA 70130
(504) 561-5858
www.hotelmaisondeville.com

Place D'Armes Hotel
625 St. Ann Street
New Orleans, LA 70116
(504) 524-4531 or (800) 366-2743
www.placedarmes.com

Andrew Jackson Hotel
919 Royal Street
New Orleans, LA 70116
(504) 561-5881 or (800) 654-0224
www.frenchquarterinns.com

Lafitte Guest House
1003 Bourbon Street
New Orleans, LA 70116
(504) 581-2678
www.lafitteguesthouse.com

Hotel Provincial
1024 Chartres Street
New Orleans, LA 70116
(504) 581-4995 or (800) 535-7922
www.hotelprovincial.com

Le Richelieu Hotel
1234 Chartres Street
New Orleans, LA 70116
(504) 529-2492 or (800) 535-9653
www.lerichelieuhotel.com

St. Louis Cemetery No. 1
425 Basin Street
New Orleans, LA 70112

Under new rules set by the Archdiocese of New Orleans, all visitors to the cemetery must be accompanied by a licensed tour guide. Check locally for listings of private guides, group tours, and entrance times. All tours are during daylight hours.

CHAPTER 18: PUZZLE AT THE PLANTATION

The Myrtles Plantation

St. Francisville, Louisiana

If you're looking to stay at a bed-and-breakfast where there's a high chance of running into an apparition, look no further than the Myrtles Plantation. There have been thousands of recorded sightings, and at least a half dozen spirits are regular guests. But which one will come looking for you?

Chloe was almost finished mixing the cake batter. Everything was in place, she thought. Just one more ingredient, and it would be ready to put in the oven.

The slave worked on a large Louisiana plantation that had been founded in 1796 by a judge named David Bradford. Just four years before that the jurist had been an up-and-coming lawyer in his early twenties in the town of Washington, Pennsylvania. By 1793, he had been appointed as deputy attorney general for the county. But then he became one of the most vocal opponents of the federal government's new excise tax on the production of whiskey, and when a warrant was issued for his arrest in October 1794 during the Whiskey Rebellion, Bradford fled down the Ohio and Mississippi Rivers.

He bought five hundred acres outside St. Francisville, a small town about twenty-five miles north of Baton Rouge, Louisiana, in what was then Spanish West Florida. In 1796, he built a two-story antebellum mansion on the highest point of the bayou property—some say on top of an ancient Tunica Indian burial ground. He called his new home Laurel Grove.

Bradford soon established himself as a judge as well as a prosperous planter. After he received an official pardon from President John Adams in March 1799, Bradford sent for his wife and children, whom he had left behind in Pennsylvania until his safety was ensured. He died at Laurel Grove in 1817; his wife remained at the plantation until her death in 1830.

One of their daughters, Sarah Matilda, caught the eye of Clark Woodruff while he was studying law under Bradford. After the judge's death, Woodruff lost no time in asking for Sarah's hand in marriage. The wedding took place in November 1817 when Sarah was just fourteen years old.

Woodruff loved his wife, but as was often the case with plantation owners in the Deep South at the time, he took one of his slaves, a woman named Chloe, as a mistress. To make his rendezvous with her easier, he moved the young woman into the main house as his children's servant.

Chloe had a bad habit, though. When she was able to sneak away from chores, she would often eavesdrop on her master's private meetings in the gentlemen's parlor. Whether it was out of simple curiosity or an attempt to overhear information that she could use against her master is unknown, but Woodruff caught the slave on several occasions and each time gave her a stern warning.

But finally Chloe went too far. Several prominent businessmen caught her listening in on one of the conversations, and the plantation owner had no recourse but to punish the slave. He not only banished her from the mansion but also ordered that her left ear be cut off.

Humiliated by the mutilation, Chloe wrapped her head in a bandanna from then on. Working back in the fields, she yearned for her days of relative ease in the big house. She finally came up with a plan to get back into her former lover's good graces.

And so, there she was, standing in front of a hot oven mixing batter. One of the Woodruffs' young daughters was going to have a birthday. Chloe would bake a cake for the celebration, but she would add a secret ingredient: oleander. Though the decorative flower was fragrant and beautiful to behold, the herb was extremely toxic. A small handful of leaves could sicken an adult; ingestion of a single leaf could prove fatal to a baby.

But Chloe's intent wasn't to kill the Woodruffs. Oh, no. She would blend just enough of the poisonous plant into the cake to make the children slightly sick. Then, claiming that she was a native healer, Chloe would offer to nurse the youngsters back to health. Once they recovered, she would be welcomed back into the house with open arms.

The cake was accepted, and it was served to Sarah Matilda and the girls. But Chloe had miscalculated how little of the shrub was necessary to be deadly, and Mrs. Woodruff and her daughters immediately fell violently ill. They began to vomit, developed diarrhea, and suffered seizures. Within hours, the mother and her children were dead.

The judge had been called away from the plantation and was absent from the party. When he returned, he discovered that his entire family was gone. Insane with grief and anger, he stormed into the slaves' quarters, certain that one of them had been responsible. Fearful for their own safety, the other slaves betrayed Chloe. Before long the murderess was captured, and Woodruff had her hanged from a plantation tree for all to see. Then, after Chloe's corpse was cut down, it was loaded down with rocks and thrown into the river.

With Chloe dead, Woodruff had every reason to believe that the slave would soon be forgotten. But that presumed she would accept her passage to the Next World quietly. Instead, Chloe's spirit almost immediately returned to the mansion.

Her ghost, wearing her distinctive green bandanna, was soon seen inside the house. Furniture began to rearrange itself overnight behind closed doors. During the day, ladies (especially those walking through the parlor where Chloe had spied on her master) would have one of their earrings pulled off by an invisible hand. Why was only one taken? Well, isn't it obvious? After Chloe was disfigured, she no longer had need of a complete pair.

It seems she also returns the jewelry after she tires of it. To this day, a single earring will turn up out of the blue in some unusual spot.

As it turns out, Chloe's not the only ghost to walk the grounds. The spectres of her victims—Sarah and the two children—show up in a large mirror that hangs in the manor. Visitors looking at their reflections sometimes see one or more of the ethereal entities standing behind them. As is usual in such cases, when the people turn, no one is there. From time to time the otherworldly guests leave their handprints behind on the glass.

The little girls can be quite mischievous, and they don't always remain indoors. They've been spotted all over the plantation. On several occasions they've surprised guests in the house who look up to see two small faces peering at them from the other side of the window—even when they're on the second floor. It's no use trying to catch the girls, though. By the time anyone goes outside to look for them, the spectres have disappeared.

As with many ghost stories, there are multiple variations of the Chloe story. One suggests that the slave was actually thrown out of the house because Sarah caught her with her husband in the children's nursery. That version doesn't mention the mutilation of Chloe's ear.

In some accounts, the poisoning was no accident. Chloe planned to do away with the family all along.

The question remains: Did Chloe exist at all? There is no record of her name in the county archives in the lists of Woodruff holdings. And there's another discrepancy in the reports as well. Sarah Matilda died of yellow fever in 1823, and her two children, a *boy* and a girl, died of the same thing a year later, *not* from a poisoned cake.

But a little thing like the truth doesn't matter when spirits are at play, does it?

In 1834, Judge Woodruff sold Laurel Grove to Ruffin Grey Stirling, whose family already owned several plantations in the area. In 1850, Stirling remodeled the mansion, adding a southern wing to the house for his large family as well as a gallery with a wrought-iron railing along the front of the building. He also increased the size of the property to more than 1,500 acres and bought about a hundred more slaves. It was during this renovation and expansion that Stirling changed the name of the manor to the **Myrtles Plantation** due to the number of myrtle trees on the grounds. Ruffin Grey and his wife, Mary, had eight sons (six of whom would perish in the Civil War) and one daughter, Sarah.

After Stirling died in 1854, Mary hired Sarah's husband, William Drew Winter, a lawyer, to manage the plantation. Eventually, she gave the young couple the deed to the property. The War Between the States was financially devastating, forcing the family into bankruptcy. They temporarily lost the house in 1868, but Sarah, as the heir to Ruffin Stirling, managed to get it back two years later.

Then, on January 26, 1871, Winter was inside the house when he heard a horse rapidly approaching. A voice from the unknown rider called out to him, and Winter walked onto the veranda to greet the visitor. Suddenly, a shot rang out, and Winter, struck in the chest and mortally wounded, staggered back into the house. He desperately tried to make it up the staircase to bid farewell to his beloved Sarah. She had heard the gunfire and by then was standing on the upper landing. Winter managed to drag himself up seventeen of the twenty steps before he collapsed, dead. Sarah lived for another seven years with the horrific memory of watching her husband die at her feet. (Although at least one newspaper identified the assassin as E. S. Webber, the man was never prosecuted.)

Many who have stayed in the house since have claimed they've heard heavy, disembodied footsteps dragging their way up the deserted staircase. But the mysterious thumping sounds never make it past the seventeenth step.

The Myrtles Plantation changed hands over the next hundred years, and much of the property was sold off. Some of the ghost stories still being told today started in the 1950s when a widow named Marjorie Munson owned the place. Many of the early tales centered on the apparition of an old woman wearing a green bonnet or beret similar to Chloe's scarf.

In the 1970s, Arlin Dease and Mr. and Mrs. Robert Ward bought the plantation. They had the mansion restored with 1850s period furnishings, including French-style furniture, stained glass, Aubusson tapestries, and Baccarat crystal chandeliers. The Chloe story, or at least the details about a poisoned cake and the green head wrap, seems to have taken hold during this period.

John and Frances Kermeen Myers purchased the Myrtles Plantation in the 1970s and lived there for eight and a half years. (Kermeen has written extensively about her time there.) The mansion came into the public eye when the Myers opened it for tours and as a bed-and-breakfast. Then in Myrtles Plantation was added to the National Register of Historic Places on September 6, 1978. John and Teeta Moss are the property's current owners. They also embrace the plantation's haunted history and continue to operate the mansion as a B&B and offer tours.

As more and more people came to visit the plantation, the number of reported ghost sightings has skyrocketed. Some guests stay there specifically in the hopes of spying a spirit, and many have been rewarded. Even when phantoms don't materialize, they sometimes show up in photographs or as streaks of light.

Some overnight visitors have reported waking up in one of the upstairs bedrooms to find the spirit of a female slave looming over their bed. Other guests have seen the ghost's shadow moving across the walls. According to an old wives' tale, when one of William Winter's daughters contracted yellow fever, he turned in desperation to the local voodoo queen. The priestess, who was a slave on the neighboring Solitude Plantation, was believed to be able to heal the sick and dying with secret herbal medicines. Despite the slave's incantations over the girl for three days, the youngster died. Winter, in fury, hanged the hapless woman from the chandelier in that very room—the same room she haunts to this day. (Some versions of this story give the slave's name as Clio, which sounds suspiciously like Chloe, or Sarah. Another variation says the girl who died of fever was Stirling's daughter instead. It's probable that over the past centuries, all of the various legends have become inextricably interwoven, and it's impossible to tell exactly where one ends and the next one begins.)

Other ephemeral figures floating around the Myrtles include a fussy maid, a little girl (who may or may not be one of the Woodruff daughters) bouncing on the bed, and a woman in a dark dress who dances in one of the parlors. A few guests who stay in the former nursery (where Woodruff had his assignations with Chloe) have even been "romanced" by an invisible incubus that may be the spirit of the judge himself.

The apparition of a sixteen-year-old Confederate soldier haunts another room. After being slightly injured, the boy hid in the Myrtles. When the locals discovered him, they were so incensed he hadn't gone back into battle that they dragged him from the mansion and hanged him.

In addition to the appearance of all the phantoms, the house has its share of other paranormal phenomena: footsteps, whispered voices, the scent of perfume wafting in the air, cold spots, lights turning on and dimming, and doors that unlock themselves. The Bridal Suite (the Stirlings' former bedroom) is particularly active.

Finally, there's one ghost on the property that's only ever seen outside. He's a caretaker dressed in khaki pants who tries to turn away visitors at the front gate to the plantation. When the startled guests try to complain, the watchman vanishes. The crabby wraith is believed to be a cantankerous worker from the 1920s who was murdered somewhere on the grounds.

So if one day you decide to tour the plantation or perhaps spend a night or two there, beware if a cranky old coot tries to shoo you off as you turn up the driveway. Take a close look. You may have already come face-to-face with one of the many wandering spirits populating the Myrtles Plantation.

The Myrtles Plantation
7747 US Highway 61
P.O. Box 1100
St. Francisville, LA 70775
(225) 635-6277 or (800) 809-0565
www.myrtlesplantation.com

CHAPTER 19: THE MENGER MYSTERIES

Menger Hotel
San Antonio, Texas

San Antonio's Menger Hotel was built in 1859, so there's been plenty of time for its more than thirty ghosts to check in. The most frequently recognized are Richard King, who once kept an apartment at the hotel, and Sallie White, a former maid and murder victim.

Myra couldn't believe it. They were here again. This was where she had met Jorge, while attending a conference in San Antonio. On their last night in town, they had managed to get away from their colleagues for a few hours and spend an hour or two walking along this very stretch.

The River Walk, wide parallel pathways set a block below street level, runs along both sides of the San Antonio River as it meanders through the center of town. It's one of the city's most popular tourist destinations, filled with great restaurants, festive bars, galleries, and kiosks overflowing with trinkets and souvenirs. And lots and lots of people. But as they made their way through the crowd, Myra barely noticed them. That night, the only thing that registered was the man strolling beside her.

Jorge felt the same way about Myra. He had grown up locally, not more than a mile or two out of the city. He'd been visiting the water path as long as he could remember. But tonight was different. Tonight he was in love.

And to think the River Walk had almost never been built. Jorge had learned all about it in elementary school. After a severe flood in 1921, plans were drawn up to dam and divert the river so that it would no longer flow through downtown. The existing channel would be paved over and turned into a giant storm drain. Work began on the project five years later, but a farsighted architect named Robert Hugman made an audacious recommendation. He suggested that, rather than convert the riverbed into drainage, a controlled stream of water should be allowed to continue to run through the city. Both sides of the river could then be developed with shops and eateries. Eventually the proposal was accepted, and money from the WPA program allowed construction to begin in 1939. The two-and-a-half-mile riverside pathway was completed seven years later. Now, after seven decades, it was impossible to imagine a San Antonio without the River Walk.

Myra and Jorge's first stroll along the waterway was one of the most magical nights that either had ever experienced. By evening's end, they knew that they *had* to see each other again, even though she'd be flying back to Denver the next day and he was headed back home to Austin. Their courtship continued, at first by phone and e-mail. But before long, there were visits back and forth, and after a year of mutually pursuing each other, they married.

Jorge made the move to Colorado. They bought a home in the upscale Greenwood Village area, just south of Denver, and two years after that, their son, Ben, was born.

As the couple's tenth anniversary approached, Myra started hinting that their boy was now old enough that she and Jorge could get away for a weekend, just the two of them. Her doting mother would be more than happy to watch the boy, and little Ben couldn't get enough of his grandma.

But where would they go? The more exotic destinations—Hawaii, Florida— were out of the question. They could only take two nights at most. Maybe one of the spas in Colorado Springs, or perhaps a resort up in the mountains.

Leave it to Jorge, still wildly romantic, to come up with the perfect idea. They would go to San Antonio. It would be their first time back since they met.

They decided to splurge and took a suite, the King Ranch Room, at the celebrated **Menger Hotel**. Now on the National Register of Historic Places, the 316-room hotel officially opened its doors on February 1, 1859. It was built by William Menger, who, after emigrating from Germany, came to San Antonio sometime in the early 1840s.

Menger founded a brewery—the first in Texas—with partner Charles Phillip Degen. The company flourished, and Menger soon set up a hotel next to the factory. The first rooms of the original two-story stone building designed by San Antonio architect John M. Fries opened in 1857. Forty more rooms were added the following year, as well as a tunnel to connect the hotel to the brewery. By the time construction was complete in 1859, the hotel was one of the grandest west of the Mississippi.

In the years following the Civil War, the Menger became the most popular hotel in the region. The city grew in leaps and bounds after the railroad arrived in 1877, so the hotel added an east annex in 1881 to accommodate visitors. The building was enlarged again in 1909 and 1951, and the entire place was completely renovated and modernized in the 1980s.

On the weekend of their anniversary, Myra and Jorge took off early on Friday, and by late afternoon they were following the bellman up to their suite. The young man quickly showed them the amenities, then left them to settle in. The rooms were exquisite, from the Victorian-style furnishings to the large four-poster bed. The suite had been named for Richard King, the founder of the fabled King Ranch. For many years he had kept those very hotel rooms as a private apartment.

King was born in New York City in 1824. He came from a poor Irish family, and his father indentured him to a jeweler when the boy was only nine years old. King fled, stowing away on a ship headed toward Alabama. Rather than putting him ashore after he was discovered, the crew adopted the lad and taught him the ropes.

King was a fast and eager learner, and he had his steamboat pilot's license by the time he was sixteen. Two years later, he was running a fleet of boats on the Apalachicola and Chattahoochee Rivers.

In 1847, at the urging of his friend Mifflin Kenedy, King traveled to the Rio Grande River to help him ferry soldiers and supplies during the Mexican-American War. The two, along with other partners, continued to transport goods on the Rio Grande all the way up to 1874. During the Civil War, they expanded their trade to ship supplies in and out of the Confederacy, which they managed to do by sailing their ships under the neutral Mexican flag.

Much of what they carried came from their own ranches. King had started buying huge expanses of land between the Nueces River and the Rio Grande in 1853. At the end of the War Between the States, King owned 146,000 acres. By the time of his death, the King Ranch had grown to more than six hundred thousand.

King married in 1854, and the couple had five children. Because his business dealings took him to San Antonio so often, King rented a suite of rooms at the Menger Hotel on a full-time basis. He spent the last several months of his life in the apartment, and he died there of stomach cancer on April 14, 1885. His funeral was held downstairs in the hotel parlor. King was buried in San Antonio, but after his wife passed in 1925, his remains were disinterred and moved to King Ranch to lie by her side.

Though well known throughout the Southwest, King was far from the most famous person to stay at the Menger Hotel. Guests have included Generals Robert

E. Lee and Ulysses S. Grant (presumably at different times), Babe Ruth, Sarah Bernhardt, and Mae West.

Theodore Roosevelt first stayed at the hotel in 1892 while in Texas on a hunting expedition. Six years later, he made the Menger Bar his headquarters when he came to town to recruit cowboys to join his Rough Riders. (The bar is a replica of the taproom at the House of Lords Club in London, right down to the cherry wood paneling and the gold-plated spittoon.) Roosevelt's final visit came in 1905, during his presidency, to be honored at a banquet.

Myra and Jorge freshened up and made their way out of the hotel. Instinctively, they turned toward the River Walk. No words had to be spoken. Where else would they spend their first night in town?

The next morning, they slept in late. After an unhurried brunch, they made their way across the plaza for the obligatory visit to the Alamo. Jorge had been there many times as a youngster on field trips, but beyond what he was forced to learn in school, he had never really thought much about the place. Myra had peeked into the mission during that conference a decade earlier—how could she not?—but it had really been checklist tourism: been there, done that. This time, however, as they ambled through the grounds, they fully appreciated the enormous sacrifice that had taken place there.

Built in 1724 as the Mission San Antonio de Valero, the structure was used until 1793 by Spanish missionaries to educate and care for the local Native Americans they converted to Christianity. In the early 1800s, it was used by the Mexican army to house a company of soldiers. The Alamo probably got its name from the soldiers' hometown, Álamo de Parras in the state of Coahuila.

During the War for Texas Independence, more than two hundred men, including co-commanders James Bowie and William B. Travis, as well as Davy Crockett, his company of Tennesseans, and a group of Hispanic volunteers, barricaded themselves in the Alamo to engage Mexican forces led by Gen. Antonio Lopéz de Santa Anna. The army laid siege to the mission beginning on February 23, 1836. On March 6, the soldiers finally stormed the fort and breeched its walls. The brave defenders fought to the very last man.

After their visit to the mission, Myra and Jorge spent the remainder of their afternoon arm in arm, leisurely poking in and out of little arts-and-crafts boutiques in the La Villita district. By six o'clock, they were back at the hotel, getting ready for their last night in Fiesta City. Then it was off for a slow boat ride on the river, followed by a light dinner on the waterside patio of Casa Rio, the first restaurant to open on the River Walk. Drinks came next at the Menger Bar— tossing back a few in memory of old Teddy—then up to the room for an intimate evening alone.

Or so they thought.

It was about midnight. The pair was lounging in the outer room, Myra standing by the window, gazing absentmindedly down at lovers passing on the street below. Jorge was flipping through channels on the TV, even though he had no real interest in watching anything. Myra turned back toward the sofa, and her mouth dropped open. The shadowy figure of a man was walking across the far side of the room, seemingly oblivious to everything around him. Jorge caught Myra's eye, then followed it until he, too, saw the spirit.

The mysterious stranger neither spoke nor acknowledged the young couple. He was handsome, ruggedly built, probably in his fifties, with wavy black hair and a long, full goatee but no moustache. He wore a jacket and vest that seemed to date to the nineteenth century. In a determined stride, the apparition walked straight toward the wall separating the room from the hallway—and passed right through!

As quickly as it had appeared, the spectre was gone.

Myra and Jorge turned to each other and simultaneously cried out an incredulous, "Did you see that?" They had heard that the hotel was haunted. It was no big secret, but they never expected in a million years that they would actually see one of the ghosts. They knew who it was from one of the old photographs they'd seen in the lobby. It was none other than the suite's longtime eponymous occupant, Capt. Richard King.

Apparently the otherworldly experience of our anniversary couple is not all that unusual. For whatever reason, whether it's because King was fond of the suite during his life or because it's where his spirit left his body, he has decided to remain behind at the Menger. His apparition has been seen all over the hotel, but it's seen most often in his namesake suite, walking through a wall where a door once stood.

King's ghost is only one of thirty-two different phantoms that have been spotted in the hotel. One is unmistakable: Teddy Roosevelt returns to the Menger Bar off the lobby, where he sits quietly nursing a drink. Bully!

Another spectre is that of Sallie White, a young maid who used to work at the Menger. Her abusive husband attacked her in the hotel on March 26, 1876, fatally injuring her. She died two days later. The hotel paid the $32 for her funeral expenses. Perhaps it's out of gratitude or loyalty that her ghost lingers in the hallways she used to service. She wears a period uniform—a long gray skirt and her hair tied back by a scarf around her forehead—and she's seen carrying clean towels and linen to the rooms.

The identity of the other spirits is uncertain. Staff members have often approached one, an elderly woman wearing wire-rimmed glasses and a nineteenth-century-style blue dress. She always sits by herself, knitting in the hotel's original lobby. If anyone tries to speak to her, she instantly disappears.

One overnight guest in the hotel reported that an ethereal intruder, dressed in gray pants and a buckskin coat, appeared by the side of his bed. The ghost seemed to be arguing with an unseen spirit. The spectral man demanded, "Are you gonna stay or are you gonna go?" three times, then faded into nothingness.

Oftentimes, the paranormal visitors don't become visible but find other ways to let their presence be known. Kitchen utensils will sometimes move themselves from one place to another or float in the air. Now and then, heavy footsteps are heard around the building, and at least one pair of weathered military boots such as the ones worn at the Battle of the Alamo have been discovered in a fourth-floor office.

Probably this last claim is just an old wives' tale: The boots would be tangible, irrefutable evidence of spectral materialization, but no one seems to know what became of them. But the story does make one wonder if a couple of restless souls from the massacre ever wandered the few hundred yards across the plaza from the mission into the hotel.

The Alamo, it seems, is haunted, too. After Santa Anna captured the make-shift fortress, he commanded that all of the defenders' bodies should be thrown into a mass grave and the mission torn down. He soon left the area, having other battles to fight. The workers who were left behind dutifully buried the dead, but they never carried out the general's second order. It's said that when they tried to break down the Alamo's walls, ghostly hands bearing flaming torches emerged from the stone to stop them. Some heard disembodied voices threatening to kill anyone who touched the building. Needless to say, the men scattered and never returned to the scene. It's been said that, to this day, phantoms occasionally pop out of the walls at night.

Remember the Alamo! As unlikely as all the ghostly tales about it and the Menger Hotel may seem, there have been too many to dismiss out of hand.

Menger Hotel
204 Alamo Plaza
San Antonio, TX 78205
(210) 223-4361
www.mengerhotel.com

The hotel is located directly across Crockett Road from the Alamo.

The Alamo
300 Alamo Plaza
San Antonio, TX 78205
(210) 225-1391
www.thealamo.org

Admission is free, but reservations are required. Visiting hours are subject to change.

PART THREE: THE MOUNTAIN STATES

CHAPTER 20: THE BIGELOW BANSHEES

Bigelow Hotel
Ogden, Utah

Some hotels can claim one or two resident ghosts. The Bigelow Hotel, formerly the Ben Lomond Suites Hotel, has at least six. Most of the spectres seem to date from the 1940s to the 1970s, but some may have been around even longer. The hotel's been there in one form or another for more than a hundred years.

Jay loved trains. All trains. Even the modern if impersonal Amtrak cars and the Bullet Train in Japan. But his real passion was the old steam engines, the smoke-bellowing workhorses that built America—so much so he only allowed trains with "steam" engines run on the tracks of the model railroad that had overtaken his garage.

Yes, Jay was a "railfan" (the one-word nickname given to real devotees), but he was no foamer (as excessive enthusiasts are sometimes known) and certainly not an FRN (a comically derisive and unprintable acronym—delicately, an "effen rail nut"—reserved for the most over-the-top rail zealots).

As he grew up, Jay had plenty of opportunity to visit the many railroad museums scattered throughout the Northeast. But his great ambition in life, his dream, had always been to one day travel west to Utah to stand on Promontory Summit, where back in 1869 a ceremonial golden spike was driven to link the United Pacific and Central Pacific rail lines, creating the first transcontinental railroad.

(Jay scoffed at those who erroneously called the site Promontory Point, which is actually thirty-five miles south of the Summit. Intellectually, he understood the mistake: Newspapermen had reported the wrong location, and the error has stuck all these years. What he couldn't comprehend was why people cared so little about such an important event in American history. Maybe, Jay mused, he was a closet FRN after all.)

When, after thirty years of working in the same office, Jay's company was downsized and he was offered early retirement and a generous severance package, he jumped at the chance. He would now be free to take his fantasy vacation: a nationwide road trip by rail. He'd head west on the California Zephyr, which passed through a spectacular cut in the Rockies between Denver and Grand Junction, and then return on the Southwest Chief.

He'd have to travel down to Los Angeles to make the loop, but he really didn't care whether he made it all the way to the coast. The only essential stop was the visit to Promontory. And so, that following spring, Jay set out. His plan was to be at the Golden Spike National Historic Site on May 10, the anniversary of the date on which the fabled spike had been driven, when there would be a reenactment of the ceremony, complete with two steam engines meeting nose-to-nose on the same track.

The national park wasn't the easiest place to get to, as least not by train. Rail service over the summit had been discontinued in 1904 when a trestle was built across the Great Salt Lake to allow locomotives to bypass a steep grade and forty-three miles of curves. The nearest city of any size is Ogden, Utah, but in order to get there, Jay first had to travel into Salt Lake City, then take a commuter rail, the FrontRunner, for the last forty miles into Ogden. After that, Jay would have to rent a car to travel the fifty-six miles west to Promontory Summit.

But for Jay, it would all be worth it.

By the time he made it to Ogden, after so much time in sleeper cars on the train, Jay welcomed a couple of nights in a real bed. He decided to spend them in luxury, in one of the city's most historic places to stay, the **Bigelow Hotel**.

In 1891, E. A. Reed built a five-story hotel, which he named after himself, at the corner of Washington Boulevard and Twenty-fifth Street. A. Perry, the president and cofounder of the Ogden Bank, rightly reasoned that a rapidly growing city like Ogden needed first-class lodgings, so in 1926 he formed a corporation with three hundred stockholders to purchase the Reed Hotel and completely remodel it.

Perry engaged Utah architects Hodgson & McClenahan to transform the building. Their first step was to raze and refurbish the interior of the Reed while letting the basic structure stand. An eight-story L-shaped tower with 350 guest rooms was added to the original hotel.

The new overall design was Italian Renaissance Revival. The exterior of the base, some of the lower floors, and the uppermost stories were faced with terracotta. The interior public rooms were adorned in a cacophony of styles, from Florentine flourishes to the LeConte Stewart murals in the sitting area known as the Shakespeare Room. Dark wood paneling was used in the English Room to re-create a chamber in Britain's Bromley Castle. The Georgian Room, located on the mezzanine, had neoclassical ornamentations associated with eighteenth-century Scottish architect Robert Adam. Even the coffee shop was festively festooned in an Arabian theme. There was enough meeting space to seat a thousand for dinner, as well as several small lounges, in-house shops, and a bank. Fireproofing was installed throughout. In all, $1.2 million was spent in the hotel's renovation. As a final step, it was rechristened the Bigelow Hotel. It opened to universal acclaim in 1927, and it instantly ranked as one of the top hotels in the state.

In 1933, Marriner S. Eccles, another Utah banker, purchased the Bigelow and renamed it the Ben Lomond Hotel. (Eccles is better remembered for his time in government than as a hotelier. He was instrumental in creating the Federal Deposit Insurance Corporation (FDIC), helped craft the Emergency Banking Act of 1933, and was head of the Federal Reserve for fourteen years, serving under both FDR and Truman.)

The Ben Lomond Hotel was a mainstay of the community for more than forty years. It then passed through a number of owners, including, for a time, Weber County, which used it for government offices. In the 1980s, the property was acquired by the Radisson chain, which converted the guest rooms into ninety-seven suites and twenty-three condos (the latter of which are all located on the tenth and eleventh floors). The hotel was listed on the National Register of Historic Places in 1990. New owners bought the building in 2016, and the following year, in a nod to history, the name was changed to the Bigelow Hotel and Residences. It now features 83 hotel rooms, 23 apartments, 15 offices, and seven banquet and meeting rooms.

After dragging himself the long three and a half blocks from Union Station to the hotel, Jay couldn't have cared less about its illustrious past. By the time he had finally entered the lobby, he barely noticed the crystal chandeliers and marble floor. All he could think about was getting a good night's sleep. He'd start out fresh first thing in the morning. He pampered himself by taking a condo for his two nights' stay, and armed with his key for 1102, he headed for the elevator. Once inside the room, he quickly showered and dropped into bed, a dead weight. He was out as soon as his head hit the pillow.

To quote a cliché, he felt like a new man the next morning. He picked up his car, then, map in hand, headed out toward Golden Spike National Park.

Jay knew that almost nothing he would see there was original. Back in 1869, as soon as the speeches were over and the press photographs were taken, the original spike was removed for safekeeping and replaced with a regular iron spike. (Jay made a mental note that one day he would visit the Cantor Arts Center in Stanford, California, where the original Golden Spike is on permanent display.) Even the mile-long track of rail in the park isn't the real McCoy. The rails across Promontory Summit had been pulled up in 1942 and reused in military depots as part of the war effort. The two steam engines at the park are also replicas of the Union Pacific's coal-burning No. 119 and the Jupiter, Central Pacific's wood-burning No. 60.

During the winter season, the new locomotives are kept in an engine house to protect them from the elements. But on Saturday during the summer months and on special occasions such as the May 10 anniversary, the engines move out onto the park's single stretch of track and cautiously approach one another until they're just a few feet apart. That year, Jay, along with railroad aficionados from all over the country, was treated to the thrill of a lifetime as the mighty locomotives steamed into view.

It was late afternoon by the time Jay got back to the hotel. The sun seemed high enough in the sky, but deep shadows had already begun to fall on the foothills. Jay looked up to the Wasatch Mountains overlooking the city. To the east he could plainly make out Mount Ogden and, to the north, the peak of Ben Lomond, from which his hotel got its onetime name.

What a beautiful setting, thought Jay. Ogden had been founded in 1846 by a fur trapper named Miles Goodyear. The settlement, which he named Fort Buenaventura, was at the juncture of the Ogden and Weber Rivers, about a mile west of the current downtown. The following year, Mormon settlers bought the budding community, by then known as Brownsville. The town's name was changed once again, to Ogden, to honor Peter Skene Ogden, a trader and expedition leader for the Hudson's Bay Company.

By 1869, the population stood at ten to fourteen thousand. Ogden quickly became a railroad hub, earning it the nickname Junction City. At the time, most passengers traveling from San Francisco to Chicago passed through Ogden rather than the much larger Salt Lake City. The Ben Lomond Suites had been built to accommodate many of those travelers.

It had been a long day. As Jay headed back to his room, he decided he needed a long, hot bath. He could use a good soak after so many days jostling across the country by train. He could already see himself drawing the water, making sure it was just the right temperature, and slipping in. It would be heaven!

But as soon as he opened the door to his room, he immediately knew something was wrong. Water was already running in the bathroom! He rushed in, and sure enough, a slow but steady stream was splashing into the jetted tub. Fortunately the drain was open. Had he left the tap on when he took off in the morning? Or had housekeeping made the error?

Well, no real harm done, Jay decided. Within just a few minutes, he had immersed himself into the generous tub and allowed his mind to drift back to what had been a perfect day. The weather, which could be tricky at that time of year, had been on its best behavior. The crowds hadn't been too large, so he had been able to take hundreds of unobstructed photographs of the engine run and the costumed actors pounding an ersatz Golden Spike into place.

Without warning, Jay felt something prod at him, pushing against his back. Was his mind playing tricks, or was it just the water jets? Then, not ten seconds later, he felt what seemed to be invisible hands pressing hard against his arm and side. Something, some unseen force, wanted him out of the tub!

Jay took the hint. He leapt out, quickly toweled off, and lay down on the bed. His mind raced. What had just happened? There had to *some* explanation for what he had felt.

He never came up with an answer. If he had only thought to ask the front desk clerk on his way out the next morning, he would have gone away with at least a few clues. It was policy not to discuss such matters, but the receptionist might have shared some of the rumors about ghosts inhabiting the Bigelow for decades, including the room in which Jay had stayed.

According to an old wives' tale—and there are no specific names or dates ever attached to the story—a woman on her honeymoon accidentally drowned in the bathtub in Room 1102. Ever since, occupants have occasionally been startled to find the water running, even though no one had turned on the faucets. Many people reported feeling unseen hands shoving them in the tub.

Another spirit, the drowning victim's son (from the woman's previous marriage), went to the hotel to pick up some personal effects his mother had left behind. He chose to stay in 1101, next door to the room where she died. Sometime in the middle of the night, overcome with despair, he committed suicide.

Guests and staff alike have heard the soft, incomprehensible voices of both phantoms in those rooms, and housekeeping has discovered unexplainable depressions on the unused beds that looked as if someone had been lying on them. According to some reports, every so often, the apparitions even materialize.

At least one other room on the eleventh floor is haunted. Receptionists have gotten telephone calls from Room 1106 at times when they knew no one was staying there. As soon as the clerk would speak, the line would go dead. Legend has it that the mystery caller is the spectre of a woman who stayed at the then-Ben Lomond while waiting for her son to return from World War II. Some sources claim she found out that he had been killed. Regardless, the woman stopped eating and eventually starved to death in that very room. (Yet another variation of the tale says that the anxious mother checked out of the hotel very much alive, but for some reason her apparition has returned to make those pesky phone calls.)

A female spirit has been caught roaming the corridors. She's thought to be Eccles's wife, presumably his first wife, Mary (also known as Maysie), to whom the tycoon was married when he bought the hotel. (Eccles and his second wife stayed more often at the apartments he maintained in San Francisco and at the Hotel Utah in Salt Lake City.) Even when Maysie isn't visible, people know when she's around by her distinctive lilac perfume. The scent is evident most often on the fifth floor, the top floor, and in the elevators.

A ghost in the lobby has never been seen, but his presence is certainly felt. He's believed to be a night clerk who was stabbed to death by a fifteen-year-old boy while the youth was robbing the hotel in 1976. The sixty-five-year-old spirit apparently hangs out by the reception desk, turning on the sound system to play music in the foyer and fiddling with the phone cords.

A security guard has run across a noncorporeal entity (thought to be female) in the third-floor gymnasium, and guests in Room 212 have been subject to spectral hands shoving them out of the way.

There's been a lot of other paranormal activity in the hotel that's never been pinned down to a particular spirit. There are strange cold spots found throughout the hotel, the sounds of footsteps and closing doors, the echo of phantom people moving around overhead, the scent of perfume, and calls to the front desk from unoccupied rooms. Then, too, the elevators sometimes act up. They'll stop on their own at the fifth or the tenth floor, despite the fact that the call button hasn't been pushed for either.

None of the spirits—and we're talking about at least six—is ever malicious, so there's never any danger to visitors. And in a way, it's nice to know they're there. They contribute yet another chapter to the long and continuing story of one of Utah's most celebrated inns, the Bigelow Hotel and Residences.

Bigelow Hotel and Residences
(formerly the Ben Lomond Hotel)
2510 Washington Boulevard
Ogden, UT 84401
https://bigelow-hotel-ascend
-ogden.h-rez.com

CHAPTER 21: "HERE'S JOHNNY . . ."

Stanley Hotel
Estes Park, Colorado

Stephen King may have been inspired to write The Shining *during his stay at the Stanley Hotel, but the paranormal activity that takes place there is anything but fictional. The whole fourth floor seems to be haunted. As are the billiards room, and the bar, and the ballroom, and the . . .*

Cameron couldn't believe it. He was actually checking into Room 217 at the Overlook—rather, the **Stanley Hotel**—in Estes Park, Colorado. This was the very same room where Stephen King stayed when he visited the hotel that featured so prominently (as the Overlook) in the author's third novel, *The Shining.* Cameron had planned the weekend a full year in advance to be sure the room was available.

Cameron was a King fanatic. As far as he could tell, he had read everything the guy ever published, including the books he wrote under the pen name Richard Bachman and the story he released as John Swithen. Cameron's favorites? Well, it was hard for him to pick, but they were probably the early ones: *Carrie,* which was King's first book, *Salem's Lot,* which followed, and, needless to say, *The Shining.*

As Cameron opened the door to the room, he was immediately struck by the spectacular sight of the Rockies on the other side of the window. (The hotel was only a few miles down the road from the entrance to Rocky Mountain National Park.) This was the view King had talked about in interviews. Soon after falling asleep, King had an unsettling dream that his three-year-old son, Joe, was running down a hotel corridor, chased by a fire hose. (*Perhaps the hallway is the one right outside my room*, Cameron thought.) King woke from the nightmare, got out of bed, lit a cigarette, sat in a chair by the window, and gazed out at the mountains. By the time the cigarette was finished, he had conceived the bare bones of what would become *The Shining.*

After the success of King's first two novels, his publisher was concerned he would be pigeonholed in the horror genre. That didn't worry King. But the stories in both books had taken place in Maine, where he lived. He figured he had to do a bit of research if he wanted to set his next novel someplace else, so he spread out a map on the table. He put down his finger randomly and found he had pointed to Colorado. King took the plunge. In 1974 he bundled up his wife, Tabitha, and their children and moved to Boulder.

After about six months, he and Tabitha wanted to have a night out without the kids, so they booked an evening at the Stanley Hotel in nearby Estes Park. The Georgian-style hotel, with its 138 rooms, white walls, red roof, and golden-dome lookout tower, had opened on July 4, 1909. It was built by Freelan Oscar Stanley, who, with his twin brother, Francis, was the inventor of the steam-powered automobile known as the Stanley Steamer.

F. O. Stanley was born into a farming family in Maine in 1849, one of seven children. Inveterate tinkerers, F.O. and Francis came up with the first model of their revolutionary vehicle in 1897. Within two years, they had opened a factory and were manufacturing up to ten cars a day. Interestingly, they sold the company to an investor, but he was unable to keep the operation profitable. The brothers bought it back and once again made it successful.

In the winter of 1903, F. O. Stanley came down with tuberculosis. The prognosis was not good: His doctor told him he would probably die within the year. He suggested that the entrepreneur move to Colorado in the hopes that the fresh mountain air would give him a new lease on life. Indeed, it did. That summer, Stanley and his wife, Flora, trekked to Estes Park and took up residence in a cottage belonging to a friend of their doctor. Within days, Stanley's condition began to reverse itself, and just a few months later he was once again his robust self. Amazingly, despite his doctor's dire prediction, he would live until 1940 to the age of ninety-one.

By the time autumn approached, the Stanleys had already decided they were going to stay in Colorado. They built a mansion similar to the one they had left behind in New England. But that wasn't all. Stanley decided to go into the hotel business.

In the early 1870s, the British Earl of Dunraven had surreptitiously bought up much of what is today Estes Park through second and third parties in order to create a private hunting reserve for himself and his friends. When the scheme became known, other settlers in the area opposed Dunraven. Although he never put his plan into effect, he held onto the property until 1907, when he was forced to sell some six thousand acres. Among the buyers was Stanley.

Many thought Stanley's dream to build a resort hotel on 160 acres in the foothills of the Rockies—7,500 feet above sea level—was foolhardy. At that time, there was no railroad linking Denver and Estes Park, and it was a difficult journey on dirt roads. To prove that guests would have no problem reaching the lodge, Stanley drove one of his own Steamers up to the property.

Stanley designed the hotel himself, and construction began in 1907. It would be a luxury getaway costing about a half million dollars to build—which Stanley was able to pay in cash. There were facilities for tennis, golf, and trap shooting as well as a power plant (also designed by the industrious Stanley) to provide electricity. There were telephones and running water in all rooms. Built for seasonal use, however, heat wasn't installed in the Stanley until around 1979. (To this day, the rooms, like many homes in the Rockies, have ceiling fans but are not air-conditioned in the summer.)

From the beginning Stanley's intent was to cater to the rich and famous. Even during the Depression, when business was slow, Stanley wouldn't allow anyone stay there who did not meet his standards. As a result of its exclusivity, the elite hotel was immediately popular with celebrities and titans of industry. Among the first visitors to the Stanley were Harvey Firestone, J. C. Penney, Dr. William Mayo, John Philip Sousa, "The Unsinkable" Margaret "Molly" Brown, and Theodore Roosevelt. More recently, Cary Grant, Doris Day, Bob Dylan, Billy Graham, astronaut Scott Carpenter, and the emperor and empress of Japan have been guests. And, of course, Stephen King.

The author and his wife arrived at the Stanley Hotel on October 30, 1974, the night before Halloween, unaware the hotel was about to close the very next day for the winter season. They were the only two guests in the entire place and were lodged in Room 217. Dinner in the Cascades Restaurant that night must have seemed awfully strange: They were the only patrons. Their table was the only one that was set, and there was only one meal available on the menu.

After dinner, King's wife went back to their room, but her always-inquisitive husband wanted to roam through the sprawling hotel. With no other guests and no activities going on, King could hear every squeak, rumble, and imagined whisper the old lodging had to offer.

Now it was Cameron's turn. He had done his research and knew that the Stanley was supposed to be haunted, just not by the spirits that appear in King's book. He had already signed up for that night's ghost hunt, led by the hotel itself.

But he also wanted to inspect the place alone, like King had. With about two hours to kill before suppertime, Cameron headed up to the fourth story. From there he would descend, floor by floor, until he reached the lobby—looking, listening, trying to catch wind of anything otherworldly that might be in the air.

But nothing. Whether it was because there were so many people around, because it was still light out, or the spirits just weren't feeling playful, Cameron didn't hear or see a thing out of the ordinary. *Oh, well*, he laughingly told himself, *I guess I just don't have the shining.*

Of course, he knew the Stanley was not the Overlook. In fact, not a single frame of the 1980 Stanley Kubrick film version of *The Shining* was shot at the Stanley Hotel, though many scenes from the 1997 TV miniseries were. (The inn also stood in for the Hotel Danbury in the movie *Dumb and Dumber,* but Cameron couldn't care less about that.)

He walked down the last flight of stairs and surveyed the broad lobby, with its gleaming hardwood floors and sumptuous decor. And there at one end was a restored 1906 Stanley Steamer, a reminder of the hotel's founder. (On his way into the hotel earlier that day, Cameron had seen a Stanley Steamer bus that was used to transport tour groups around the grounds. Originally, the vehicles had been used to ferry guests up the mountain from Lyons.)

As Cameron strolled through the foyer, a light strain of music caught his ear. Soft piano music. It wasn't being piped in over a sound system. No, someone was playing it live. He couldn't make out the melody exactly, but it was sweet, wistful. Thinking the music must be coming from a piano bar—he needed a drink after his tiring walk wandering through the entire building—Cameron followed the sound.

Unexpectedly, it led him not to a cocktail lounge but to an open doorway, on the far side of which was the hotel ballroom. It wasn't set up for an event that night, so he was able to see the entire room at a glance. It was empty. Nevertheless, there was that music. Eventually Cameron's eyes fell on a grand piano at one end of the room. The notes were coming out of it all right, but no one was sitting on the bench. Then his eyes dropped to the keyboard: The keys were moving by themselves in time to the piece of music.

Was it possible?!

Cameron stepped into the ballroom, and the instant he crossed the threshold the music stopped. The keys stood still. Whoever or whatever had been playing was gone. Cameron staggered out of the deserted room and headed back upstairs to think over what he had just seen, or rather heard. Just two hours later, however, he was back in the lobby joining about twenty other intrepid ghost hunters. As the tour progressed, their guide assured them that—as opposed to the ghosts in *The Shining*—none of the spectres currently inhabiting the Stanley Hotel is evil or malicious.

The most frequently seen is F. O. Stanley himself. He most often shows up in the lobby or in the billiards parlor, which was his favorite room in the hotel. Several bartenders have also spied him walking through their lounges, but whenever they tried to intercept the spectre, he vanished.

And as it turned out, Cameron wasn't alone in what he had experienced in the ballroom. Many people have had the exact same thing happen to them. Always, the spectral music and the moving piano keys stop the instant anyone passes through the doorway. Although no apparition has ever materialized there, it's been decided that the invisible musician is none other than Flora Stanley, who liked to play for guests at the hotel. Her ghost isn't the only one to visit the ballroom. Workers in the adjoining kitchen have heard the noise from a phantom party in full swing when the room was actually empty.

Unexplainable footsteps and noises have been heard all over the building, but nowhere do they occur more often than on the fourth floor. When the hotel first opened, adults stayed on the first three floors, but their children and the nannies were lodged on the fourth floor. (Cameron suddenly recalled reading somewhere that, during his single night in the hotel, King had seen the ghost of a little boy calling for his nanny.) Today, guests whose rooms are on the top floor sometimes are disturbed by the sound of children laughing or playing in the hallway, but if the occupants open their doors to complain, there's no one in the passage.

Inside the rooms, children's handprints occasionally appear on the mirrors. Guests have returned to their rooms to discover that their personal belongings have moved around on their own. Some rooms are more active than others. In Room 401, children have been heard singing in the closet, and the windows sometimes fly open by themselves. Lights flick on and off for no reason in Room 407, and the closest elevator has a life of its own. People standing outside the hotel have looked up to see the face of a man staring out a window of 407 even when the room was unoccupied. For some reason, legend has it that the nameless stranger is Lord Dunraven.

The room that has the most paranormal activity on the fourth floor is 418. Guests who stay there are frequently bothered by the sound of phantom children on the other side of the door, and when the room is empty, the youngsters' noise often emanates from inside. Maids will enter the vacant room to discover indentations on the bedcovering, as if someone had been sitting or lying on it. The place has another strange anomaly: If anyone who is sick walks into the room, his or her symptoms will become more acute. Perhaps that's because, according to rumor, Room 418 used to be set aside for children when they were ill.

The hazy spectre of an unidentified man has been spotted in rooms all over the hotel at night. Sometimes guests will awaken to find him looming over them. When discovered, the ghost runs into the closet or simply vanishes. From time to time, the spirit has been blamed for stealing jewelry and baggage, though there's no known reason why he would do so.

The identity of the spectral housekeeper in the room where Stephen King slept is. Her name is Miss Wilson, and there are suggestions the author may have seen her. She was working in Room 217 during the early years of the hotel when she was injured in a gas explosion. After her recovery, Stanley employed her for the rest of her life. She remained in the hotel's service until she died of an aneurism forty years later—again, in Room 217. She has gone to her mortal end, but her spirit has stayed at the Stanley, hard at work. Guests find their covers turned down or their luggage unpacked and placed in the closet even though housekeeping hasn't been in the room. Miss Wilson can be mischievous as well. Sometimes she pulls the blankets off visitors in the middle of the night. Room 217 was once on the ghost tour when no one was staying there, but Cameron had it all to himself that night. Or did he? Would Miss Wilson be watching over him as he slept?

After crawling into bed, he turned on the TV to help him nod off, but wouldn't you know it? The Stanley Hotel certainly knew its chief claim to fame: There on the in-house cable, playing over and over in an endless cycle, was the film version of Kubrick's *The Shining*. Cameron turned up the sound. An ax head was splintering a door. A maniacal Jack Nicholson popped his face through the hole. "Here's Johnny . . ."

A perfect end to a perfect day, Cameron thought as he fell into a deep, contented sleep.

Today, the Stanley Hotel is on the National Register of Historic Places, with eleven buildings set on fifty-five acres. In addition to its accommodations for overnight guests, the hotel offers sixteen thousand square feet of space for meetings and special events. Plus, as many a visitor can attest, there is plenty of room for the ghosts.

Stanley Hotel
333 E. Wonder View Avenue
Estes Park, CO 80517
(970) 586-3371 or (800) 976-1377 (reservations)
www.stanleyhotel.com

The lodgings conducts its own in-house ghost hunt called The Stanley Hotel Spirited Night Tour. The 60-minute group walking tour never goes onto guest floors or into guest rooms. Reservations are required: The tours often sell out weeks in advance. Guests taking the tour must be at least eight years old. The tour route varies depending upon the time of day, the season, and the availability of the public rooms. To book a tour, contact the Tour Office, which is located on the lower level of the Stanley Hotel. Phone: (970) 577-4111. Email: StanleyTours@StanleyHotel.com.

CHAPTER 22: COLORADO CURIOSITIES

The Brown Palace Hotel & Spa, Oxford Hotel
Denver, Colorado

Hotel Colorado
Glenwood Springs, Colorado

Tourists flood to Colorado for its endless natural attractions, with majestic, snow-capped Rockies, forests, and canyons, and giant, inland sand dunes. Of course, all of those visitors need places to stay, and there are ghost hosts to greet them at many of state's top hotels.

The **Brown Palace Hotel**, built by Henry Cordes Brown, opened on August 12, 1892. Today, it's part of Marriott's Autograph Collection of hotels and offers 241 guest rooms and luxury suites.

From its earliest days up until 1985, the hotel had several permanent residents. One of these, Mrs. Louise C. Hill, was a mover and shaker of Denver society from the late nineteenth through the early twentieth century. After her husband's death and with difficulty finding domestic staff, she moved into the Brown Palace Hotel in or around 1942. She lived quietly in Suite 904 until her death in 1955.

Her presence can still be felt in her old room, however. During a period that the hotel gave historical tours, which included a visit to the former Hill suite, the front desk would get calls from the room even though it was unoccupied. Oddly, there was only static at the other end when the receptionist picked up. Stranger still, the suite was undergoing a complete renovation at the time, and its phone line was disconnected. The calls stopped after the tours were discontinued, so perhaps Louise's spirit just didn't like being disturbed.

Another otherworldly visitor to the Brown Palace is an unidentified male phantom who stands just outside (or sometimes a few steps within) the dining room. The spectre usually wears a uniform of some sort—it's often compared to those once worn by train conductors—but occasionally he's garbed in a plain, dark suit instead. The ghost has been seen walking through the wall and out of sight.

When lights turn themselves off or on in the hotel, people generally blame it on the age of the building, but there are also strange sounds and disembodied voices heard throughout the Brown Palace. For instance, in the past, the dining area was the San Marco Room, where dancing took place to the music of visiting big bands or the hotel's house band, the San Marco Strings. According to an old wives' tale, a floor manager once heard music coming from the former ballroom after hours, and when he entered the hall he encountered four formally clad musicians—all ghosts—practicing away.

Paranormalists think some of the spooky activity may be from a 1911 double murder that took place in the hotel. A man named Frank Henwood fatally shot Tony Von Phul, a rival for the affections of Isabel Springer, who was already married to a Denver politician. During the incident, a bystander named George Copeland was also killed. (Such hauntings that recur frequently, recreate incidents from the past without change, and do not interact with the living are known as residual hauntings.)

The five-story, redbrick **Oxford Hotel** opened in downtown Denver in 1891. Perhaps its most interesting feature is the ground level bar, which is a single, windowless room off the lobby. Locals were already enjoying the bar's signature martinis long before the Prohibition Era, and they weren't going to let a federal law get in the way of their fun. During the nation's dry years, the room operated as an illicit speakeasy. (There are allegedly still secret tunnels and moving walls to get in and out of the room.) The day after Prohibition ended, the bar officially opened as the Cruise Room.

By the 1950s, the hotel's glamor had faded, and the place had become a run-down boarding house. Despite that, it was placed on the National Register of Historical Places in 1979. A new owner in the 1980s engineered the hotel's comeback. In 2012, the Cruise Room was restored to its original Art Deco décor.

The most frequently seen ghost at Oxford Hotel is the easily recognizable apparition of a postal worker in uniform. Local lore says he went missing one winter during the 1930s, and his frozen corpse wasn't found until the spring thaw. His spirit now visits the Cruise Room. He sits at the bar, stays to himself, and quietly sips a beer. It's only after he's left the building that other patrons notice that his glass of beer, which they had watched him drink, is still full.

Overnight guests at the hotel have reported having the feeling that someone was always watching them or walking behind them. They've also heard the inexplicable sound of wood snapping, but no damage is ever discovered.

One guestroom in particular, Room 320, has a gruesome ghost story connected with it. Legend has it that a woman killed her lover in the room and then committed suicide beside him. A variation claims exactly the opposite: The man murdered the woman because she was cheating on him. Either way, Room 320 is now haunted, but the phenomena are very specific: They only happen to single men staying there alone. Invisible, disembodied hands will grab at the man's arms or rip the sheets and blankets off the bed while he is sleeping.

Hotel Colorado opened in 1893, built by silver baron Walter Devereaux to accommodate visitors to the nearby Glenwood Hot Springs. The hotel's in-house spa and swimming pool were also fed by the healing waters of the mineral springs. The hotel's nineteenth-century Italian-style interior furnishings complemented the building's exterior, which was designed to resemble a Renaissance-era villa. It was the first hotel in the area to be lit by electricity, and it famously had a courtyard fountain that shot water 185 feet into the air. Hotel Colorado went through several owners, including a stint as a US Naval Convalescent Hospital during World War II. Beginning in the 1990s, it underwent a complete restoration and is now listed on the National Register of Historic Places. Of the original 191 guest rooms, 131 are still available for overnight guests.

Hauntings at the hotel occur at all hours, but most of them take place between 2 a.m. and 4 a.m. They include the unmistakable scent of cigar smoke in the lobby, thought to be from Devereaux's unseen spirit. Unoccupied elevators move from floor to floor despite not being called, and the sound of clattering dishes and the aroma of perfume waft through the Devereaux Dining Room long after guests have gone and work is done for the night.

People throughout the hotel have heard a woman screaming, but no source for the bloodcurdling cries has ever been found. The shrieks are said to come from a phantom maid who, while alive, was allegedly involved in a love triangle. In the end, she was killed by one of her lovers in a guestroom. The murder triggered so much paranormal activity in the room that it was taken out of service and is now used for storage. A version of the story says that the incident took place during the hotel's time as a naval hospital.

There are a few visible apparitions in the Hotel Colorado as well. One is an unidentified woman who likes to wake up men in the middle of the night. Another is a little girl in Victorian garb who is spotted in public areas playing with a ball.

Perhaps the most active guestrooms, paranormally speaking, are on the third and fifth floors. Phenomena include lights that switch on and off by themselves, televisions that change channels on their own, and knocks at the door when no one is in the hall. There are also bizarre sounds and unrecognizable smells.

One last ghost story. Supposedly, when Room 551 was refurbished in 1982, it needed new wallpaper. The workers applied it but, when they returned the next day, they found the paper had somehow been removed from the wall, rolled up, and laid out on the floor. Puzzled at how it occurred, the crew nevertheless repeated the process of replacing the wallpaper. Once again, the next morning they found the curled paper back on the floor. After a few more attempts, the workers decided to let the phantom decorator choose the wallpaper. Before leaving, they placed samples of several different patterns and colors on the bed. The next day, all but one of them had been tossed onto the floor. The remaining roll was pasted on the wall, where it stayed.

The Brown Palace Hotel and Spa
321 17th Street
Denver, CO 80202
(303) 297-311
https://www.brownpalace.com

Hotel Colorado
526 Pine Street
Glenwood Springs, CO 81601
(970) 945-6511
https://www.hotelcolorado.com

Oxford Hotel
1600 17th Street
Denver, CO 80202
(303) 628-5400
https://www.theoxfordhotel.com

CHAPTER 23: ARIZONA APPARITIONS

Copper Queen Hotel
Bisbee, Arizona

Jerome Grand Hotel
Jerome, Arizona

The mining of copper was one of Arizona's early major industries, but when demand (and prices) fell, mines began to close, as did supporting businesses such as hotels. Some of those lodgings now have a second life, with their ghostly guests still in residence.

Located in southeastern Arizona less than ten miles from the Mexican border, Bisbee was once a major center of copper mining, especially from the massive Queen Mine. The **Copper Queen Hotel**, built by the Phelps Dodge Mining Company and opened in 1902, housed visiting investors and other VIPs as well as regular travelers. The hotel had 78 guest rooms spread over four floors and a fifth story to hold the elevator machinery. There was also an adjacent courtyard building, which originally held law offices. Today, the completely refurbished lodging has 48 guest rooms in the main hotel with an additional five in the courtyard structure.

There are several spirits roaming the halls of this historic hotel, but the best known is that of Julia Lowell, a "lady of horizontal employment" who "worked" there in the 1920s and 1930s. She had the misfortune to fall in love with one of her gentleman callers, and when he refused her requests for more than a professional relationship, she committed suicide. Her body was found in her bathtub in Room 315, which the Copper Queen has now officially named "The Julia Room." Her spectral presence is felt in the western end of the second and third floors in the old section of the hotel. Now and then, male guests and staff in that area have heard a disembodied woman's voice, presumed to be Julia's, whispering to them. She occasionally materializes at the foot of a man's bed and dances suggestively. She also seems to enjoy fiddling with men's feet.

Other ghosts at the Copper Queen include Howard, a former front desk clerk, who likes to make his presence known to the employees doing his job now. Another phantom is the spectre of a little boy who's drawn to the hotel because his mother or perhaps some other relative used to work there. It's believed he drowned in the San Pedro River nearby. Then there's the apparition of a mature, distinguished-looking man who has long hair and a beard and wears a black cape and top hat. His dim form usually manifests itself in rooms or doorways on the fourth floor. There's always the telltale scent of a burning cigar just before or after his revenant is seen.

Constructed by the United Verde Copper Company, **Jerome Grand Hotel** started life as the United Verde Hospital in January 1927. It sits on a plateau on the side of Cleopatra Hill, and at an elevation of 5,200 feet there's a magnificent view of the Verde Valley.

The hospital replaced another clinic that had stood on the site since 1917. The new, 30,000 square foot structure was built entirely of concrete because the earlier hospital had been severely damaged when a ground fault shifted. State-of-the-art equipment was installed in the medical wards as well as throughout the building itself, including an advanced heating system and the first self-operated Otis elevator in the state. In 1930, United Verde Hospital was named the most modern hospital in all of Arizona.

Unfortunately, copper prices plummeted during the Great Depression, and United Verde Company ceased operations in Jerome. Its mines and other holdings were acquired by Phelps Dodge Mining Corporation in 1935, and the medical facility's name was changed to Phelps Dodge Hospital.

Over the next twenty years, with few jobs available, most residents left town. There was no longer a need for a large hospital, so Phelps Dodge closed it in 1950. By the end of the sixties, the company realized the space would never reopen as a hospital, so over the next two decades all of the medical equipment and major furnishings were removed. During that time, a caretaker or family was hired to live in the building, just to keep it occupied and free of vandalism, but after a caretaker hanged himself in the boiler room in 1980, the place was boarded up.

The ornate Spanish Mission Style, five-story structure sat there empty, high on a mountainside plateau above town, until Larry Altherr, along with his family, bought the property in 1994. Sensing the area was ripe for tourism, he renovated the former hospital top to bottom and opened it as the Jerome Grand Hotel in 1996.

At the same time, the new owners also debuted an upscale eatery, the Grand View Restaurant and Lounge. Although run as a separate business with its own entrance, the restaurant occupied the area on the ground floor that once held a dispensary and handled hospital admittance. In the end, the hotel decided to lease out the space instead. The Asylum Restaurant, unaffiliated with the Jerome Grand other than sharing part of the building, has been in operation there since 2001. (The restaurant's cheeky name comes from the oft-repeated but erroneous claim that at some point the hospital was a mental institution or tubercular sanatorium.)

There have been rumors for years about the Jerome Grand Hotel being haunted, and the management isn't shy about acknowledging its ethereal guests. The hotel mentions some of the ghost stories on its official website and keeps a journal at the front desk for people to record any paranormal experiences they had during their visit.

Those who stay overnight sometimes catch unexpected whiffs of cigars, whiskey, or flowers, and they hear disembodied coughs, strained breathing, and muffled voices spilling in from adjacent, empty rooms. Doors open and slam shut on their own, and lamps and television sets have been known to turn themselves on or off, sometimes becoming unplugged in the process. People have woken up in the morning to find their phones or other electronics under their beds. A few folks have seen objects in their rooms move, especially small items like bathroom toiletries. The occasional but distinctive sound of a hospital gurney can be heard rolling down the hallways, even on the padded carpets and particularly on the third floor where the operating theater was located.

As for the actual ghosts, one of them is Claude Harvey, a maintenance man whose body was found on April 3, 1935, with his head pinned under the elevator car. Was it suicide? A tragic mishap? Or was it a murder staged to look like an accident? The coroner reported that, although Harvey's neck was indeed broken, the elevator could not have caused the fatal injury.

Whatever happened that night, the United Verde Copper Company didn't want to be involved in a scandal, so the incident was quickly and quietly settled, with no autopsy and no x-rays allowed. The cause of death is still listed as undetermined—which could cause a ghost to become restless. The phantom is blamed for any problems with the elevator, especially if it's an electrical issue. Odd noises have been heard echoing from the empty shaft as well, and the car will change floors without being called. It's thought that Harvey rides the lift whenever the mood strikes him.

Harvey's ghost appears on the stairs and in the boiler room, oblivious to everyone around him. Staff members on night shift assume that the spectral male form they've seen in the laundry room is Harvey. They've also heard the revenant sneeze and cough.

Another ghost in the Jerome Grand Hotel was a mineworker before he became confined to a wheelchair. During a stay in the hospital, he was placed into a room—now numbered Room 32—that had a balcony. The man killed himself by crawling over the railing and dropping to his death. His spirit is spotted primarily on the second and third floors. By the way, the miner is not the only person to commit suicide in that room. It was also the scene of a businessman shooting himself.

Not much is known about the other spirits haunting the Jerome Grand.

One is the ghost of an elderly lady in a white gown, who may or may not be the woman whose unintelligible voice is heard at the other end of phone calls to the front desk from unoccupied rooms.

Still roaming the hotel from its time as a hospital, there's the apparition of a woman wearing a nurse's uniform as well as a doctor or nurse seen in a long, white lab coat and carrying a clipboard.

And then there are the children. Guests on the third and fourth floors have been known to call down to the front desk to report a presumably unattended baby crying in the next room. When the specified room is checked, it's empty. The inexplicable scents of baby powder and zinc oxide ointment are also common.

The footsteps and voices of phantom children playing together float down from the fifth floor. The apparition of one of the kids, maybe four or five years old, has been seen and heard running down the corridor on the third floor. On occasion, the youngster can also be heard crying or giggling. Sometimes the ghost materializes at the foot of the bed inside an occupied room and simply stares at the guest lying there. (Sources disagree about the intrusive juvenile's gender, but most say the spectre is a little boy.)

There's even a phantom cat! It's been heard throughout the hotel but seems to be partial to the third floor, scratching and meowing at doors. Both visitors and staff have felt the invisible feline rub up against them. Often its outline can be seen pressed into the bedspread upon entering a room, and some guests swear that the cryptic kitty has curled up next to them as they slept. On rare occasions, the cat becomes visible, and it's even been caught on film! A guest staying in Room 20 in 2008 captured a photo of the cat sitting on a table. Purportedly, the hotel has a copy of the picture at the front desk.

The town of Jerome is undergoing somewhat of a renaissance. It's drawn a close artisan community that owns about 30 studios and galleries. The biggest surprise was the discovery that the soil and weather are similar to that of Loire Valley in France, where some of the world's best wines originate. Several wineries and vineyards have now opened in Greater Jerome, so who knows? Maybe Jerome will one day be as famous for wines as it is for its historic past . . . and its ghosts.

Copper Queen Hotel
11 Howell Avenue
Bisbee, AZ 85603
(520) 432-2216
https://www.copperqueen.com/

Jerome Grand Hotel
200 Hill Street
Jerome, AZ 86331
(928) 634-8200 or (888) 817-6788
www.jeromegrandhotel.net

CHAPTER 24: SHADES OF THE OLD WEST

St. James Hotel
Cimarron, New Mexico

At least two of the ghosts that inhabit the old St. James Hotel in Cimarron, New Mexico, are holdovers from its raucous Wild West days: one, an inveterate gambler gunned down after winning his biggest stake ever, the other, the wife of the original owner. There may be a phantom cowboy and a diminutive spectre known only as "the Imp" as well. But then, who's counting?

Cheryl *was* Annie Oakley. Well, obviously not literally, but she was going to play the famous sharpshooter during what she hoped would be a fun yet spooky murder-mystery weekend in Cimarron, New Mexico.

Cheryl lived in Taos, the ski resort and arts community, about fifty miles southwest of Cimarron. She'd been reading about the getaway staged at the **St. James Hotel** for a couple of years, but (as often happens) she didn't think seriously about doing it until she heard rumors that it might be discontinued. New owners would be taking over the 125-year-old former saloon and completely refurbishing it, and who knew whether the "games" would continue?

About two weeks before the event, participants received a "subpoena" in the mail, ordering them to appear to take part in an inquest regarding a murder at the lodgings. They were each given a specific character to play throughout the entire proceedings, many of whom, like Cheryl's, were actual historical people who had some tie to the joint. The twenty or so players—and, indeed, they would be role-playing throughout—were expected to provide their own wardrobe, appropriate to whomever they would be portraying.

Everyone would arrive at the hotel early Friday, get settled, and then gather downstairs with the others, in costume, for the festivities to begin. They would be given clues (including lots of red herrings), act out prepared scenes, and have a chance to search for evidence. Finally, the killer would be revealed late Saturday night.

Cheryl made the turn off US 64 and traveled about a half mile down NM 21 into the center of the dusty town just after noon. The rooms were already prepared, so she was able to check in early. She had deliberately chosen to stay in one of the hotel's original thirteen rooms rather than in the ten-room annex that was added in the 1980s. If she was going to do this thing, she was going to do it right. By two o'clock, she had made her way to Room 17. Except for the modern bathroom facilities and bed, the room probably looked very much the way it did back in the 1870s.

The room really was in a time warp: There was no phone and no TV. They *were* available in the newer rooms, but what would be the adventure in staying in one of those? She hung up some clothes, unpacked her toiletries, opened the window to let in the midday breeze, and laid out her cowgirl outfit on the bed for later. Time to go out and explore.

With only nine hundred or so year-round inhabitants, Cimarron is little more than a village. Its roots date back to the western migration of the pioneers in the nineteenth century. Up until the beginning of the 1800s, the land was occupied solely by Native Americans, primarily the Anasazi, the Jicarilla Apaches, and the Utes.

Between 1821 and 1880, the Santa Fe Trail was established as the main wagon trail for those hoping to make the exhausting nine-hundred-mile journey from Missouri down to New Mexico. The "highway" was also used by traders, the federal army during the Mexican-American War, fortune seekers heading to the California gold rush, and, later, stagecoaches. The dirt path fell into disuse after the railroad reached Santa Fe in 1880.

One of the main legs of the trail, the Mountain Branch, crosses today's US 64 and passes right through present-day Cimarron. (The Cimarron Cutoff passes farther south.) Many parts of the old trail remain visible. Ruts can be seen out near Philmont Ranch and about thirteen miles south of town off NM 21. The closest section to Cimarron is a thirty-yard-wide basin visible from US 64 near where Cheryl had made the turnoff to Cimarron. She made a note to check it out on her way home on Sunday.

The town also dates to the mid-nineteenth century. In 1842, a trapper named Lucien Bonaparte Maxwell fell in love with a local woman named Luz Beaubrien. Her father, Charles, along with Guadalupe Miranda, the secretary of the territory's governor, owned the 1.7-million-acre Beaubrien-Miranda Ranch in northern New Mexico—the result of a land grant from the governor. As a wedding present, Charles gave the couple fifteen thousand acres of property, on which, in 1858, Maxwell built a two-story mansion on the site of what is today Cimarron. The community, nestled in the foothills of the Sangre de Cristo Mountains, received its official charter four years later and took its name from a Spanish word for "wild" or "unbroken."

Charles Beaubrien died in 1864, naming Maxwell as his heir. Maxwell later bought out all of his father-in-law's partners and other family members to ultimately own all of the original ranch. He welcomed settlers onto the property and did little or nothing to discourage squatters, even after gold was discovered in nearby Elizabethtown. In 1870, Maxwell sold everything (by then known as the Maxwell Land Grant Company) except for his house and 1,200 surrounding acres. He moved shortly thereafter to eastern New Mexico, where he died in 1875.

Meanwhile, Henri Lambert, who had been President Lincoln's personal chef, was working in Elizabethtown. He had come west to get rich after hearing about the gold strike but wound up going into the restaurant trade. The new Maxwell Land Grant Company convinced Lambert to move to Cimarron to open a saloon and restaurant to serve the town's rough-and-tumble mix of cowboys, miners, and frontiersmen.

The Lambert Inn was an immediate success, and it soon became one of the most notorious bars in the Southwest. And one of the most dangerous. Twenty-two bullet holes still riddle the ceiling of the saloon, now the St. James Hotel's dining room. When the pressed-tin roofing was removed during a refurbishment in 1901, more than four *hundred* bullet holes were found in the beams underneath. (The only reason people weren't killed in the overhead rooms was the double layer of wood between the saloon ceiling and the floorboards above.)

Sensing that Cimarron needed a comfortable place for travelers to stay overnight—and for hungover cowpokes to sleep off a night's revels—Lambert added guest rooms to the adobe structure in 1880. At the time, it was considered deluxe accommodations, one of the first hotels west of the Mississippi to have running water.

By the time the railroad bypassed Cimarron in favor of Santa Fe, gold had been depleted in the area mines, and the boom times were over. The population and the number of visitors to the town immediately declined. The hotel struggled on, however. Lambert died in 1913, his wife thirteen years later. Over the next sixty years, the landmark passed through a number of hands and was vacant for several long periods. Along the way, there had also been a name change to the St.

James Hotel. Finally, in 1985, a new owner took over, and the hotel was completely restored with heavy carpets over the hardwood floors, plush velvet drapes, crystal chandeliers, and other period furnishings.

The legacy of the St. James Hotel cannot be disputed. The list of occupants and visitors reads like a Who's Who of the Old West: Wyatt and Morgan Earp, Doc Holliday, Jesse James (who always stayed in Room 14 under his pseudonym R. H. Howard), Robert Ford (who had been a member of the James gang before turning against the outlaw and shooting him), Bat Masterson, Kit Carson, Billy the Kid, Pat Garrett, train robber Black Jack Ketchum, and Gen. Philip Sheridan.

Among the most frequent patrons was gunfighter Clay Allison, who liked dancing naked on the bar after having one drink too many. (That bar can still be found in the dining room.) Allison also liked shooting people. According to most accounts, he personally killed nineteen of the twenty-six men who died in gun-fights at the saloon.

Rumor has it that William "Buffalo Bill" Cody once worked for Maxwell and, years later, after his time as an American Indian scout, returned and befriended Lambert. By all accounts he became the godfather of the innkeeper's son, Fred.

Supposedly, Cody also met Annie Oakley for the first time in the old Lambert Inn, but the tale isn't true. Their initial encounter was in New Orleans in 1884 when the *Buffalo Bill Wild West* show was playing the Crescent City. Oakley was also in town, performing in the Sells Brothers Circus. But the story about the two circus legends meeting in Cimarron persists, so Cheryl was more than happy to masquerade as Little Sure Shot for three days—even though Oakley may never have set foot in the St. James.

Cheryl spent most of her afternoon visiting the fifteen buildings and other sites in the Cimarron old historic district, all of which date from the 1860s and 1870s. Following a map she had picked up at the visitor center, she started out at the old well in the town plaza. Next came the Colfax County courthouse, the offices of the *Cimarron News,* a placard marking the site of Lucien Maxwell's homestead, and the Old Mill Museum, which had once been a gristmill named the Aztec Mill, built for Maxwell in 1864.

Having "done the city tour," Cheryl hurried back to the crown jewel of Old Town: the St. James Hotel. It was time to get dressed.

A few hours later, with introductions and instructions for the weekend out of the way, Cheryl enjoyed an early dinner with the other participants. This was the second mystery weekend for one of them, and two others, a husband and wife, were already making plans to return in the future.

Cheryl decided to turn in early. The next day would be a long one. She slowly climbed the wooden staircase to the second floor, the boards audibly creaking in a way only heard in old buildings. She made her way down the short hallway to 17, opened the door, clicked on the light, and walked in.

As she undressed, being careful not to tangle the fringe on her buckskin skirt and jacket, Cheryl slowly became aware of the strong scent of roses in the room. *How strange*, she thought. There were no fresh flowers in the room, and roses were definitely out of season. Nevertheless, the odor was unmistakable.

She crossed to the open window and bent forward across the wide sill. She took a deep whiff, filling her lungs with the clean night air. No, not even a hint of roses. The flowery scent wasn't coming from outside. She leaned back into the room.

Though puzzling, the smell wasn't overpowering. In fact, Cheryl decided, it was kind of nice. She walked to the bed, turned the lights out, and within minutes was fast asleep. An hour passed, then two, then three.

Suddenly, Cheryl found herself wide awake, her eyes unseeing in the dark. It took her a moment to remember where she was. Cimarron. *This town must really close up at night*, she thought to herself. There wasn't a hint of light coming through the window.

The window. Something was tapping on the open glass. That's what had woken her up: a barely audible yet persistent rapping! Not like a twig scraping along the surface. The sound was more precise, measured, like fingers tapping on a desk.

Reflexively, Cheryl pulled her blanket in close for protection. Was someone trying to sneak into the room? But no, the sounds weren't menacing. The soft, rhythmic beats continued . . . one . . . after . . . the other. Finally, she could stand it no longer. Cheryl jumped out of bed, her eyes now acclimated to the darkened chamber, and rushed to the window.

As she crossed the few steps, the raps became more persistent and pronounced. The taps were also getting louder. And louder. Cheryl reached out, grabbed hold of the latch, and pulled the window shut.

Instantly, the sound stopped.

Dead silence.

Cheryl backed away from window in surprise. How could whatever was causing the disturbance have ceased so abruptly? And why? She ran her hand across the pane, then tested its mounting on the frame. Nothing was loose or rattling. There seemed to be no explanation for what she had just experienced.

And, although Cheryl didn't know it, there wasn't one—at least not an *earthly* explanation. But there was a supernatural one. The next morning, when she casually mentioned the incident to the clerk working the front desk, the woman said matter-of-factly, "Oh, you were visited by one of our ghosts, Mary."

It turned out that the St. James Hotel was, indeed, haunted by not one but several spirits from its bygone days. And Cheryl had met one of the inn's most frequent otherworldly tenants: Henri Lambert's wife, Mary. Room 17 used to be her bedroom. It was also where she died.

Mary's apparition never appears, but guests who have stayed in the room have reported the unambiguous, unexplainable scent of roses (the flower that Mary favored) permeating the premises. And if the occupants left the window open at night, invariably they would be awakened by the sound of an invisible hand—Mary's—rapping on the glass. The noise would continue unabated until the window was closed tightly.

There have been lots of other paranormal goings-on in the hotel. Mysterious cold spots are felt all over the inn. Folks in the dining room as well as a former owner have claimed that every so often the reflection of a cowboy appears in the mirror over the bar. There are also rumors that the unidentified phantom of a short, pockmarked man nicknamed "the Imp" prowls the halls.

Most of the spectral phenomena take place on the second floor. Electronic equipment often goes haywire, especially cameras. Lights turn on and off without warning, and personal items will sometimes move by themselves or fall off tables and shelves. Smoking isn't permitted in the hotel, but somehow the clearly identifiable aroma of cigar smoke will occasionally drift down the corridor.

By far, the most intriguing spectre at the St. James Hotel belongs to T. J. Wright. According to legends surrounding his malevolent spirit, the twenty-two-year-old cardsharp was staying in Room 18 when he won the deed to the hotel in a high-stakes poker game. But he never collected. Wright was found in his room, shot to death, the next morning. Ever since, dangerous, poltergeist-like activity has broken out whenever anyone tries to go inside. People say a fresh glass of whiskey is left in the room to placate the vengeful wraith. Otherwise, the room is kept under lock and key, and no visitors are allowed to enter, even for a quick peek.

The St. James Hotel is open year-round. But Cimarron, despite its rich past, is not exactly on the tourist trail. You have to want to go there. As a result, if you do stay at the inn, it's possible you may be the only overnight guest—at least, among the living. You can rest assured you will not be alone.

St. James Hotel
617 S. Collinson Ave.
Cimarron, NM 87714
(575) 376-2664 or (888) 376-2664
https://www.exstjames.com

The St. James Hotel is located in the Cimarron Historical District, about a mile south of US 64 (the Kit Carson Highway). Collinson Avenue is NM 21. The hotel's popular Murder Mystery Weekends do continue, but there are only four or five per year. The dates change from year to year, so check the hotel's website. Make reservations well in advance if you wish to attend the themed, costumed event or if you want to reserve a particular room at any time of the year. Room 18 is usually closed to guests.

PART FOUR: THE WESTERN STATES

CHAPTER 25: THE HEATHMAN HAUNTINGS

Heathman Hotel
Portland, Oregon

For some reason all of the rooms in Portland, Oregon's Heathman Hotel that end in the numbers 03 seem to be home to supernatural phenomena. But the most active of all is the dreaded Room 703. Does it really house the returning spirit of a long-forgotten suicide?

It felt good to be home. Portland, Oregon. Max hadn't been there in years.

After high school, he'd gone east for college and then moved to New York to work for a small travel agency right after graduation. When his parents died he returned briefly to Oregon, packed up what few mementoes he thought might fit into his East Village apartment, discarded the rest, and sold the old homestead. This was his first time back.

A wan smile crossed his lips. Now he lived in Manhattan. But when he was growing up, Portland was the Big City. He had actually been raised seven miles west in Beaverton, itself a fair-size metropolis—the sixth-largest city in the state. But if he and his friends wanted to have real fun come weekends, they headed into Portland.

Max realized that most of the country probably thought the place had little to offer. Sure, there were great views of Mount Hood and a lot of city parks and flowerbeds. (Not for nothing is Portland known as the City of Roses.) But excitement?

Well, people who felt that way had obviously never been to Portland. Its youth embraced punk early on, making Portland a center for hip, underground music. Counterculture chic led to Portland establishing the world's only H. P. Lovecraft Film Festival. And how many cities take part in the annual World Naked Bike Ride?

For the jocks, Portland has an NBA team, the Trail Blazers. And the city has more strip clubs per capita than anywhere else in the United States—some say even more than in Vegas. (Max always politely demurred when his friends back in New York asked if the saying "If you don't know any strippers, you can't be from Portland" was true.)

And then there's the beer. Portland has not one, not two, but *five* annual beer festivals—which shouldn't be all that surprising since there are twenty-eight microbreweries in town, earning the city the nicknames Beervana and Beertown. Party animals can visit any number of "theater pubs" where movies are free as long as the customers keep buying brewskies. The drinking age is twenty-one, just like everywhere else in the country, but Max and his high school buds had, shall we say, lots of friends who could help them out on a Saturday night. Ah, memories.

And now, thanks to contacts he had established in the Big Apple over more than a decade in the industry, he was able to pursue a dream and start a new career: writing freelance travel articles.

Most recently, he had talked to both Southwest and Alaska Airlines, proposing a series of stories highlighting the secret joys to be found in often-overlooked destinations on their regional maps. To his amazement, both airlines were interested and wanted him to submit a sample piece for their editors.

Write what you know. That's what they always told you in class, Max thought. He decided he might as well go back to the beginning: Portland.

As he flew west, childhood capers had flooded back to mind. Before long, the plane had made its final approach to the airport following the Columbia River. Max picked up his rental car and headed south on I-205 and I-84 toward the city. Within forty-five minutes of touching down, he had pulled up in front of the **Heathman Hotel**.

Max knew it well, or at least its public areas. He had attended functions in several of their eight meeting rooms, and now and then, when the family had something special to celebrate, his parents would treat him to dinner in its main restaurant, which was renowned for its collection of fine wines—not that Max was ever allowed to partake. (He was a bit upset that on this trip he had just missed the hotel's annual Beaujolais Nouveau Festival celebrating the season's new harvest.)

Other than a clumsy failed attempt to book a room at the Heathman on prom night—an embarrassing faux pas that was probably best forgotten—this would be Max's first time staying overnight in one of the grand hotel's 150 guest rooms and suites. It was also his first time there since a $16 million renovation had been completed in 1984 as part of a major redevelopment of downtown Portland.

He had forgotten how central the place was to everything Portland had to offer: It was in the heart of the business and entertainment districts, literally next door to the Portland Center for the Performing Arts and the Arlene Schnitzer Concert Hall (the former Paramount Theatre). Even when the hotel was brand new, the street on which it's located—Broadway—was nicknamed Portland's Great White Way.

The hotel had been a local landmark since its opening on December 17, 1927, and was added to the National Register of Historic Places in 1984. At the beginning of the twentieth century, as American timber interests moved westward to take advantage of the land's plentiful natural resources, George E. Heathman Jr., a real estate developer, saw the need for upscale residential lodging in the city.

Mind you, there were already several fine hotels downtown at the time: the Imperial Hotel (built in 1894), the Seward Hotel (constructed in 1909 and later renamed the Governor Hotel), the Benson Hotel (dating to 1912), and the more recent Commodore Hotel, which was completed in 1925. Heathman himself owned two other hotels in the city: the Roosevelt and another Heathman Hotel, both built between 1925 and 1927.

But George Heathman had given up control over those two properties almost as soon as they were finished. By 1927, he had envisioned a "New Heathman Hotel" that would cater to a more discriminating clientele. In addition to its deluxe accommodations, it would boast a restaurant with the finest cuisine in town.

The ten-story, Italian Renaissance–style structure, designed by local architects DeYong and Roald, was built in record time—just seven months. The facade was faced with brick, and windows were set off by ornamental stone. Inside, the lobby was paneled with dark, expensive woods. On the mezzanine level, freestanding plaster columns and mock half columns set into the walls were decorated with painted acanthus leaves.

Heathman insisted that his new hotel also be accessible to the public at large. From 1927 until 1953 when the television era began, KOIN radio aired its popular broadcasts from the mezzanine of the Heathman. The ground floor of the building housed one of the largest coffee shops in the entire Pacific Northwest.

Heathman invited all twelve hundred laborers who worked on the hotel to a huge party to celebrate its completion. A formal opening and dedication followed, attended by the state governor, the city mayor and commissioners, and heads of the business community.

In the 1950s and 1960s, people throughout America deserted its city centers and moved into the suburbs. It was no different in Portland, and for three decades the Heathman Hotel, along with the rest of downtown, suffered the consequences. George Heathman died in 1930 at the age of forty-nine, but his wife, Katherine, and two of his four children retained an interest in the hotel until the 1960s. One son, Harry, managed the property until two years before his death in 1962.

Finally in the 1980s, far-sighted civic leaders in an alliance with citizens, investors, and the art community began to turn around the city's fortunes. The hotel's refurbishment was critical to the revitalization plan. Although it had been luxurious by 1930s standards, the Heathman was completely remodeled into an upper-end boutique destination hotel. A sense of the original decor was maintained throughout. The elegant Tea Court was reopened, with eighteenth-century French landscapes by Claude Lorrain on the walls and an antique Czechoslovakian chandelier overhead. Throughout the hotel, original artworks, including several lithographs from Andy Warhol's Endangered Species series, were put on display in the hallways. Guest accommodations were redecorated in a variety of nineteenth-century styles, including Empire, Regency, and Biedermeier. The Heathman also expanded its library, adding several first editions signed by contemporary writers who had stayed at the hotel, and it instituted a Books by Your Bedside program for overnight guests.

Indeed, upon check-in that first night, Max was both surprised and delighted to find that the concierge had had a travel book by a local author placed on his nightstand. Surprised because Max didn't remember telling anyone what he did for a living; delighted because, well, it was a really nice, personal touch.

Unless the book was put there by a ghost, Max laughed to himself as he settled beneath the covers.

His first morning walking the streets of downtown reawakened memory after memory. Sure, the skyscape had changed, but each block recalled faces and events that he hadn't thought about in years. And, for the most part, all of them were happy. None of the remembrances of things past made him want to pack up and move back to Oregon, but it was very satisfying to let the warm glow of reminiscences wash over him.

Making his way back to the hotel, Max hoped he could capture what he was feeling with pen and paper. He crossed the lobby, made his way to the elevator, and headed up to 703. As he dipped his keycard into the slot on the door to his room, an odd sensation suddenly hit him, a premonition. He wasn't sure *how* he knew, but there would be something out of place, something *wrong,* on the other side of the door.

He snapped on the light switch as he entered and immediately turned to look into the bathroom. No one there. It was empty. As was the rest of the room. Housekeeping hadn't been in that day, so everything seemed to be right where he left it. And yet . . .

Max closed the door warily behind him. *What is wrong with this picture?* he thought. That old cartoon puzzle came to mind where you had to compare two drawings: One showed what the scene is supposed to look like. The other had been slightly altered. The challenge was to figure out what was different.

His eyes scanned the room, moving first from the bed to the dresser. His suitcase lay open on the stand, his clothes and toiletries undisturbed. The TV was off, the remote sitting to one side.

Then it hit him: the table. He hadn't sat down at the table the night before, but the chair, which he hadn't moved, was pulled out, turned to one side. And resting on the table were the two water glasses from the bathroom. He didn't remember putting either of them there.

He walked into the bathroom and reached down to pick up the towel he had dropped on the floor after showering. Now he was *sure* something weird was going on. There were not one but *two* towels at his feet. He might have stumbled into the bathroom half asleep and carried out a couple of glasses the night before, but he knew for certain that he had only used *one* towel to dry himself that morning. Where had the other one come from?

Someone had been in his room!

Max raced over to the phone and punched at the keypad.

"Hello, front desk. How may I help you?"

"Yes," said Max, trying to keep his voice calm. "This is 703. Has housekeeping been in my room today?"

"Just a minute, sir. Let me check." The receptionist put him on hold briefly, then came back to report, "No, sir. I just spoke with the head of housekeeping. We're very sorry, but they're running a little behind today. She'll come over immediately."

"No, no, that won't be necessary. I mean, that's not the problem. It seems that someone's been in my room."

There was a long pause at the other end of the line. Then, "We'll send someone right up."

Max set the phone back into the cradle and immediately began to wonder whether he had done the right thing. Had he simply forgotten moving the chair and the glasses and using an extra towel? If anyone else had been in the room, it certainly wasn't a robbery. No one had rummaged through his suitcase. In fact, it seemed that none of his stuff had been touched.

The hotel manager showed up at his door within seconds, accompanied by security, who thoroughly checked out the room. They assured Max that electronic records showed no one else had been in the room that morning—at least not by using a key. Then they dropped the bombshell.

It may have been the ghost. It seemed the Heathman was haunted.

Ever since the renovations back in the early 1980s, all of the rooms in the hotel ending in 03 have experienced paranormal activity. Some spectre must have been disturbed, and it has now attached itself to all of the rooms in a vertical column from the top floor down to the lobby. And the phantom was most active in 703.

The most frequently reported ghostly phenomena were objects moving on their own or a mussed-up towel here and there. But some guests have felt sudden chills and cold spots in their rooms; others have heard tapping noises or disembodied heavy breathing. One man swore he was temporarily trapped beneath the sheets of his bed when they pulled themselves taut around him. And a few people have seen dark shadows moving around the room or on the walls, though there's never been a complete manifestation of an apparition.

The hauntings are attributed to a woman who, years earlier, committed suicide by throwing herself down the emergency stairwell adjoining Room 703. Of course, there's no record of such a death ever having occurred, but details like that don't usually matter when it comes to ghost stories, do they?

The manager offered Max his sincere apologies and offered to change his room immediately. But Max decided to stay put, partly in the hopes that his spectral visitor would return. Wouldn't *that* be something to write about: meeting the Heathman haunter face-to-face?

Unfortunately, the rest of Max's stay was uneventful—as least as far as the playful spirit was concerned. Still, Max was able to come away with a tale that was much better than anything he could have hoped for. The only problem was, he wasn't sure whether anyone would believe him.

Heathman Hotel
1001 SW Broadway at Salmon Street
Portland, OR 97205
(503) 241-4100 or (800) 551-0011
www.heathmanportland.com

CHAPTER 26: THE MARINA MANIFESTATION

MGM Grand Hotel and Casino, Bally's Las Vegas Hotel and Casino, Flamingo Hotel and Casino, Westgate Las Vegas Resort & Casino
Las Vegas, Nevada

Even before it became part of the MGM Grand Hotel and Casino, the old Marina Hotel in Las Vegas had a reputation for being haunted—at least according to eight-year-old Roxana, who clearly saw the apparition of a man in golf attire standing at the foot of her bed.

I woke up—dead awake—something I don't remember ever having happened before. I knew immediately that something strange was going on in the room.

I must have been seven or eight at the time; I'm not sure. My parents had taken my grandmother and me on vacation with them to Las Vegas, and we were staying at the old Marina Hotel located right on the Strip. My folks were in one bed; my grandmother and I were in the other.

It must have been the second or third night there. I remember being sound asleep; then the next thing I knew I was sitting upright in my bed. It was around three in the morning, certainly well after midnight. It took me a couple of seconds to figure out where I was, since I didn't get to stay in hotels all that often. But then it all came back to me.

The room was dark, but there was a soft glow of light coming in from underneath and around the edges of the heavy drapes. (Even with thick curtains, there was no stopping the giant neon signs from shining through the window.) I looked down to the end of the bed, and standing there—I'll never forget it—was a man. A stranger.

And though I was just a kid, I somehow knew he was a ghost. I mean, he didn't look like ghosts in the movies or cartoons. I couldn't see through him or anything. He looked real. Or real enough. But there was just *something* about him that didn't add up.

I'd never seen him before. He was an older man, I would guess in his sixties, very tall and very thin. I don't recall what he was wearing other than he had on a small hat. The type that newsboys or, I guess, golfers wear.

I must have been afraid. My heart was racing. But I didn't scream. He was standing sideways to the bed, but his head was turned toward me. I don't know how long we stayed like that, staring at each other. Then, for no reason, his eyes squinted up and he started laughing. His mouth opened wide, but no sound came out of him. There was complete silence.

I couldn't understand what he found so funny. I hadn't done anything. I hadn't moved an inch from the moment I spied him. After what seemed like hours— though I'm sure it was only a couple of minutes at most—he started to fade away. At first, his entire body, then everything but the head gradually turned translucent and disappeared. The last thing to vanish was his face, his eyes locked on mine to the very last second.

With the spell broken, I pulled the covers up over my head and pressed myself down into the bed. I didn't know what to do. Should I wake my grandmother? My parents?

But I was afraid to peek out from under the blankets in case he was still there. I started crying, careful not to make any noise. I told myself that it would soon be morning. It would be over. Once it got light out, everything would be all right.

I don't think I even dozed off the rest of the night. I just lay there, waiting. Eventually I heard my parents moving around, so I knew it would be safe to look out. Sure enough, they had opened the curtains, and the room was flooded with light. Grandma had gotten up, too, and they were beginning to go over their plans for the day.

I jumped out of bed and ran over to my mom. I grabbed ahold of her, and the words started tumbling out, one over the other. I doubt if I made any sense. I knew my parents wouldn't believe me. Why should they? A ghost? In *our room?*

"Now, Roxana," my mother cautioned. (I knew she was being serious, because she only called me "Roxana" when I was in trouble. Otherwise I was "Rox" or "Roxie.") "It must have been your imagination."

And so it went. I pleaded with them to move to another room. I didn't want to stay there another night. What if the man came back? But they were having none of it.

I'm not sure how I got through that second night. I suppose I just willed myself to sleep. And, fortunately, the spirit *didn't* come back, or I slept soundly and missed him. Anyway, the next day none of us said another word about my encounter, and over the years I put it out of my mind.

Until one day in November 1990, when I was around eighteen. My mom and I were watching the news on television, and a reporter announced that the Marina Hotel would be closing its doors at the end of month. The year before, Kirk Kerkorian had bought it and changed its name to the MGM Marina. But now he was planning to tear it down to build a new MGM Grand on the property.

"And you know," the guy on TV told the anchor, "they say the place is haunted. I wonder where all of the ghosts are going to go."

In an instant, all of my memories from that night in the hotel came back to mind.

"See, Mom. Did you hear that?" I called triumphantly. "I told you I wasn't making it up. That's where I saw the ghost."

"Of course you did," she said in that dismissive tone of hers I'd come to recognize. I never spoke to her about it again.

But the broadcast made me curious. If a news program said the hotel was haunted, even in passing, then other people must have run into the apparition, too. What were *their* stories?

This was years before the Internet, so the only thing I could think of was to call the chamber of commerce in Las Vegas. The lady who answered the phone was very sympathetic (and very patient) and gave me the number of a man who owned a souvenir shop who was "really into that sort of thing." I don't remember his name. I talked to him for about ten minutes, then he had to go because of some customers. We played phone tag back and forth a few times, but we never connected and I finally lost interest.

It's funny you should ask me about this now. It all happened—what?—thirty years ago? Still, sometimes I wonder. How many other little girls in that hotel woke up in the middle of the night to find a ghost standing at the foot of their bed?

The Marina Hotel and Casino opened in Las Vegas in 1975 on Las Vegas Boulevard (aka the Strip) just north of Tropicana Avenue. It was a tiny hotel by today's standards, a mere 714 rooms. In addition to the ubiquitous slots, the casino held a sports and racing book and four poker tables. Its main restaurant, decked out in a nautical theme, was aptly called Port of Call.

Two years before the Marina was built, Kerkorian had opened the doors to his **MGM Grand Hotel and Casino** less than a mile down the Strip at Flamingo Road. When it first greeted guests on December 5, 1973, the hotel, set on forty-three acres with 2,084 rooms on twenty-six floors, was one of the largest and certainly one of the most luxurious in the world. It contained two showrooms, the Ziegfeld Stage for spectacular revue shows and the Celebrity Room for headliner acts.

On November 21, 1980, around seven in the morning, with approximately five thousand people in the MGM Grand, a fire broke out in the Deli, a restaurant adjacent to the casino on the second floor. The flames were mostly contained to that level and the lobby, but toxic fumes and smoke billowed up the elevator shafts and stairwells, all the way to the roof. Eighty-five people were killed in the disaster, most of them from smoke inhalation and carbon monoxide poisoning, and another 650 were injured. Only seven people died in the casino itself. Most of the victims were found in stairwells on the upper floors.

Despite the severity of the damage, the hotel was renovated and reopened in just eight months. A second residential tower was added in 1981. Five years later, the casino hotel was sold to Bally Entertainment Corporation, and it became **Bally's Las Vegas**.

In 1989, Kerkorian bought the Marina Hotel and renamed it the MGM Marina. He next acquired the hundred-acre Tropicana Country Club, which was next to the Marina. His original plan was to raze them both, then build a brand new MGM Grand Hotel and Casino on the site. But after consideration, he decided to incorporate the old Marina tower into his design for the new megaresort.

When it was finished in 1993, the sprawling MGM Grand was the biggest hotel in the world, with just over five thousand rooms. (With the addition of several guest residential areas in recent years, the hotel's room total now tops 6,800.) Kerkorian, a former owner of Metro-Goldwyn-Mayer, took advantage of his association with the studio to work many of MGM's most famous images into the decor, including the MGM lion and characters from *The Wizard of Oz*.

The original Marina rooms, though smaller than the new rooms, were completely remodeled to blend in with the rest of the hotel. Once the outside of the former Marina was painted emerald green to match the other sections, it was hard to tell where one structure ended and the other began. The Marina tower has since been revamped once again and is now promoted as the MGM Grand's exclusive West Wing.

Rumors have circulated for years that both Bally's and the current MGM Grand Hotel are haunted. The former comes as no surprise to paranormal specialists. It just makes sense that there are unsettled spirits among the dozens who perished in the catastrophic fire.

Why phantoms turn up in the West Wing of the new MGM Grand is more of a quandary. The spooks definitely date back before the Marina rooms became part of the present resort, but there doesn't seem to be enough information about the apparitions for anyone to identify them or figure out why they're hanging around.

There have been numerous reports that at least two other Las Vegas casino hotels, the **Flamingo Hotel and Casino** and the **Westgate Las Vegas Resort & Casino**, are also haunted. The Flamingo's ghosts date back to the earliest days of the city, when it first became a desert getaway.

In the latter months of 1945, organized crime figures including Benjamin "Bugsy" Siegel traveled west to check out the fledgling Nevada town where gambling and off-track betting were legal. Siegel's first investment was the purchase of the El Cortez Hotel on Fremont Street, in what is now downtown Las Vegas.

Seven miles away on what would one day become the Strip, William R. "Billy" Wilkerson, the owner of the *Hollywood Reporter* as well as Ciro's and the Cafe Trocadero nightclubs on the Sunset Strip, had started work on a hotel of his own. He quickly became strapped for cash, however, and he had to turn to Siegel and his partners for financing. In the end, Wilkerson wound up with only a one-third interest in the property.

Siegel knew nothing about hotel construction, but he muscled his way into the day-to-day operations. Soon there were delays and enormous cost overruns, neither of which enamored him to "the boys" back East. Finally, the 105-room Pink Flamingo Hotel and Casino opened the day after Christmas, 1946. Folklore has it that Siegel named the place for his girlfriend, Virginia Hill, whom he had nicknamed Flamingo because of her long legs.

The hotel had cost $6 million, an astronomical sum at the time. That would have been acceptable if gamblers had immediately flocked to its doors as promised. But they didn't. Then, from January to March 1947, the hotel had to be closed while construction was completed.

To say that Siegel's "investors" were not pleased would be an understatement, and there was talk that Siegel was skimming money. By spring, the casino was starting to turn a profit, but it was too little too late. In a mob hit that continues to be shrouded in mystery, Bugsy Siegel was gunned down on June 20, 1947, while sitting alone in the living room of Hill's Beverly Hills mansion.

Siegel is buried in the Hollywood Forever Cemetery in California, but that's not where his spectre has chosen to spend eternity. His apparition, sometimes accompanied by that of Hill, has been spotted back at the Flamingo, walking through the rose garden in the central outdoor courtyard or upstairs in one of the presidential suites. Perhaps the hotel is where Bugsy's heart and soul really lie, but his materialization is a bit puzzling. The Flamingo Hotel and Casino that's standing today is an entirely different structure (or, more precisely, collection of structures) than the one built by Siegel.

In 1967, Kirk Kerkorian purchased the property. Six years later, he sold it to the Hilton Corporation, which rechristened the hotel the Flamingo Hilton in 1974. Over the next twenty years, additional hotel towers were added. In December 1993, the last remaining section of the original Pink Flamingo was torn down to make way for the hotel's famed garden oasis. After another change of ownership in 1998, the Hilton name was dropped, and the following year the hotel adopted its current moniker, the Flamingo Las Vegas.

As for Siegel's ghost still holding court at the current incarnation of the Flamingo, it's not unheard of for a spirit to show up in a new building constructed on a site it was already haunting.

The Westgate Las Vegas Resort & Casino, located a mile or two east of the Strip on Paradise Road, was built by Kirk Kerkorian and opened in 1969. First known as the International Hotel, it was sold the following year and reopened as the Las Vegas Hilton in 1971. The hotel operated under the Hilton banner until 2012. It then became the LVH—Las Vegas Hotel and Casino—until 2014, when it took its current name.

The hotel has just shy of 3,200 rooms and was the first "mega-resort" in Las Vegas. From its inception, the place was known for its star showroom, which was inaugurated by Barbra Streisand. The shows by the lounge's next headliner, Elvis Presley, are mythic: fifty-eight sold-out performances, followed by equally exciting appearances in 1970 and 1972. For most of the rest of the 1970s, the Hilton's resident superstar was Liberace.

On February 10, 1981, just three months after the devastating fire at the MGM Grand, an arsonist set flames to the Las Vegas Hilton. Because of safety procedures introduced at all of the city's casino hotels after the MGM misfortune, only eight lives were lost at the Hilton.

The hotel was haunted long before it became the Westgate Las Vegas, but not by any of the people who died there. Instead, one of the spectres belongs to a very recognizable Elvis. No less than Wayne Newton, himself synonymous with the Vegas Strip, claimed he saw the King of Rock and Roll's apparition backstage at the hotel. Liberace's spirit has turned up, too, and apparently he's quite a prankster. Stagehands say they sometimes hear him singing or the sound of his distinct laughter, and they blame Mister Showmanship, as the flamboyant entertainer was known, when their tools disappear and turn up later somewhere else.

They say what happens in Vegas, stays in Vegas. Apparently that goes for its ghosts, too.

MGM Grand Hotel and Casino
3799 Las Vegas Boulevard S.
Las Vegas, NV 89109
(877) 880-0880
www.mgmgrand.com

Bally's Las Vegas Hotel and Casino
3645 Las Vegas Boulevard S.
Las Vegas, NV 89109
(800) 634-3434
https://www.caesars.com/
ballys-las-vegas

The Flamingo Hotel and Casino
3555 Las Vegas Boulevard S.
Las Vegas, NV 89109
(702) 733-3111
https://www.caesars.com/flamingo
lasvegas.com

Westgate Las Vegas Resort & Casino
3000 Paradise Road
Las Vegas, NV 89109
(702) 732-5111
https://www.westgateresorts.com

CHAPTER 27: THE MARILYN MIRROR

Hollywood Roosevelt Hotel, Knickerbocker Hotel (now the Hollywood Knickerbocker Apartments), the Oban Hotel (now the Hotel Hollywood)
Hollywood, California

Santa Maria Inn
Santa Maria, California

The Georgian Hotel
Santa Monica, California

At least three hotels in Hollywood, California, can claim resident ghosts, including two haunted by screen siren Marilyn Monroe. In one, the Hollywood Roosevelt, she often showed up in an unlikely way: as a reflection in a giant mirror. And she's not the only celebrity to return to the hotel from the Next World.

"Mirror, mirror, on the wall. Who's the fairest one of all?"

Kristen couldn't resist. *Snow White and the Seven Dwarfs* was her favorite Disney film, and here she was in Hollywood! Could there be a more perfect place to find a magic mirror? Of course, she knew the narrow, six-foot-tall glass wasn't magical at all. But it *was* located on hallowed ground. It was mounted on a landing overlooking the grand lobby of the fabled **Hollywood Roosevelt Hotel**, which opened its doors back in 1927.

The grande dame had been built by a consortium of business folk and film royalty, including Douglas Fairbanks, Mary Pickford, and Louis G. Mayer. The twelve-story hotel, with more than three hundred rooms, was intended to complement Grauman's Chinese Theatre, the movie palace catty-cornered across Hollywood Boulevard that opened only three days after the hotel. Given the landmark's proximity to where so many red-carpet movie premieres would take place, it was only right that the first Academy Awards ceremony was held in its banquet hall, the Blossom Room.

As much as Kristen appreciated the historic significance of the Hollywood Roosevelt, she really wasn't there to bathe in the ambience. She was waiting to meet up with a friend of hers, Tamara, who was working as a Marilyn Monroe look-alike in front of the Chinese.

On any given day in the tourist season, there would be at least a half dozen look-alikes on that block-long stretch of Hollywood Boulevard, offering to pose with sightseers in exchange for a small gratuity. There were perennials like Batman and Superman, and there were usually a few imitators dressed as screen icons in their most famous roles, like Charlie Chaplin as the Little Tramp or Johnny Depp looking all the world like Jack Sparrow. And always a Marilyn.

Kristen's friend Tamara had been portraying Monroe for about three years, primarily at special events, private parties, and industry functions. And in between, she tried to spend a few hours each week on Hollywood Boulevard.

Tamara actually had fun with all the out-of-towners. She realized that they knew she wasn't actually Marilyn, but for a few minutes, all of them were able to forget about reality and enter the world of fantasy that is Hollywood. She knew exactly how to pose with the tourists, how to pucker her lips and bend slightly forward in her pleated white skirt. She'd coo, purr, pout, talking the breathy, husky Marilyn voice she had practiced for years—whatever it would take to bring Marilyn back to life for a moment or two. Tamara would do almost anything not to break the spell for visitors to La La Land, which is why she was meeting Kristen over in the hotel lobby rather than out there on the street.

While waiting, Kristen wandered from the lobby up to the gift shop on the mezzanine. She grabbed some juice and a PowerBar—it might be an hour or more till she and Tamara got some solid food. On the way, she encountered the mirror.

As Kristen stared into the glass and recited the wicked queen's incantation, she became aware of her friend standing behind her. Tamara was smiling, staring straight into the mirror, not acknowledging Kristen or making eye contact. "Marilyn" fluffed her hair, dabbed a fingertip against her beauty mark, and licked her reddened lips to moisten them, all without making the slightest sound.

Kristen, surprised at Tamara's sudden appearance and a bit annoyed that she was toying with her, spun on her heels. "What's the deal, girl? I'm hungry!"

No one was there.

Kristen was stunned. She had seen her friend over her shoulder only seconds before. Where had she gone? And how could she get away so quickly?

Kristen scanned the mezzanine. It was empty. There wasn't a soul in sight. She peered over the railing and caught sight of a girl all in white rushing into the lobby from the street door to Hollywood Boulevard. It was Tamara. Kristen ran down the stairs and hurried up to her friend.

"How did you do that? How did you get all the way down here?"

"What are you talking about?" Tamara asked, truly baffled. "I just walked in the door." Then she added: "Is everything okay? You look like you've seen a ghost."

Maybe Kristen had.

According to legend, the Hollywood Roosevelt Hotel did indeed own a mirror that was haunted by Marilyn Monroe. Supposedly one of the housekeeping staff was the first one to see the ghost. While she was polishing a head-to-toe mirror in one of the rooms, she noticed the reflection of the instantly recognizable blonde bombshell standing behind her. (Some versions of the story have the discovery being made in a suite where Marilyn used to stay; others place the mirror in a manager's office.)

The tale soon became common knowledge among employees, and pretty soon it was leaked to the public. Before long, everyone wanted a peek at the shiny surface. For many years the Roosevelt hung the mirror by the downstairs elevators located near the valet stand at the rear of the hotel. Tongue-in-cheek, the hotel placed two large posters of the sex symbol on the walls opposite the lifts so that, either by accident or with a bit of deliberate finagling, people could catch a glimpse of Monroe in the glass. Around 2000, the mirror was moved to a spot near the gift shop, where it stayed for about a decade. It was placed into storage when the mezzanine and gift shop underwent restoration, and it was never put back on public display. Rumor has it that the mirror has been sold and is now in private hands.

Interestingly, Marilyn's ghost still shows up at the Hollywood Roosevelt, just not in the mirror. She allegedly appears in Room 229 and Suite 1200, two of her favorites at the hotel, as well as in one of the cabanas and on deck chairs in the pool area, where she did her first modeling shoots.

Monroe is not the only celebrity spectre in the Hollywood Roosevelt Hotel. Upstairs, Room 928 is haunted by Montgomery Clift, who stayed there for four months while shooting the movie *From Here to Eternity*. In fact, the actor walks the entire ninth floor. Guests hear the disembodied sound of a bugle coming from his former room (even when no one's staying there) and in the hallway where Clift used to pace while practicing.

Some sort of strong residual essences, thought to belong to Clark Gable and Carole Lombard, can be detected in the twelfth-floor penthouse where the couple honeymooned. A thirty-inch-diameter column of icy air, a typical paranormal "cold spot," can be felt in the Blossom Room, the hotel's ballroom. The ghost of an unidentified man has also been spied there. Usually he's described as being dressed all in black, although a few sources have him in white instead.

People staying at the hotel have found themselves dead-bolted out of their own suites. Invisible children can sometimes be heard playing in the halls. Now and then, apparitions manifest in the rooms, often as reflections in the mirrors. (Shades of Marilyn!) And then there are the phone calls to the switchboard that come from unoccupied guest rooms.

You know, the usual stuff.

Marilyn Monroe, it should be noted, has a few other hangouts in Greater Hollywood. People have claimed they've seen her standing on the sidewalk outside the Brentwood house where she died. Her spirit also manifests by her crypt in Pierce Brothers Westwood Village Memorial Park in Westwood.

For several years her spectre also used to return to the **Knickerbocker Hotel** on Ivar Avenue until renovations at the hotel around 2000 forced the lobby nightclub to close. The building opened as an apartment building in 1925, but within a few years it had been converted into a hotel for overnight to long-term occupancy. Among the celebrities who stayed there were Milton Berle, Bette Davis, Cary Grant, Laurel and Hardy, Jerry Lee Lewis, Elvis Presley, Frank Sinatra, Red Skelton, Barbara Stanwyck, Lana Turner, and Mae West, among many others.

The hotel has seen its share of tragedy and notoriety. In 1943, police dragged actress Frances Farmer, half naked, kicking and screaming from the hotel on assault and DUI charges. Director D. W. Griffith, who kept an apartment at the Knickerbocker, died of a cerebral hemorrhage under the grand chandelier in the lobby in 1948. The MGM costume designer who went by the single name Irene, despondent after her marriage broke up, committed suicide in 1962 by jumping from a fourteenth-story window. William Frawley, best known for his role as Fred Mertz on TV's *I Love Lucy,* was also a longtime resident. He was walking back to his small studio apartment in 1966 when he suffered a heart attack and died.

(Reports vary. Some have him collapsing on the sidewalk in front of the hotel; others place him on the outside staircase or on Hollywood Boulevard.)

During the height of the Jazz Age, Los Angeles police often looked the other way as a notorious speakeasy operated in the hotel just off the lobby. In time, the Art Deco, dark-wood-paneled Lido Room became a popular Hollywood watering hole for the famous and well connected.

Marilyn Monroe's association with the Knickerbocker started when she began seeing baseball great Joe DiMaggio. She used to enter the hotel through the service entrance to avoid the press and then meet up with the slugger in the nitery. After the two got married, part of their honeymoon was spent at the Knickerbocker. In the last few years of the nightclub's operation, women visiting the ladies' room were sometimes surprised to see a golden-haired phantom powdering her nose in front of the mirror. It was Marilyn! Once spotted, Monroe would quickly disappear.

The nightspot is also of particular interest because its lobby bar was the longtime postmortem haunt of Rudolph Valentino, one of Hollywood's greatest stars of the silent screen. While he was alive, the Latin Lover would often tango into the wee hours on the tiled dance floor of the nightclub in the lobby, and he apparently returned to do so long after his demise. For a time Valentino's apparition was reported at his former beach house up the Coast and at Falcon Lair, his Beverly Hills estate. (Both are now private residences.) He had a favorite hideout some 150 miles north at the **Santa Maria Inn**, where his spirit sometimes returns to visit his preferred room, Suite 210. Valentino's presence is also felt—and his shadow is occasionally seen—by his crypt in the Cathedral Mausoleum at Hollywood Forever Cemetery.

By the 1960s, the Lido Room in the Knickerbocker Hotel had ceased operation. The nightclub was reopened in 1993 by entrepreneur David Fisher as the All-Star Cafe and Speakeasy. It was mostly during Fisher's tenure there, up until the venue lost its lease in 2001, that Monroe's and Valentino's spectres were spotted.

The hotel has been transformed once again, this time into senior housing, the Hollywood Knickerbocker Apartments. With the nightclub out of business and access to the building limited to tenants and their guests, there's no telling if either of the legendary spirits is secretly cutting a rug behind closed doors.

Before leaving the Knickerbocker completely, it's worth noting that the hotel has at least one more connection with the Beyond. Magician Harry Houdini lived during the heyday of Spiritualism, and for the last third of his career he actively debunked fraudulent mediums both on and off the stage. It's unclear why. Perhaps Houdini was incensed that such con artists were preying upon those who had lost loved ones. Or, it may have been a personal crusade: He was very close to his mother, and it's believed that he desperately wanted to find a true medium who could contact her after her death. Then again, maybe the showman simply realized that it would be good business to include something so topical in his act.

Regardless, Houdini made a pact with his wife, Bess, that whoever died first would try to get in touch with the other from the Beyond. Any message had to contain a specific, secret word (*believe*) to be proof of actual spirit communication. Attempts to contact the master illusionist began almost immediately after his death on Halloween 1926.

Ten years to the day after Houdini's death, Bess attended a séance conducted by spirit medium Edward Saint on the roof of the Knickerbocker Hotel. The event, billed as the final official Houdini séance, was broadcast on radio. Houdini never came through. Or did he? As soon as the séance ended and before the group could disperse, there was an unexpected cloudburst, with rain falling only on the Knickerbocker and its immediate surroundings. Was it Houdini giving a sign after all?

Another haunted hotel in Tinseltown deserves mention: the **Oban Hotel**. Now known as the Hotel Hollywood, the small, three-story peak-roofed structure was built beginning in 1922 and had its grand opening in 1927. It stands on Yucca Street, one block north of Hollywood Boulevard and around the corner from the Knickerbocker.

For many years, Hollywood wannabes stayed there during their struggle to the top. Among the Oban Hotel's many guests were James Dean, Clark Gable, Fred MacMurray, Glenn Miller, Paul Newman, Orson Welles, and, yes, Marilyn Monroe. (That lady did get around!) The rooms were simple, with a bed, desk lamp, dresser, ceiling fan, desk and chair, and private bath with a toilet, sink, and stand-up shower. But it was enough for those just starting out.

Times have changed. The former Oban Hotel was completely remodeled in 2002 with up-to-date amenities including flat-screen televisions, DSL, and Wi-Fi.

It also has at least two ghosts. Possibly more.

One of the spirits belongs to an early resident of the hotel, a Hollywood hopeful named Charles Love. For whatever reason he never "made it." Love did manage to be seen on-screen, but only as a double for silent film comedian Harry Langdon.

In the end, Love settled for the life of a props manager. It's an essential job on any movie set, but still . . .

On February 15, 1933, after a fight at the studio followed by a long drinking spree, the thirty-three-year-old Love returned to his tiny flat. According to the *Los Angeles Times,* he composed a "note of farewell" to Langdon, then shot himself to death with a single bullet to the head.

Suicides are particularly prone to becoming earthbound entities, and Love was no exception. The unusual part, though, is that his spectre has not been trapped in the room where he died. Rather, he seems to have retired to the basement, the stairs leading down into it, and the landing immediately above. Most often, his presence is indicated by an intense cold spot hovering outside the door leading down to the cellar. In their classic book *Hollywood Haunted,* Laurie Jacobson and Marc Wanamaker say that Love also makes himself known by emitting an incredibly foul, pungent stench that reeks of methane gas.

Love's spectre has become visible from time to time, but only in the form of a shadow. The foggy apparition turns from black to dark brown and finally rust colored. Some believe that his spirit is sometimes joined at the top of the stairwell by the phantom of a former owner of the Oban. And at least one psychic has suggested that the second floor is haunted by a resident female ghost who stays near the room she occupied at the front of the hotel.

About ten miles to the west is the seaside city of Santa Monica, where, in 1933, a Mrs. Rosamond Borde opened the Lady Windermere Hotel. Although not located in Hollywood itself, the place soon became a quick getaway for folks from the film industry. The place was perfect to escape from the glare of the spotlights and the press, and movie stars mingled with mobsters in the downstairs Prohibition-era speakeasy. Regulars included Gable and Lombard, Stanwyck, Humphrey Bogart, Frank Capra, and, it's said, Bugsy Siegel.

The inn was remodeled and renamed the **Georgian Hotel** in the 1950s, and it was refurbished and modernized again in 2000. Today, a mix of Old and New Hollywood can be seen in the hotel's restaurant and lounges along with tourists visiting the West Coast. There also appears to be a goodly number of spectral guests staying on from the days gone by.

Most of the reports of hauntings come from the hotel staff. Disembodied voices have been heard in the lobby, the bar, on the main staircase, and back in the kitchen. The sounds are usually unintelligible murmuring, but every so often a recognizable phrase will pop out. More than one waiter cleaning up after hours or setting the tables for breakfast has come into the restaurant to see the room filled with phantoms dressed in 1930s-style clothing. After a beat or two and the blink of an eye, the apparitions vanish. Individual spirits have also been spotted by housekeepers and service personnel. And eerie music will float through the air long after any bands have ceased playing for the night.

The ghosts don't limit themselves to the ground level. Unexplained footsteps on hardwood floors, including the sound of women wearing high heels, are sometimes heard upstairs—even in hallways and rooms that are carpeted. The third and fourth floors seem to be especially active. The Georgian Hotel, née the Lady Windermere, has always been a relaxed, comfortable place for friends to meet and greet. Perhaps that's why so many phantoms haven't wanted to let the good times go.

Hollywood Roosevelt Hotel
7000 Hollywood Boulevard
Hollywood, CA 90028
(323) 466-7000 or (800) 833-3333
www.hollywoodroosevelt.com

Hollywood Forever Cemetery
6000 Santa Monica Boulevard
Hollywood, CA 90028
(323) 469-1181
www.hollywoodforever.com

Knickerbocker Hotel (now the Hollywood Knickerbocker Apartments)
1714 Ivar Avenue
Hollywood, CA 90028
(323) 463-0096

The former Oban Hotel (now the Hotel Hollywood)
6364 Yucca Street
Hollywood, CA 90028
(323) 466-0524
www.thehotelhollywood.com

Santa Maria Inn
801 S. Broadway
Santa Maria, CA 93454
(805) 928-7777

The Georgian Hotel
1415 Ocean Avenue
Santa Monica, CA 90401
(310) 395-9945 or (800) 538-8147
www.georgianhotel.com

CHAPTER 28: THE RIDDLE OF THE BLACK DAHLIA

Millennium Biltmore Hotel, Alexandria Hotel
Los Angeles, California

The mystery surrounding the unsolved murder of Elizabeth Short, nicknamed the Black Dahlia, has been the subject of dozens of books, magazine articles, films, and television documentaries. The ill-fated twenty-two-year-old's naked and mutilated corpse was found dumped in a vacant lot in Los Angeles, but her ghost walks the halls of the luxury hotel where she was last seen alive.

It was good to get back to the hotel. It had been a grueling day on the floor—Ryan hated attending trade shows—and he was ready to collapse. As head of his sales force at the L.A. Convention Center, he not only had to be the public face of his company, the glad-hander, but he was also the final arbiter of any deals that might be closed that week. And if that weren't stressful enough, it was the first sales meeting for most of his team, and they had to be trained on the spot.

The Biltmore was Ryan's oasis.

Built in 1923 by John McEntee Bowman, the **Millennium Biltmore Hotel**, as it's now known, takes up the better part of a city block in downtown Los Angeles. At the time of its construction, the residential palace was the largest hotel west of Chicago. (Even today it has 683 guest rooms, including seventy-six suites.)

The renowned architectural firm of Schultze and Weaver—they had previously designed the Breakers Hotel in Palm Beach as well as the Waldorf Astoria in New York—used Italian-Spanish Renaissance and Beaux-Arts influences to create their West Coast masterpiece. Its three-story Renaissance Court off the Pershing Square entrance, where the lobby originally stood, was modeled after the court of Queen Isabella of Spain, and it boasted marble floors and a replica of the elaborate Escalera Dorado (or Golden Staircase) in Spain's Burghos Cathedral. Italian artist Giovanni Smeraldi, whose work also appeared in the White House, the old Grand Central Station, and the Vatican, painted the fresco ceilings throughout the lobby.

Perhaps the hotel's pièce de résistance—for which it became justly famous— is its thirty-foot-high, 11,500-square-foot Crystal Ballroom on the Galleria level. Gold leaf and giant backlight panes of stained glass adorn the ceiling, accented by enormous Austrian crystal chandeliers.

Ryan was first drawn to the Biltmore by its beauty and lavish accommodations. What always brought him back was the palpable sense of history that pervaded the premises. Film buffs recognized parts of the hotel from scenes in *A Star Is Born, Chinatown, The Fabulous Baker Boys, Vertigo, Ghostbusters,* and *The Sting* among many other movies that were shot there. And they knew that eight Academy Awards ceremonies were held there in the 1930s and 1940s. JFK made the Biltmore his L.A. headquarters during the 1960 presidential campaign. When the Beatles stayed there in 1964, the streets around the hotel became so crowded that the band had to arrive by rooftop helicopter. And in 1984, the International Olympic Committee worked out of the Biltmore when the games were in town.

But, unknown to Ryan as he crossed the lobby that fateful night, there was also a sinister footnote in the hotel's legendary past. Back in 1947, it was the last place anyone remembered seeing Elizabeth Short before she died.

The notorious tale of the young lady known as the Black Dahlia is heartbreaking. The gruesome manner of her death, luridly described in detail by the *Los Angeles Examiner* and other newspapers, as well as the inability of police to solve the crime, made the case a national sensation.

Elizabeth Short was born in the Hyde Park section of Boston in 1924 and was raised in nearby Medford, one of five daughters. When she was six years old, her father, Cleo, who had been wiped out in the stock market crash, deserted the family. Her mother, Phoebe, managed to keep the family together by working a variety of odd jobs. Elizabeth was prone to asthma and bronchitis, so starting when the girl was sixteen, her mother began to send her to Florida for the winter to stay with family friends.

About that time, Cleo surfaced in Vallejo, California, and wrote his wife, asking to be allowed to return. She refused. But when Elizabeth was nineteen, the young woman traveled alone by train to stay with her father. Before long, they moved to Los Angeles.

Elizabeth's relationship with her father was tumultuous from the start. He expected her to play the docile and obedient daughter, but she was having none of it. She got a job at Camp Cooke (today's Vandenberg Air Force Base), and, surrounded by soldiers, the attractive teenager blossomed. She was flirtatious and soon spent evenings out on the town. That came to a stop in 1943, when Elizabeth was arrested for underage drinking in Santa Barbara, and police sent her back to Medford.

From there she moved to Florida, where she met an airman, Maj. Matthew Michael Gordon Jr. He was deployed to Southeast Asia, but they remained in touch, and he proposed marriage by letter from a hospital bed in India. Elizabeth accepted, but before he could get back to the States, Gordon died in an airplane crash.

In 1946, Elizabeth returned to Los Angeles to visit an ex-boyfriend, Lt. Gordon Fickling, who was stationed in Long Beach. Her attempt to get back together with him didn't work out, but she decided to remain in Southern California. According to most sources, it was during this period that friends nicknamed her the Black Dahlia—a play on the title of a then-current movie, *The Blue Dahlia*—because of Elizabeth's penchant for dressing all in black. (Other reports say an unknown newspaperman covering her murder created the sobriquet.)

Elizabeth never seemed to have a job or a permanent residence. With little money, she was forced to move from one fleabag hotel or boardinghouse to another, basically surviving on the goodwill of others. Her longest period in one place in 1946 seems to have been one month, from mid-November to mid-December, when she stayed in a two-room apartment with eight other young women. Even at a dollar a day for her share of the room, she found it too expensive.

Despite reports to the contrary, Elizabeth never resorted to prostitution, nor did it appear from later investigation that she was particularly sexually active. But she was quite aware of her physical allure, and she knew that by frequenting bars and clubs she could meet people—men—who would provide her with a meal or two and perhaps a night's lodging in return for a few hours of friendly, though usually platonic, companionship.

Sometime in late December 1946, Elizabeth began living with a family in San Diego. A concessions girl at a twenty-four-hour movie arcade found her sleeping in the theater, took pity on her, and invited Elizabeth to stay with her at her mother's house. Elizabeth accepted, but she was far from an ideal guest. What was supposed to be a brief stay stretched into weeks. She didn't find work, laid about the house all day, and stayed out all night.

Whether Elizabeth left on her own or was eventually asked to leave is unclear. She had been seeing a twenty-five-year-old married salesman named Robert "Red" Manley whenever he was in town for business, and she begged him to take her back to Los Angeles, where he also lived. On January 8, 1947, he picked her up around noon, but rather than head north immediately, he rented a local hotel room for the night—although, according to his later testimony, they slept separately.

They set out for L.A. the next morning. They stopped at the downtown Los Angeles bus station so that Elizabeth could check her luggage, then continued to the Biltmore Hotel. Elizabeth claimed she was going to meet her sister, who would be taking her to live with her in Berkeley. Manley walked Elizabeth into the hotel through the Olive Street entrance; the two said good-bye and parted company around 6:30 p.m. Hotel staff later reported seeing Elizabeth in the lobby for a time, but for all intents and purposes, that was the last that anyone remembered seeing the Black Dahlia alive.

That was more than fifty years ago. Ryan stepped into the elevator, pressed the button for his floor, and breathed a sigh of relief as the doors closed in front of him. In less than five minutes he would be back in his room, with his shoes and tie off and a drink from the minibar in hand. What did he want to do tonight? He *should* spend an hour at the gym, and he could check to see if anything was going on at the Staples Center just a few blocks down the street. But he was so exhausted he would probably just call room service and crash.

The elevator was passing the second floor when Ryan realized that the button to another floor was also glowing on the panel. He looked quizzically over his shoulder and there, standing silently in the corner, staring straight ahead, was a woman—a stunning woman, in her early twenties, dressed head to toe in black, with piercing blue eyes and dark, wavy hair swept back high over her head.

She's beautiful enough to be a movie star, Ryan thought. He wondered if a motion picture was being shot in the hotel because the stranger's hairstyle and wardrobe made her look like a femme fatale straight out of a 1940s film noir.

The elevator slowed to a stop, and the doors quietly opened. Ryan instinctively stepped to one side to let the woman by, and as she passed, he was enveloped by a sudden chill. The woman had gotten no more than a few steps out onto the landing when she turned and stared straight at Ryan. What was he seeing in her eyes? Panic? An unspoken cry for help? Was she in some kind of trouble?

But before either could say a word, the doors slid shut. Ryan frantically punched the open door button. It seemed like it took an eternity, but after just the slightest hesitation, the elevator reacted, and the doors slowly began to slide apart.

The girl was gone!

Ryan rushed out of the lift and peered down the long hallway in both directions. The corridor was empty. There was no way that anyone could have gotten into a guest room in that amount of time. The woman had been out of sight for mere seconds. It was as if she had evaporated.

Ryan stood there, hoping she would show herself. Anything to prove that he hadn't been hallucinating. But when no one turned up in the hall after ten minutes, Ryan resigned himself to the fact that the woman's identity and how she had disappeared so quickly would remain a mystery.

And so it was, for several days. While nosing in a bookstore on his last night in town, however, Ryan ambled into a section for works about Los Angeles and the Southland. As his eyes scanned the titles, he was suddenly riveted in place. There, staring out at him from the cover of one of the books, was the smiling face of the bewitching siren he had seen in the elevator. It was the Black Dahlia!

What little Ryan recalled of the murder flooded back to mind, and the book, which he hurriedly bought, told him the rest. Elizabeth's body was discovered in a scruffy lot in Leimert Park in the Crenshaw district of Los Angeles on January 15, 1947. The corpse was so pale that, at first, the woman who came across it thought that she was looking at a discarded department store mannequin. The victim's torso was naked and had been sliced cleanly in half at the waist. The lower part of the cadaver lay with its legs spread wide. The upper half was posed with the arms bent at ninety-degree angles and raised above the head. Cords attached to the wrists and ankles suggested that the woman had been held in bondage, and there were cigarette burns all over her body. Her mouth had been slashed from the corners up toward the ears, and most of her fingertips had been sliced off. Partial prints positively identified her as Elizabeth Short.

Despite the macabre way in which she was disfigured, she had died from internal bleeding caused by repeated blows to the head. It was also *not* a sex crime: There was no evidence that she had been violated, nor were any bodily fluids from the killer found.

A couple of days after Elizabeth's body turned up, a note arrived at the *Examiner* offices, its message written in letters that had been cut and pasted together. Enclosed with the letter were Elizabeth's Social Security card and birth certificate, various photographs, the claim check for her baggage, and her address book with a page torn out.

Over the days, weeks, and months that followed, the police interviewed thousands of people. There were about two dozen serious suspects, but after a thorough investigation they were all eliminated. Manley, initially the prime suspect, passed repeated interrogations and two lie detector tests. Incredibly, almost sixty people, men and women, confessed to committing the crime! But all of the leads eventually led to a dead end.

To this day, the murder remains unsolved.

Elizabeth Short, the infamous Black Dahlia, is buried in Mountain View Cemetery in Oakland, California. But her spirit obviously prefers the Biltmore Hotel. Over the years, her ghost has been spotted in the main lobby, the hotel's ground floor public areas, the elevators, and some of the residential hallways. In many versions of the Black Dahlia haunting, including one popularized by Troy Taylor (author of *Beyond the Grave* and *Field Guide to Haunted Graveyards*), Short's apparition leaves the elevator on the sixth floor. As is the case with so many ghost legends, there is no proof of any of the sightings.

There are many reasons the ghosts of murder victims are said to return from the Other Side. Some may not be aware they are dead; others are trapped in the venue where they met their violent end. It's thought that some spectres come back to search for their killers.

But Elizabeth Short left the hotel alive: There was no sign of struggle or blood from her vicious vivisection found in any of the rooms. So why has the Black Dahlia reappeared in the building where she was last seen? And why in the elevator? If, as legend suggests, her ghost gets off the lift at a particular floor, is it because that was where she met her killer?

More than a half century after Elizabeth Short's death, the murder may have to be solved before the many questions surrounding her haunting can be answered. In the meantime, look around you the next time you visit or stay at the historic Biltmore Hotel. That silent stranger dressed all in black standing next to you in the lobby just may be the Black Dahlia herself.

The Biltmore is not the only haunted hotel in downtown Los Angeles. Only four blocks away, a ghost walks the corridors of the **Alexandria Hotel**. When it was built in 1906, the eight-story structure was the most elegant lodging house in the city. It became *the* place to hold social events, especially after the addition of its magnificent Palm Court ballroom in 1911. Receptions were held there to honor President Woodrow Wilson and Gen. John J. Pershing, and Rudolph Valentino regularly danced to its orchestra under the baton of Paul Whiteman. Charlie Chaplin, Mary Pickford, and D. W. Griffith met at the Alexandria in 1919 to found United

Artists, and other celebrity guests of the hotel included Sarah Bernhardt, Humphrey Bogart, Enrico Caruso, Winston Churchill, Jack Dempsey, Clark Gable, Greta Garbo, Mae West, and Presidents Theodore Roosevelt and William Howard Taft.

When the luxurious Biltmore opened its doors in 1923, the Alexandria Hotel lost its appeal. By 1932, it was bankrupt. The hotel closed two years later, and its furnishings were auctioned off. In the 1950s, it reopened as a transient hotel, and for about two decades the former Palm Court was used as a training ring for boxers.

The Alexandria was refurbished in the 1980s, though it was never restored to its original splendor. In 2007, its rooms were converted into studio apartments as affordable urban housing, and Company of Angels, the city's oldest repertory theater company, relocated to the third floor of the hotel.

It was during the 1980s renovations that a spectral Lady in Black began to appear at the Alexandria Hotel. In their book *Hollywood Haunted*, Laurie Jacobson and Marc Wanamaker describe the unidentified apparition as dressing completely in black and wearing a large black hat. The spirit's clothing suggests she lived in the early part of the twentieth century when the hotel was in its heyday. The Alexandria may not be the splendid palace it once was, but it must hold enough memories for at least one of its former residents to still call it home.

Millennium Biltmore Hotel
506 S. Grand Avenue
Los Angeles, CA 90071
(213) 624-1011
www.millenniumhotels.com

The Alexandria Hotel
501 S. Spring Street
Los Angeles, CA 90013
(213) 626-7484
www.thealexandria.net

CHAPTER 29: THE GRAY GHOST

The *Queen Mary*
Long Beach, California

A transatlantic liner gained its spectral nickname the Gray Ghost, because wartime camouflage allowed it to elude the enemies' sight. But now, out of service and permanently docked as a tourist hotel, the Queen Mary*'s name has become associated with a different type of ghost—the all-too-human kind.*

Nick wasn't sure what to expect. He knew that the **Queen Mary** was supposed to have ghosts onboard—he and Jody *were* taking its Haunted Encounters tour—but he didn't know whether people were still seeing things around the ship. He was sure that the chances a phantom would show up while he and his girlfriend were there were slim to none.

It didn't matter to them. They weren't really there to try to see spirits. They were interested in getting down into the bowels of the ship, and guests were only admitted there if they took one of the daily guided tours.

Nick had learned all sorts of new things about the *Queen Mary* in the brief introductory film that started out the tour. In 1930, Cunard Line began construction of the ship to provide weekly express service between Great Britain and New York City. After a delay caused by Depression-related financial difficulties, work was resumed on the vessel in 1934.

Cunard intended to christen the ship the HMS *Queen Victoria*, but there was a misunderstanding when they asked King George V for royal permission to name the ocean liner for England's "greatest queen." He enthused that his consort, Queen Mary, would be pleased to accept the honor. Needless to say, *Queen Mary* it was.

The ship's maiden voyage was on May 27, 1936. Traditional in many ways, but with modern Art Deco interior design, the vessel soon became the most popular transatlantic cruiser afloat. She was also one of the fastest. In August 1936, the *Queen Mary* won the prized Blue Riband by capturing the record for the quickest Atlantic Ocean crossing to date—just three minutes short of four days. (The honor would go to the *Normandie* the following year, but the *Queen Mary* recaptured it in 1938 and held on to the prize until 1952.)

Its speed came from four giant propellers turned by enormous steam turbines. Nick and Jody marveled as they walked the metal catwalk through the engine room. The long, narrow stretch was known as Shaft Alley, no doubt because it was located directly above the propeller shafts. The young couple couldn't imagine how horrendous the heat and noise must have been when everything was going full blast.

Back in 1940, the *Queen Mary* was en route to New York when England and France declared war on Germany. After dropping off its passengers, the ship diverted to Australia, where it was painted battleship gray and remodeled into a transport ship to carry troops. During the last two weeks of July 1943, it would set a record for carrying the most people ever aboard a single ship—16,683—15,740 of whom were in the armed services.

The ocean liner was so fast it could outrun any German U-boat. That capability, along with its camouflage color, allowed it to appear almost invisible as it floated by, earning it the nickname the Gray Ghost.

Despite its speed, the *Queen Mary* was a big target, so she was always surrounded by protective escorts. On October 2, 1942, one of them, the HMS *Curacoa*, cut in front of the *Queen Mary*'s bow. The megaliner sliced the smaller vessel in half, instantly flooding the *Curacoa*'s lower decks. The *Queen Mary*, under orders not to stop for any reason whatsoever, helplessly watched as 338 of the 400 men onboard sank to their deaths.

Some of those guys are probably haunting this baby, thought Nick. *I wonder if anyone's ever seen them?*

"C'mon, Nick," called Jody. "Everyone's heading up to the pool."

Indeed, he was lagging behind. The tour had started at the stern of the ship on G, one of the bottom decks. They were about to head up to C, the lowermost deck that would have been accessible to passengers.

After the war, the *Queen Mary* was completely restored. There were standard second and tourist classes, of course, but the first-class accommodations could only be described as luxurious, at least for its day. Every room was paneled with the richest woods available and was individually designed to take advantage of the unique layout of the suite. Each cabin had its own phone and toilet facilities.

The ornate first-class dining room, known as the Grand Salon, was gigantic, two stories high supported by massive columns. It was so large that all three ships from Columbus's first voyage to the New World could have been squeezed inside. For a more private evening, guests could dine on the Sun Deck in the intimate Verandah

Grill, which sat eighty. At night, the cozy cafe was transformed into the Starlight Club, which acted as an alternative to the popular Observation Bar located above the bow.

First-class passengers also had access to shops and a full wraparound Promenade Deck, plus the exclusive use of a library, smoking salon, children's nursery, kennel, and on-deck tennis court. And, there was the spacious indoor swimming pool. (Second-class passengers had a separate, smaller and less elegant indoor pool, but it was removed after the ship was taken out of service.)

Located slightly forward of midship on the former C and D decks, the first-class pool was on two levels completely enclosed by four walls decorated with brown, tan, and beige rectangular tiles, accented with stripes of seafoam green. A double staircase at one end of the pool led up to dressing rooms on a balcony that overlooked the bathing area.

For about two decades after the war, the liner was the transatlantic ship of choice for the rich and famous. But the golden era of transoceanic cruising came to an end. The first commercial jet flight took place between London and New York on October 4, 1958, and, before long, the well-to-do were choosing to fly to Europe rather than spend days at sea.

Cunard held out for seven years, but in 1966, the line was forced to sell the vessel (along with its sister ship, the *Queen Elizabeth*). A consortium of buyers brought the *Queen Mary* to Long Beach, California, in 1967 with the intent of turning her into a hotel and maritime museum. She was eventually moored permanently at Pier J, where she became completely dependent on onshore utilities and services. (The *Queen Elizabeth* was sold for scrap in Hong Kong the following year.)

To refit the *Queen Mary* for the next phase of her life, almost everything below what is now R (for *restaurant*) deck was razed. The boilers, engines, and all but a short, representative piece of the propellers were removed. Initially, the indoor pool was saved for use by hotel guests, but it was soon determined to be structurally unsound. Although the pool was never taken out, its water was drained.

Cabins on A and B decks were turned into hotel rooms. The library, music room, and several other public spaces were made into a shopping arcade, and additional retail venues were opened on Sun Deck. Most of the passenger lounges and dining rooms became banquet rental halls.

On November 2, 1972, the first 150 hotel rooms were opened to the public. While the number has varied under different owners, there are currently more than 300 staterooms and suites onboard.

Nick and Jody caught up with the rest of the group at the side of the pool, which had been drained for years. The guide allowed people to poke around for a few minutes on their own, and while Nick shot photographs on the lower level, Jody took the opportunity to explore. She walked up the stairs behind the diving board and made her way back to the old changing rooms. As she walked into the ladies' facilities, she felt an odd presence, almost as if there were someone standing there watching her. But no, no one had followed her inside.

Confused by the sensation, she stepped back out onto the upper walkway overlooking the pool and stared down. Nick and most of the group were at the far end of the pool. But then a small motion almost directly below her caught her attention. She walked halfway around the balcony to get a better look. There, on the pool level, was a girl, about nine years old, quietly laughing and playing by herself. Jody was sure she hadn't been with them on the tour. Where had she come from?

And why did no one else seem to see her?

Jody stood transfixed as the youngster ambled back and forth, so close to the edge of the empty pool that she was afraid the child would fall in. Then Jody saw it: Trailing behind the girl on the smooth tile was a line of wet footprints.

Jody caught Nick's eye to point out the girl, then glanced down to make sure the youth was standing in the same place.

But she was gone.

In fact, she wasn't anywhere. The girl had dissolved. Only the damp imprints of her soles were left behind.

The old first-class pool may very well be the most haunted area of the ship. In addition to the little girl, a sad-looking boy has also been seen from time to time. Several adult female phantoms have been reported in the two-tiered room, including a woman wearing a 1960s miniskirt, a petite brunette in everyday wear, an elderly swimmer in a 1930s-era one-piece bathing suit and bathing cap, and (seemingly out of place) a blonde woman in white evening gown with long sleeves. Sometimes one of the spectres would appear standing on the balcony; other times one would be seen on the diving board ready to plunge in. None of the ghosts stick around for long, however, and they'll fade from view if anyone tries to watch them.

There are other paranormal phenomena in the area as well. The pool hasn't had water in it for decades, but the sound of splashing sometimes echoes off the walls. Many visitors to the changing room cubicles have felt some unexplainable aura within the closed quarters. (Some psychic investigators have suggested that the facilities may be a vortex or portal to Beyond the Veil.) Small circular orbs of light often show up in both digital and regular photographs, even though the glowing circles weren't visible when the pictures were taken.

There seems to be an endless stream of otherworld entities throughout the *Queen Mary,* but interestingly none of them was reported until after the ship was docked in Long Beach.

One of the most famous spooks is John Pedder, who haunts Shaft Alley around watertight door 13. His tale is gruesome. On July 10, 1966, during one of the ship's last voyages, the *Queen Mary* entered a fog bank. The captain took the usual precaution of closing all watertight doors to prevent flooding if, heaven forbid, the ship collided with an unseen vessel in the mist.

Eighteen-year-old Pedder, from Skipton, Yorkshire, England, had joined the ship's crew the previous March. He had finished three tours as a fireman in the boiler room and was on his second sailing as a bilge pump operator in the engine room. No one knows precisely what actions Pedder took that morning when he heard the unmistakable sound signaling the closure of the several-ton steel door. But his lifeless body was discovered about 4:00 a.m., crushed between the hydraulic door and its frame.

Had the door malfunctioned? No, it was tested three hours later and was found to be in perfect working order. Had he slipped? Unlikely. He was found in a standing position, his head and shoulders thrust halfway through the opening. The massive door takes a full six seconds to travel the three feet to its closed position, so the most probable solution was that Pedder had tried to run or jump through at the last moment and was, well, just too late.

People have seen the lad's phantom at the doorway, wearing a beard and dressed in his overalls (variously reported as white or blue). Security dogs supposedly refuse to pass through the space, and some people have reported feeling a rush of air pass by them in the "tunnel." Is it Pedder, desperately trying to make it through the door before it closes in on him?

The ghosts of two other crew members have been spotted nearby. Although unidentified, one is a man in a white boiler suit; the other has black hair and a long beard and wears bluish gray coveralls. Both tend to go about their business oblivious to present-day staff and those on tour. In addition to seeing the men's apparitions, people hear inexplicable banging on the metal pipes.

Also below deck, there's spectral activity all around the area of the hull that was repaired after the *Curacao* collision. People have heard loud sounds of knocking on the metal, ripping steel, and rushing water. Most disconcerting are the ghostly cries of the men who were killed in the accident.

A phantom crewmember named Senior Second Officer William Eric Stark manifests in his old living quarters and out on deck. On Sunday, September 18, 1949, the staff captain told Stark that he had a bottle of gin in his cabin and that he and two other officers were free to go there and have some after completing their shift at 10:00 p.m. Stark got there before the other two men. While waiting, he found what he believed to be the proffered gin in a closed cabinet, poured himself a drink, and downed it.

Because he had a cold, Stark didn't notice the liquid's unusual odor, but he knew that something was wrong as soon as it hit his tongue. Upon closer examination, he discovered that someone had filled an empty gin bottle with the poisonous cleaning solvent carbon tetrachloride.

After his initial panic, Stark was relieved when there were no immediate consequences. He joked about the accident with his friends and the staff captain, but his flippancy was premature. He felt a bit queasy the next day, but the ship's doctor only recommended bed rest. By Tuesday, Stark's condition had deteriorated, and he was admitted to the hospital. Within hours he had sunk into a coma and died.

A little relaxation, a simple mistake, and the result was death. No wonder Stark's soul has never come to rest.

Other than the unknown ladies by the pool, the best-known female ghost on the *Queen Mary* is the Lady in White, who always appears dressed to the nines in a long, white, backless evening gown. Her spirit used to sweep into the Queens Salon, which had once been the ship's main lounge. She would make her way to the grand piano or, sometimes, stay on the dance floor and sway in time to the music. Regardless, after a few minutes, she'd startle onlookers by instantly disappearing.

When Sir Winston's restaurant was opened in the hotel, the piano was moved to the new, elegant eatery. And wouldn't you know it? The mysterious Lady in White moved right along with it. She's not seen very often these days, but that doesn't mean she's not around.

Behind crew doors, another presence has been seen, heard, and felt in the main kitchen. One old wives' tale says that it's the ghost of an unpopular cook who was thrown into an oven, either by angry staff or troops. Another suggests it's Leonard "Lobster" Horsborough, who was a chef onboard for fifteen years before dying from heat stroke or heart trouble on November 13, 1967, during the ship's final voyage. His body was buried at sea, but perhaps his spirit prefers to spend its time in his old kitchen rather than Davy Jones' Locker!

Of course, the ship's wraiths don't keep to the public and crew areas. They infest the hotel staterooms as well. Dozens of guests have reported seeing spectres in their "cabins." Many have gotten up to answer knocking at their doors, only to discover that there was no one in the hallway. In some of the rooms, the showers and other fixtures have a way of working by themselves. Guests who stay in the suite that Winston Churchill occupied during his crossings on the *Queen Mary* have reported smelling and seeing cigar smoke in the room.

These hauntings are only the tip of the iceberg. The sounds of children laughing and playing ring out in the old nurseries and out on deck. The barking of an unseen dog has echoed out of the former first-class kennel. Plates, trays, and other objects move on their own in the lounges, dining rooms, and corridors. And front desk personnel have looked up to see people vanish while standing in the middle of the lobby.

For more than forty years now, hundreds of sightings have occurred on the *Queen Mary,* and the manifestations continue to this day. Few hotels embrace their reputation for being spook-ridden as wholeheartedly as the *Queen Mary.* If you want to see one of the spectres, your best bet may be to stay overnight. That stranger who greets you as you take a midnight stroll on the Promenade Deck may not be another hotel guest. He may be sailing for eternity on the Gray Ghost.

The *Queen Mary*
1126 Queen's Highway
Long Beach, CA 90802
(562) 435-3511 or (800) 437-2934
www.queenmary.com

As of this writing, the *Queen Mary* is temporarily closed for necessary repairs. Plans are underway for its restoration and eventual reopening for hotel guests and the public.

CHAPTER 30: THE PHANTOM IN THE DEL

Hotel del Coronado
Coronado, California

Was it suicide that killed Kate Morgan at the famed Hotel del Coronado in 1892? And was that really her name? She's been gliding down the hotel's hallways for decades, and spectral phenomena still plague the room where she stayed in the days leading up to her death.

"Will there be anything else, sir?"

"No thanks. I think everything will be fine."

"I hope so, sir. Good luck."

Tim tipped the bellhop, then locked and chained the door behind him. The well wishes might have seemed odd under any other circumstance, he mused, but he *was* in Room 3327.

Tim had been trying to stay there for years, but the room had always been booked when he had vacation. Ordinarily, management at the **Hotel del Coronado** in Coronado, California, doesn't even rent the room unless it's specifically requested, but that hasn't diminished its popularity.

After all, it's haunted.

The sightings date back to the turn of the twentieth century. In the 1880s, a tremendous land boom sprang up on the West Coast, and as people began to flood south from Los Angeles, railroad magnate Elisha Babcock and Hampton L. Story (of the Story & Clark Piano Company) decided the time was right to build a luxury, seaside resort in San Diego. Rather than place their hotel in the downtown Gaslamp Quarter of the city, they decided to purchase Coronado Island, which sat just offshore in San Diego Bay. They would subdivide the land and position the hotel at the island's southernmost tip along a wide sandy beach.

In 1969, a tall, modern bridge was raised to connect the island to the mainland, but up until that time the only way to reach Coronado was by boat. That automatically added a veneer of exclusivity and a certain mystique to the venue.

Work on the new hotel began on twenty-eight acres of beachfront property in March 1887. The original plans for the Del, as the Hotel del Coronado is nicknamed, called for just under four hundred rooms. The main lodge has been significantly expanded over the years, though, and today, with the addition of the Ocean Towers and California Cabanas, the total is up to 679 rooms, plus an additional seventy-nine cottages and villas.

The suites in the original structure, now known as the Victorian Building, were elegant, and the hotel was the first on the West Coast to be wired for electricity. There were tennis courts, a tea garden—even a saltwater pool (despite the fact that the ocean was mere steps away across a broad lawn and beach). Perhaps the inn's most outstanding feature was its 23,500-square-foot main dining room, the Crown Room, with its high, arched, pine wood–paneled ceiling. The entire exterior of the Del was painted a pristine white, set off by deep maroon roofs.

Building costs far exceeded estimates. It turned out that almost all of the necessary resources had to be brought from outside the area during the hotel's construction, including the lumber and the labor force. Plus, fresh water had to be pumped over from the city. A real estate bust threatened to sink the endeavor, but at the last minute John D. Speckels, the sugar king, offered a welcome infusion of cash. By 1890 he had bought out the other partners completely.

The Hotel del Coronado, now a U.S. National Landmark, opened to great fanfare in February 1888. By the Roaring Twenties it had become a popular vacation spot for Hollywood celebrities. Among the film stars who dropped in during its early days were Tallulah Bankhead, Charlie Chaplin, Tom Mix, Mary Pickford, Rudolph Valentino, and Mae West. The hotel would also become a backdrop for many movies, most notably the 1959 Marilyn Monroe–Jack Lemmon–Tony Curtis motion picture *Some Like It Hot.*

Other major figures to visit included Sarah Bernhardt, Thomas Edison, Charles Lindbergh, Babe Ruth, and L. Frank Baum (who may have used the hotel's Queen Anne–style turrets as inspiration for his description of the Emerald City). Political figures such as Edward, Prince of Wales (later King Edward VIII) and eleven U.S. presidents, beginning with Benjamin Harrison, have also been drawn to its doors.

But perhaps the Del's most frequent guest—a five-night stay that has stretched into forever—is Kate Morgan.

On November 25, 1892, a wan woman in her mid-twenties walked into the lushly furnished foyer and inquired about a room. She was later described by a coroner as being five foot six, with a fair but sallow complexion, two moles on her left cheek, medium-length black hair and brown eyes, and weighing about 150 pounds.

A female traveling alone, especially one without suitcases, certainly drew suspicion and was frowned upon in Victorian times. But the woman assured the desk clerk that she'd been traveling with her brother, a Dr. M. C. Anderson. He had gotten off the train in Orange on their way south from Los Angeles, but he would be arriving shortly. She had no luggage because he was holding the claim tickets.

The sympathetic clerk took the woman at her word, registered her under the name Mrs. Lottie A. Bernard of Detroit, and showed her to Room 302 on the north side of the building. (In later years, the room's number was changed to 3312. It is currently 3327.) Over the next few days, she repeatedly asked the staff about her brother. Had he arrived? Had he sent a message? The answer was always a polite but regrettable no.

Meanwhile, her worsening health was obvious to anyone who saw her. Several people, including the pharmacist who ran the hotel's drugstore, recommended that she visit the house physician. She assured them that she had already been diagnosed. She suffered from neuralgia, and her brother would treat her as soon as he arrived. Later, when the hotel manager pressed her further, she confessed that she had stomach cancer. (At the same time, he discreetly asked as to how she was planning to pay for her stay, and she told him to wire a G. L. Allen in Hamburg, Iowa. Indeed, money arrived by wire the morning her body was discovered.)

Despite her sickly condition, on November 28 "Lottie" managed a trip into San Diego, where she purchased a handgun and ammunition. That night, she was seen by guests on a hotel veranda, looking out across the bay as an impending storm approached.

The next morning, a hotel electrician found the secretive woman, dead, on a small set of stone stairs leading down to the beach on the west side of the building. There was a gunshot wound in her right temple and a forty-four-caliber pistol beside her on the steps.

According to police, there was no doubt the mysterious person had committed suicide. But why had the "Beautiful Stranger," as newspapers dubbed her, done it? Was she merely ending the pain of a fatal disease? And why had her brother abandoned her? In fact, was anyone really supposed to meet her at all?

No one was sure. Only one thing became certain: The woman was not Lottie Bernard. After almost two weeks of inquiry, it was determined that her real name was Kate Morgan.

She had been born Kate Farmer sometime around 1865 in Iowa, and on December 30, 1885, she married Thomas Morgan. At the time of her death, Kate was employed as a domestic by the L. A. Grant family of Los Angeles, working under the assumed name of Mrs. Katie Logan. She had told the Grants and her coworkers that she had fled from her husband, who was an inveterate gambler. Other than that, she never talked about her past.

On November 23, Kate had told the Grants that she was going to take a one-day trip to San Diego. When she didn't return, they contacted the police, who in turn connected her disappearance with the news reports coming out of San Diego. When Kate's trunks were opened back at the Grant residence, papers found inside confirmed that she was living a double or triple life.

But why was she heading to San Diego? And what was the true manner of her illness? An autopsy was never performed. Clues to the reason for her suicide may have been destroyed when Kate burned a large stack of papers in the fireplace of her hotel room. And the unclaimed suitcases, purportedly left behind at the train depot, were fictitious.

An anonymous "prominent physician" suggested in the *San Diego Union* newspaper that the early symptoms of pregnancy were almost identical to stomach cancer. It was his conclusion that Kate was "enceinte" and was using the medications found in her room, including camphor and quinine pills, to induce a miscarriage.

An eyewitness reported that he had seen Kate arguing with an unidentified male on the train heading to San Diego. The man got off in Orange, just as Kate claimed her brother had, but to the observer it seemed to be more of a lover's spat than a squabble between siblings. Had Thomas Morgan unexpectedly come back into Kate's life? Or was it, perhaps, a boyfriend who had gotten her pregnant and then, after a final quarrel, deserted her?

And there was the question of the missing day. Even in 1892 it was only a few hours' journey between the two cities, but she didn't arrive in San Diego, or at least at the Coronado, until two days after she left her employer's house.

While officials decided what to do with the remains, they were held by a local mortuary, Johnson & Company. Given the notoriety of the case—indeed, it drew national press—and no family to object, they put Kate's body on display. Eventually Morgan was buried in Mount Hope Cemetery just east of downtown San Diego.

But it seems that her spirit wanted to return to the Del.

Which leads us to the question: Why? According to paranormal investigators, sometimes when a life is snuffed out abruptly the person doesn't even know that he or she is dead. Also, people like Kate Morgan whose lives have been cut short or who die violently sometimes find it difficult to find eternal rest. On the other hand, perhaps she's still waiting for her "brother" to arrive. Then, too, Kate was certainly pampered at the hotel during her last days. Maybe she enjoyed the service so much she never wants it to end.

Regardless, hundreds of people have reported spotting Kate's ghost in Room 3327. But Tim wanted to see her for himself. Or, if not her ghost, he at least wanted to experience some of the other strange paranormal phenomena that take place there.

It's been said that personal items left lying out would go missing, then turn up elsewhere in the room. Guests might wake up in the morning to find the place a complete mess, as if some unseen intruder had picked up stuff at random and thrown it around the room. People have heard the sound of disembodied footsteps in the dark or caught brief whiffs of a flowery perfume in the air. There might be sudden drops in temperature. Blankets have been ripped off guests as they slept, and the television and ceiling fan have been known to turn on by themselves.

Sometimes the main attraction herself showed up: a dark-haired woman dressed in 1880s clothing. Even when she didn't appear, people often entered the room to find an impression on the bed as if someone had been lying there. No wonder maids prefer to service the room in pairs!

Kate doesn't like to stay in her room. She's been encountered floating down the third-floor hallway, and she's manifested outside in the garden, on the stairs where she breathed her last, and on the beach. Even when she doesn't choose to materialize, some people will nonetheless get the impression that she is watching them. "Sensitives"—as people who can discern the presence of invisible spirits are called—have reported being overwhelmed by feelings of hopelessness and despair when they walk down the stairs where Kate's body was found.

Tim, who wanted nothing more than to cross paths with a visitor from the Other Side, had been adamant about staying in 3327. Unfortunately, it turned out to be a quiet night at the hotel. No moving curtains over the windows, no shifting blankets on the bed. No filmy phantom passing by the nightstand or inanimate objects flying about the room. Not even the creak of a sagging floor board. He forced himself to stay awake until three, but finally Tim drifted off to sleep.

He woke with a start—wide-awake—at 5:00 a.m. There was just a hint of predawn light peeking through the drapes. What had disturbed him? He looked around the room cautiously, but, no, he was alone. Yet something was telling him, *compelling* him, to get dressed and head down to the beach. Within minutes, he was walking through the lower lobby toward the sand.

Then it dawned on him: Whatever spirit had told him to go to the beach had done so because it knew he would walk in this direction. It knew he would run into . . . Kate Morgan!

Lost in thought, Tim started down the infamous set of stairs where Morgan's lifeless body had been found more than a hundred years earlier. Halfway down he felt something brush against his arm, passing him by. It was almost imperceptible. The touch was brief. The briefest. But it had definitely happened.

Tim instinctively spun around to look around, but the staircase was empty, of course. He stood there, transfixed, unsure whether he could believe what had just occurred. Slowly he became aware of the opening of windows overhead and the rattling of service trays down nearby hallways. The hotel was coming back to life.

The sun was up, and early risers were already jogging on the beach. Content, Tim began an unhurried walk back to his room—her room—running through his mind every detail of a morning he would never forget.

"Thank you for coming through, Kate," he mumbled. "It was worth the wait."

Skeptics say that all of the spooky goings-on at the Hotel del Coronado can be attributed to the natural creaks and groans of any century-old seaside hotel. But after his experience, Tim knew better. So, too, does the staff. Every year when they celebrate their employee Christmas party, they make sure there's an extra name on the guest list: Kate Morgan. Their resident ghost is always welcome.

But it turns out, Kate's not the only spook haunting the Del.

Burning, iridescent eyes, thought to be those of a different woman, have startled guests in Room 3312 as they glowed in the darkened chamber. Other visitors have had to endure flickering lights, had the windows open and shut by themselves, seen the curtains sway even when the windows were closed, heard unnatural sounds emanating from the plumbing, or had the bed shake. Many just felt a general restlessness and anxiety.

Sometimes, passersby in the hall have seen unusual lights radiating out from under the door. In the summer months, the maintenance crew finds it almost impossible to keep the room's window screens from falling off. And what causes the light bulb at the bottom of the nearest stairwell to burn out after only one or two days?

It's said that 3312, which was once numbered 502, was where Elisha Babcock clandestinely met his mistress. She supposedly committed suicide in the room after finding out she was pregnant. The gossip was impossible to verify: By the time police arrived, her body had somehow disappeared.

Then there's Room 3502. During a visit to the Hotel del Coronado by Vice President George H. W. Bush, one of the men from his Secret Service detail was assigned to the room. In a single evening, the agent suffered shifting drapes, cold gusts, and a strange luminescence filling the room. At one point he called down to the front desk complaining about the loud talking and footsteps from the guests overhead. The receptionist, puzzled, assured him there wasn't anyone in the room directly above him. Then the spectral form showed up. The agent asked to be transferred to another room before morning.

Even more phantoms infest the Hotel del Coronado. The ghost of the Crown Room's first maintenance supervisor appears, testing the dining room's floor with his cane. An ethereal woman in period dress gaily dances across the hotel ballroom. The spirit of a terminally ill young girl who was rushed to a hospital in 1950 has returned to roam the corridors looking for the doll she left behind. There are other phantom children as well: The spectres of a little boy and girl are seen throughout the property, either racing in the halls or running up and down the stairs.

Finally, paranormal activity took place for several months in a shop with the name Established in 1888, it specialized in hotel-related souvenirs. Several people reported seeing a dark form moving behind the locked doors after hours. One shop manager arrived in the morning to discover that all of the books on a lower shelf near the register had been disturbed. Some were on their sides; others were scattered on the floor and lying open. Memorabilia concerning the filming of *Some Like It Hot* not only fell but sometimes literally flew off the shelves. Oddly, once the shopkeepers moved any Marilyn Monroe collectibles to back behind the counter, the tchotchkes never moved another inch.

Hotel del Coronado
1500 Orange Avenue
Coronado, CA 92118
(619) 435-6611 or (800) 468-3533 (800-HOTEL-DEL)
www.hoteldel.com

The Hotel del Coronado is on Coronado Island, just a few minutes from downtown San Diego. The island is linked to the mainland by a 2.1-mile bridge that towers two hundred feet over San Diego Bay.

The haunted rooms at the Del are all within the hotel's original section, now called the Victorian Building. Those who wish to stay in Room 3327 must specifically request it.

CHAPTER 31: SAN DIEGO SPIRITS

US Grant Hotel, Horton Grand Hotel
San Diego, California

As cities grow, there are always real estate developers who are happy to provide lodging for tourists and those in town for business. Sometimes existing hotels are restored or upgraded; sometimes they are razed and new ones built. But that doesn't necessarily mean the hotels' old ghosts are going anywhere.

In 1910, Ulysses S. "Buck" Grant Jr. opened an elegant, eleven-story hotel in San Diego and named it after his father, the eighteenth president of the United States. Today the palatial hotel is part of the Marriott Luxury Collection. Located in the moody, historical area of downtown referred to as the Gaslight Quarter, it's little wonder that the place has attracted guests—and kept a few ghosts—over the past century.

There's the usual assortment of paranormal activity that occurs in haunted hotels, such as strange, unrecognizable sounds, flickering lights, self-moving objects, and disembodied footsteps. But in the middle of the night, guests have been known to wake and see the phantom of a plump gentleman in a black suit leaning over them. Even before the person can react, the spectre instantly vanishes. The spook's identity and reason for being in the **US Grant Hotel** remains a mystery.

The name of the apparition that's seen most often is Frances Josephine "Fannie" Chaffee, the daughter of a U.S. senator from Colorado and the first wife of U. S. Grant Jr.

The Grants married in 1880 and had five children over their twenty-nine years together. In 1893, Fannie's health began to fail, so the couple moved from New York to sunny San Diego, where Grant's younger brother already lived.

Grant soon took up real estate, and in 1895 he bought the old Horton House hotel, primarily as an investment. He tore it down in 1905 and five years later built the US Grant Hotel in its place. The undertaking was successful, as were other property ventures, and Grant soon found himself on the boards of several banks and recognized as one of city's brightest citizens.

Unfortunately, Fannie's constitution continued its slow decline. She passed away in 1909 at the age of fifty-two and was buried in San Diego's Greenwood Memorial Park. In 1913, Grant married Emerica Rosa "America" Workman Will, a divorcée from her first husband and a widow from a second.

Meanwhile, Fannie's phantom moved into the US Grant Hotel. When she materializes, she's wearing a white dress of early twentieth-century design. Oddly, whenever she appears, things go missing or get moved out of place. Folks who get a good look at her say Fannie looks sad and weary.

Perhaps there's a bit of bitterness as well. Although it pure conjecture, some paranormalists suggest Fannie hasn't returned to the hotel to relive whatever happy times she may have had there but to show her annoyance or disapproval that her husband remarried so soon after her death—or that he remarried at all.

Not to be confused with Horton House, which was razed to make way for the US Grant Hotel, the **Horton Grand Hotel** began life during the Victorian era as two separate structures, the Grand Hotel and the Brooklyn Hotel.

In 1885, San Diego was linked to a transcontinental railroad. This led to a building frenzy of homes for the increasing number of people moving to San Diego as well as hotels for visitors. The Grand Hotel, a luxury accommodation built in the Italianate Baroque Revival style, opened on F Street in 1886 or 1887 (sources vary). The Grand's name was changed to the Horton Hotel in 1907.

The Brooklyn Hotel, also on F Street, opened about the same time as the Grand Hotel. It had a contemporary Western design and a more casual atmosphere. Its name was changed to the Brooks-Kahle Saddlery Hotel after a harness and saddle shop by that name leased the ground floor in 1912. Tom Mix and Roy Rogers were said to be regular customers. The store remained open until 1960.

The two hotels were slated for demolition in the 1970s so that a downtown shopping mall, Horton Plaza, could be constructed. Local developer Dan Pearson had other plans. He bought both buildings, had them dismantled brick by brick, marking and cataloguing everything, and then warehousing it all for future use.

In the mid-1980s, he had the hotels reassembled side by side on Island Avenue, just a few blocks from where they originally stood, with a courtyard and a shared lobby linking the two buildings. (Looking at the Horton Grand Hotel from Island Avenue, the tower to the left is the former Grand Hotel; the one to the right was the Brooklyn Hotel.) Both hotels underwent historical restoration as well as refurbishment for modern use. Remarkably, the architectural styles meshed, and the Horton Grand Hotel was born.

When it opened to the public in 1986, apparently some of the ghosts from the original two hotels returned—and new ones soon joined them. One of the latter is the spectre of Ida Baily, the madam of a brothel that once stood where the Horton Grand sits today. Her spirit takes many forms. In addition to her human visage, she sometimes appears as a white fog or floating mist. Guests sometimes claim to sense her warm, affable presence even when she doesn't materialize. A few folks reported having had an entirely different encounter with Ida, however: They say they felt her icy aura approach them and then pass directly through their bodies.

The spirit that's seen most often—or at least the one that receives most of the blame for paranormal activity in the hotel—is Roger Whitaker, who was a professional gambler. He regularly made the rounds of San Diego's card rooms and casinos in the 1880s and 1890s. Although there are several variations to the story of his death, most of them agree that he was shot and killed while hiding in the armoire in Room 309 at the old Grand Hotel.

In some versions of the story his assailants were trying to collect on old gambling debts; in another, he was caught (uncharacteristically) cheating during a card game to pay off what he owed. After being roughed up and possibly being shot and wounded, Whitaker managed to escape. They tracked him down to his room at the Grand shot him dead through the closed cabinet doors. (Some sources say the shots were fired through the door to his room instead.)

An old wives' tale that's heard less frequently says Whitaker was shot to death in 1843 in the prostitution and gambling district of San Diego known as the Stingaree. (Large portions of the Stingaree neighborhood would be transformed and incorporated into the Gaslamp Quarter a century later.) In that version of the legend, Whitaker's killer was a father determined to prevent the rogue from marrying his daughter. He tossed Whitaker's body into a local bog. Some forty years later when the original Grand Hotel was built, Whitaker's revenant moved in.

Even though the hotel's location has changed, Whitaker still resides in Room 309. Lights turn on and off "by themselves," and the doors of the current armoire swing open "on their own." He's also been known to move stuff around while guests are sleeping. Sometimes the room's temperature will instantly and unexplainably become very hot, and, on these occasions, even the air conditioner won't cool it down. Perhaps the phenomenon that frightens guests most is being woken up in the middle of the night because Whitaker's spirit is shaking the bed violently.

Hotel staff passing by Room 309 have reported hearing someone inside handling playing cards when the room is unoccupied, and maids are occasionally shocked to find a human-shaped indentation on the comforter of the bed they had just made up.

Although it doesn't happen very often, Whitaker does become visible from time to time, either in the hallway or in Room 309. Those who have seen the apparition say the ghost is friendly and looks to be solid flesh and blood. A story goes that a woman who was staying at the hotel saw Whitaker in the corridor and asked him where she could find the ice machine. She didn't realize she was talking to a ghost until it suddenly disappeared.

There are more spectres in the Horton Grand Hotel besides Ida Baily and Roger Whitaker. Although they've been seen throughout the buildings, their usual haunt is descending the main staircase. You'll know them when you see them: They're always well attired in garb from the nineteenth century.

US Grant Hotel
236 Broadway
San Diego, CA 92101
(619) 232-3121
https://www.marriott.com

Horton Grand Hotel
311 Island Avenue
San Diego, CA 92101
(619) 544-1886 or (800) 542-1886
www.hortongrand.com

HAUNTED HOTELS

CHAPTER 32: NORTH TO ALASKA

Alaskan Hotel & Bar
Juneau, Alaska

Golden North Hotel
Skagway, Alaska

The Historic Anchorage Hotel
Anchorage, Alaska

Passage to Alaska from the Lower 48 didn't begin in earnest until the Klondike Gold Rush of 1896, where mere survival was often difficult. Little wonder that there are so many ghostly revenants and haunted hotels from that era.

The **Alaskan Hotel**, built in 1913, is Juneau's oldest continuously operating hotel, and it was placed on the National Register of Historic Places in 1978. Centrally located, the Alaskan is on the city's main street near the downtown wharf. Among the hotel's early residents was a young woman named Alice who was left behind when her husband departed for the Yukon. After three weeks, she was destitute and was forced to enter the world's oldest profession in order to survive. Her husband finally did return, a full month late, but when he discovered how his wife had been making ends meet, he killed her in her hotel room. Many believe that it's her troubled spirit that haunts the hallways of the Alaskan Hotel.

The old hotel is filled with cold spots, and guests have reported feeling an invisible spirit, presumed to be female, stroke their faces or sit beside them on the bed. The phantom's reflection has also been spotted in several of the hotel's mirrors. For some reason, the rooms on the south side of the hotel seem to have the most paranormal activity. The room that figures most in the hotel's ghost legends is 219, but 218 and 308 are also frequently mentioned as well.

The **Golden North Hotel** in nearby Skagway closed to overnight guests in 2002, but ghost stories about it have appeared in paranormal literature for so long that it has to be mentioned. Currently, the ground floor of the building houses shops for tourists. When the hotel was in operation, its second story had sixteen rooms. The room in which Mary supposedly died, number 24, was the most haunted. It was located along the back wall of the hotel and was one of fifteen guest rooms on the third floor.

According to legend, sometime in 1898, a fearless eighteen-year-old woman named Mary traveled to Skagway to meet her fiancé, who had sent for her. She stayed in Room 24 at the Golden North Hotel and waited for his return from the Klondike, where he was panning for gold. Days turned into weeks, but the young man never returned. (His fate is unknown, but conditions on the trail were brutal. Many men died in their search for sudden wealth.)

Sadly, it may not have mattered even if he had made it back. Mary was already frail when she got to Skagway, and she fell sick with tuberculosis (or possibly pneumonia) soon after her arrival. When the hotel manager looked in on her one morning, he found Mary dead, lying on her bed in a lace-trimmed bridal gown.

Over the ensuing years, hotel guests were always aware when Mary was around. In addition to hearing her footsteps and seeing light orbs, visitors occasionally sensed an unseen presence sit on the bed next to them. Some guests were inexplicably overcome with nausea, felt faint, or experienced a choking sensation. A very few people saw Mary's apparition: a female figure in a long, white nightgown walking the hall outside Room 24.

Ghostly phenomena were experienced in Rooms 9, 13, and 14. Room 14, especially, was known for the frequent appearances of illuminated orbs or entities.

Though seldom mentioned by storytellers, the Golden North Hotel in which Mary died was a different building than the one sitting at Third and Broadway today. There was an earlier Golden North Hotel in Skagway, but it was torn down after the Gold Rush ended. According to a 1910 map, it stood at Fourth Street between State and Main and was owned by George Dedman and Edward Foreman. Unfortunately, no guest records of the original Golden North Hotel have been preserved.

In 1908 or 1909, Dedman and Foreman bought another building in Skagway. It once housed the Klondike Trading Company, which supplied folks heading off to the gold fields, but the operation went out of business after the bust. The two-story structure was lifted off its foundation and moved to the southwest corner of Third Street and Broadway. Dedman and Foreman added a third floor and remodeled the building into their new Golden North Hotel. (It's unclear whether the ground level remained a store or was made into a hotel lobby.)

So why has Mary's ghost turned up at a hotel she never visited? It's rare for a spirit to hop from one venue to another, but it's not unprecedented. The lodgings where she actually died is gone, but with the new hotel having the same name and owners, apparently there was enough of a connection for Mary's spirit to make the transition.

Anchorage, Alaska's largest city by population, was founded in 1914. Shortly thereafter, the original Anchorage Hotel was built at the corner of 3rd Avenue and E Street. The accommodation was expanded in 1936 by constructing a second structure, the Anchorage Hotel Annex, on the other side of the alley behind the building. The two were then connected by an elevated walkway. In time, the building in front was sold and demolished. Today the Hilton Anchorage stands in its place.

The Annex continued to operate on its own, however. After many years it became shabby and dilapidated, and the lodgings went through many hands and changed names multiple times. Eventually, a set of new owners recognized the hotel's worth, saw its potential, and completely refurbished it in 1989. The Anchorage Hotel Annex was placed on the National Register of Historic Places in April 1999.

Several famous figures have stayed at what is now called the **Historic Anchorage Hotel**, including forester and wilderness activist Bob Marshall; Alaskan landscape painter Sydney Laurence, who had his studio in the lobby and also lived upstairs; and Will Rogers and Wiley Post, who were guests there just two nights before their fatal flight to Barrows

The hotel also has a number of otherworldly residents. The Historic Anchorage Hotel doesn't shy away from the spooky legends about the place, and it even mentions some of the stories on the home page of its website. Overnight guests regularly report paranormal activity in their rooms, such as rustling drapes even when the windows were closed and shower curtains that move on their own. In fact, hotel personnel hear so many first-person accounts from visitors that they keep a "ghost log" at the front desk for those who want to share their brushes with the Beyond.

Apparitions at the Anchorage include the city's first police chief, Jack J. Sturgus, who was gunned down in front of the hotel the night of February 20, 1921. Somehow, "Black Jack" Sturgus was shot in the back with this own gun. The case remains unsolved. His spectre returns to the scene of the crime every year on the anniversary on his death, hoping to find his assailant.

The apparition of a little girl, her identity unknown, frequents the second floor. Many visitors have seen her in the hallway, and her spirit is particularly drawn to Rooms 215 and 217 for some reason. She makes their TVs turn on and off "by themselves," and she loves to open the taps in the bathroom sink and tub. So far, no electrician or plumber has been able to find a "real world" explanation for any of these anomalies.

A phantom bride still wearing her wedding gown startles people with some frequency. It's believed she committed suicide in the hotel after she was left standing at the altar. Now she returns in the hopes of finding the man who jilted her. She's supposedly responsible for artwork falling from the walls and for shadows and ghostly faces that appear in the hallway.

Alaska is nicknamed "The Land of the Midnight Sun" and "The Last Frontier." Its state motto is "North to the Future," and its autumn and winter skies are often emblazoned with the aurora borealis, the eerie (though natural) Northern Lights. All of these seem apt for such a vast, barely-explored territory where it's possible that people may be outnumbered by ghosts.

Alaskan Hotel & Bar
167 South Franklin Street
Juneau, AK 99801
(907) 918-9470
www.thealaskanhotel.com

The Historic Anchorage Hotel
300 E Street
Anchorage, AK 99501
(907) 272-4553
www.historicanchoragehotel.com

Golden North Hotel
Third Street and Broadway
Skagway, AK 99840
(907) 983-2451

CHAPTER 33: MURDER AT THE MOANA

Moana Surfrider
Honolulu, Hawaii

The phrase a hui hou *is Hawaiian for "until we meet again," but the phrase took on a whole new meaning for Jane Sanford after she was fatally poisoned in a Honolulu hotel. Her ghost has been meeting people ever since.*

The **Moana Surfrider**, which began life as the Moana Hotel, was built by Walter Chamberlain Peacock in 1901. It was the first hotel to be located in the Waikiki area of Honolulu and was added to the National Register of Historic Places in 1972. The building has had numerous renovations and expansions, and it's also gone through several owners. Today, the original structure is part of a complex known as Moana Surfrider, A Westin Resort & Spa.

The hotel's primary and best-known ghost is that of Jane Stanford, who was a co-founder of Stanford University in California. She was on vacation, staying on the second floor of the Moana, when she died from ingesting strychnine. Not by accident. She was murdered.

On January 14, 1905, Stanford had been in her Nob Hill home in San Francisco when she noticed the mineral water she was drinking inexplicably tasted bitter. Whatever her suspicions, she was quick-thinking enough to regurgitate the liquid. She took the water that remained to a pharmacy for analysis and discovered that the water was laced with strychnine—enough to have killed her. Stanford immediately fired the maid, despite there being no evidence against her and no motive for her to kill Stanford. In the end, charges were never filed against her or anyone else. Shaken by the incident and suffering a lingering winter cold, Stanford sailed to Hawaii to recuperate with plans to continue on to Japan.

On the evening February 28, Stanford suffered an upset stomach and had her personal secretary, Bertha Berner, bring her some bicarbonate of soda. Later that night, about 11:15 p.m., she called out to Berner in panic. Stanford believed she had been poisoned again and wanted help to induce vomiting. The pair was unsuccessful, and Stanford died on the scene. There were three days of testimony following the subsequent investigation, but the coroner's jury delivered its ruling after just two minutes of deliberation: Sanford had died of strychnine that had been placed in the bottle of bicarbonate soda with "felonious intent" by person or persons unknown. Suspicion fell on Berner, of course—especially since she had also been at the Nob Hill address the evening of the first attempted murder—but she had been a trusted and loyal employee for more than twenty years. Again, there were no arrests.

The case remains unsolved.

Jane Stanford's spirit has been seen by staff throughout the hotel ever since, including in the basement. She also appears to guests. They spot her wandering the hallways, seemingly lost, and on rare occasions, the spectre comes up behind visitors, taps them on the shoulder, and asks them for help locating her room.

Moana Surfrider
2365 Kalakaua Avenue
Honolulu, HI 96815
(808) 923-3111
https://westin.mariott.com

APPENDIX A

BOOKINGS

Even a cursory visit to a bookstore or library will offer the reader dozens of books that can provide information on the hundreds of haunted hotels found worldwide. These range from general listings, such as *Haunted Places: The National Directory,* to more specialized volumes that deal with a single city, state, or local region. What follows is a representative sampling of the ones I've consulted while writing *Haunted Hotels.*

I've also visited websites too numerous to mention, primarily for historical background about a hotel, its builder, or the city where the venue is located. I have listed, however, several metasites that contain directories of haunted locations and provide links to other Internet sites dealing with ghosts, the occult, and the unexplained.

BOOKS

Austin-Peters, Tracie. *Welcome to Haunted Las Vegas, Nevada.* Atglen, PA: Schiffer Publishing, 2009. The book's 160 pages explore the paranormal playgrounds located on the Strip and elsewhere in the desert city.

Christensen, Jo-Anne. *Haunted Hotels.* Edmonton, AB: Ghost House Books, 2002. Thirty-six hotels and inns are profiled by region, including America's Northwest and South, California, Canada, and Great Britain.

Cobb, Todd. *Ghosts of Portland, Oregon.* Atglen, PA: Schiffer Publishing, 2007. Cobb traces the footsteps of many of Portland's most famous spectres, including the screaming girl beneath St. John's Bridge, self-moving furniture in the White Eagle Bar, and the restless spirits in the Shanghai Tunnels.

Coulombe, Charles A. *Haunted Places in America.* Guilford, CT: Globe Pequot Press, 2004. Its fifty chapters include ghost legends from a variety of venues, from theaters and college campuses to churches, restaurants, and private homes. There are also haunted hotels, including five that appear in this volume: the Golden North Hotel, the Stanley Hotel, the Menger Hotel, the 1886 Crescent Hotel and Spa, and Florida's Biltmore Hotel.

Dresbeck, Rachel. *Insider's Guide to Portland, Oregon.* 5th ed. Guilford, CT: Globe Pequot Press, 2007. Includes information on Portland's Heathman Hotel.

Dwyer, Jeff. *Ghost Hunter's Guide to Los Angeles.* Gretna, LA: Pelican Publishing Company, 2007. Dwyer provides short sketches of about a hundred haunted venues in Southern California, from Santa Barbara down to San Diego. They include such sites as the Hollywood Roosevelt Hotel, the Knickerbocker Hotel, the Oban Hotel, the Georgian Hotel, the Alexandria Hotel, the *Queen Mary,* the Hotel del Coronado, Marilyn Monroe's crypt in Pierce Brothers Westwood Village Memorial Park, and Hollywood Forever Cemetery.

Guiley, Rosemary Ellen. *The Encyclopedia of Ghosts and Spirits.* New York: Facts on File, 1992. This one-volume encyclopedia is a classic. It collects stories about phantoms, primarily ones from America and the United Kingdom, along with essays on important figures in ghost folklore, paranormal research, and Spiritualism.

Hauck, Dennis William. *Haunted Places: The National Directory.* New York: Penguin, 1996.

———. *The International Directory of Haunted Places.* New York: Penguin, 2000. Hauck's national directory and its smaller international companion volume together, list almost three thousand haunted locations, plus sites where UFOs and mysterious creatures have been sighted around the world. The books are considered essential to any ghost hunter's library.

Hotel del Coronado Heritage Department. *Beautiful Stranger: The Ghost of Kate Morgan and the Hotel del Coronado.* Coronado, CA: Hotel del Coronado Heritage Department, 2002. The book delves into Kate Morgan's life and incidents that may have led up to her death.

Jacobson, Laurie, and Marc Wanamaker. *Hollywood Haunted.* Santa Monica, CA: Angel City Press, 1994. A time-honored work on Haunted Tinseltown. Chapters include investigations of the Alexandria, Hollywood Roosevelt, and Oban Hotels.

Jonas, Shirley. *Ghosts of the Klondike.* Skagway, AK: Lynn Canal Publishing, 1996. A collection of ghost stories about the colorful characters who populated the Alaskan Panhandle during the days of the Yukon gold rush, including "Mary" at Skagway's Golden North Hotel.

Kermeen, Frances. *Ghostly Encounters: True Stories of America's Haunted Inns and Hotels*. New York: Warner Books, 2002. Kermeen profiles forty haunted hotels and bed-and-breakfasts, including (in great detail) the Myrtles Plantation, which she owned, lived in, and operated as an inn for almost a decade.

————. *The Myrtles Plantation: The True Story of America's Most Haunted House*. New York: Grand Central Publishing, 2005. This 336-page paperback by a former owner of the Myrtles Plantation details the many ghost legends surrounding the antebellum mansion.

Matsumoto, Carol. *The Ghosts of Captain Grant's Inn: True Stories from a Haunted Connecticut Inn*. Woodbury, MN: Llewellyn Publications, 2017. Paperback. 264 pages. See chapter 1 to learn more about this book.

Oberling, Janice. *Haunting of Las Vegas*. Gretna, LA: Pelican Publishing, 2008. A 224-page paperback surveying the haunted hotels, parks, and landmarks of Sin City. This new book supplants her earlier *Las Vegas Haunted* (2004, self-published under the Thunder Mountain Productions Press banner). Oberling is also the author of *Haunted Nevada* (Boca Raton, FL: Universal Publishers, 2001) and maintains the website www.hauntednevada.com.

Parvis, Sarah. *Haunted Hotels (Scary Places)*. New York: Bearport Publishing, 2008. This thirty-two-page illustrated hardbound edition introduces young readers to eleven hauntings.

Revai, Cheri, and Heather Adel Wiggins. *Haunted New York*. Mechanicsburg, PA: Stackpole Books, 2005. A series of short sketches detail sixty-one haunted sites in New York State.

Schoenberg, Dr. Philip Ernest. *Ghosts of Manhattan*. Charleston, SC: Haunted America, 2009. Schoenberg's book is based on his own walking ghost tours of New York City. He discusses legendary haunts in the Big Apple, including the Hotel Chelsea.

Smith, Barbara. *Ghost Stories of the Sea*. Edmonton, AB, Canada: Ghost House Books, 2003. This collection of spooky tales includes the story of the *Queen Mary*.

Williams, Docia Schultz. *History and Mystery of the Menger Hotel*. Plano, TX: Republic of Texas Press, 2000. Williams, a city guide and resident of San Antonio, traces the 150-year history of the Menger, profiles its famous guests, and follows its many phantoms. She is also the author of *When Darkness*

Falls: Tales of San Antonio Ghosts and Hauntings (1998) and coauthor with Reneta Byrne of *Spirits of San Antonio and South Texas* (1997), both published by Republic of Texas Press.

Wlodarski, Robert, Anne Nathan-Wlodarski, and Richard Senate. *A Guide to the Haunted Queen Mary.* West Hills, CA: G-Host Publishing, 1995. This small paperback goes into greater detail than many other tellings of the hauntings at the ship-turned-hotel located in Long Beach, California.

VIDEOS AND DVDS

America's Most Haunted Inns. Ardustry Home Entertainment, producer, and Luminence Films, distributor, 2004. This documentary by Robert Child looks at several ghost-ridden spots in Bucks County, Pennsylvania. Owners and managers of the various hotels and bed-and-breakfasts are interviewed on camera, and psychic Cathe Curtis is seen doing ghost investigations.

Ghosts Among Us. Crystal Home Video, 2007. DVD. In this 180-minute, two-disk DVD set, host Patrick McNee relates ghostly goings-on across America. In the Hollywood section, he takes a close look at the murder of Elizabeth Short, the so-called Black Dahlia, and the hotel she is said to haunt.

Haunted History: Haunted Hollywood. A&E Television Networks, 2000. VHS. This show originally aired as a one-hour program on the History Channel on August 25, 2000. The tape describes ghosts sighted at the Roosevelt Hotel, the Knickerbocker Hotel, Hollywood Forever Cemetery, and Raleigh Studios in Hollywood as well as the Georgian Hotel in seaside Santa Monica. Expert commentary is provided by author Laurie Jacobson (*Hollywood Haunted*) and paranormal researchers Dr. Barry Taff and Dr. Larry Montz, among others.

Hollywood Ghosts and Gravesites. Delta Entertainment Corporation, 2003. DVD. This sixty-one-minute program surveys hauntings by Marilyn Monroe, Rudolph Valentino, Harry Houdini, and Bugsy Siegel, among others. Also covered are the ghost phenomena on the former transatlantic liner, the *Queen Mary.*

The Search for Haunted Hollywood. Tulsa, OK: Video Communications, 1992; originally released by Gold Key Entertainment, 1989. VHS. Ninety-two minutes. First aired as a TV special. John Davidson, host; starring Patrick Macnee. On-screen personalities Norm Crosby, Susan Ollson, and Jack Carter provide first-person ghost encounters. Mentalist Max Maven conducts an on-screen séance.

Haunted legends that are investigated include those involving the famous Hollywood sign and spectral appearances by Marilyn Monroe and Montgomery Clift in the Roosevelt Hotel. Ghost investigators Hans Holzer, Nonie Fagatt, Daniel Hobbit, Richard Senate, and Barry Taff are also interviewed.

WEBSITES

www.bnbfinder.com/haunted.php

This site is designed to help vacationers plan, locate, and reserve appropriate bed-and-breakfasts for their travels. The particular page noted above lists more than two hundred inns that are purportedly haunted. Almost all of them are located in the United States. There is not a large international selection, just one or two in Canada, and another in India.

www.haunted-places.com

Besides offering state-by-state and international listings, Haunted-Places.com provides information on books, TV, and radio programming devoted to the paranormal and the supernatural. It also offers a subscription to a newsletter, the *Haunted Places Report.*

www.theshadowlands.net

Founded by Dave Juliano in 1994

Dave Juliano and Tina Carlson, codirectors

The Shadowlands lists more than thirteen thousand haunted places located all over the world. There are brief descriptions—usually two to five sentences—of each venue, categorized by the country, state, and city in which the sightings occur. The website also offers links to information on UFOs and mysterious creatures such as Bigfoot and the Loch Ness monster.

www.hauntedrooms.com

Haunted Rooms America lists hundreds of haunted hotels throughout the United States, searchable by state or the hotel's name. The site can assist you in booking a stay at any of the accommodations, and also offers special tours, guided ghost hunts, and sleepover events at several locations.

The Speakeasy Channel on https://www.youtube.com

YouTube's Speakeasy Channel has more than two hundred short videos posted (each less than twenty minutes long) detailing hauntings, paranormal phenomena, cryptids, and urban legends from around the world. Some of them are just plain scary stories. The site warns viewers, "It's not our fault if you don't sleep tonight." Because of conflicting URLs (at the time of publication), perhaps the best way to access the spooky videos is to go to YouTube.com and then do a site search for The Speakeasy Channel.

ABOUT THE AUTHOR

Tom Ogden is one of America's leading experts on the paranormal and, as a professional magician for almost fifty years, he has a special insight into ghost phenomena, hauntings, and all things that go bump in the night.

Ogden's first book, *200 Years of the American Circus*, was released in 1994. The American Library Association and the New York Public Library named it a "Best Reference Work," and Ogden was subsequently profiled in Writer's Market. His other early books include *Wizards and Sorcerers* and two magic instructional books for the Complete Idiot's Guide series. In 1998, Tom Ogden released *The Complete Idiot's Guide to Ghosts and Haunting*. His first book for the Globe Pequot "Haunted" series followed in 2008. This second edition of *Haunted Hotels* is his thirteenth book of ghost stories for Globe Pequot.

Nicknamed "The Ghost Guy," Ogden has been interviewed by numerous radio programs, podcasts, and periodicals, and he's in demand as a speaker on the Spirit World. His original ghost videos can be found on his "Hauntings Channel" on YouTube, and he is a member of the Paranormal Investigation Committee of the Society of American Magicians.

Tom Ogden resides in haunted Hollywood, California.